PADDIES

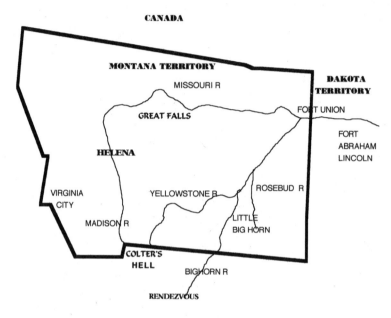

CANADA

MONTANA TERRITORY

DAKOTA
TERRITORY

MISSOURI R

FORT UNION

GREAT FALLS

FORT
ABRAHAM
LINCOLN

HELENA

VIRGINIA
CITY

YELLOWSTONE R

ROSEBUD R

MADISON R

LITTLE
BIG HORN

COLTER'S
HELL

BIGHORN R

RENDEZVOUS

WYOMING TERRITORY

PADDIES

by

J. PATRICK MULROONEY

CREATIVE ARTS BOOK COMPANY
Berkeley • California 1999

Paddies is published by Donald S. Ellis and
distributed by Creative Arts Book Company.

For Information contact:
Creative Arts Book Company
833 Bancroft Way
Berkeley, California 94710
(800) 848-7789

ISBN 0-88739-206-7 Paperback
ISBN 0-88739-194-x Hardcover
Library of Congress Catalog Number 97-78499

Printed in the United States of America

My deepest thanks to Bernadette Lorenzini for typing the manuscript; to Pam McDiffett for transfering it to disk and helping with the correspondence; to my secretary, Jacque Zehner (many thanks).

Special thanks to Victoria Gill for editing a rather wordy version of the story; and Jenny Malnick at Creative Arts for her wit and guidance.

My deepest gratitude to Don Ellis, a publisher willing to take a chance on a first-time author; to my old buddies Bud Burch, Herb Helbig, and Dick Nusser for reading it and their advice and encouragement to get it published; to Tom Knaphurst and Patricia Irvine for advice on how to get the book published; to Dr. Peter J. McCaffrey, my English professor, who encouraged me to write after medical training.

I'm forever grateful to Mom and Dad for their support and love; to my daughters, Michelle Overholtzer for proofreading, and Dr. Amy Mulrooney for her love and encouragement; to my sweet wife, Carol, for putting up with me and doing a lot of driving in Montana while I wrote various parts of the story.

Lastly, I thank our forefathers who settled this rugged, unforegiving, yet soothingly beautiful place called Montana.

To Nate

PADDIES

1

The fifty-four caliber ball tore through the air on its cushion of hot gases and split the buckskin over the trapper's upper thigh. It went deep into the muscle, just missing his femoral artery, and exited below his left buttock. Seared buckskin and flesh stuck to it as it splashed into the Rosebud River. As it hit the water, Ned O'Grady felt a strange tearing sensation in his left leg and only then heard the report of a fifty-four caliber Hawken rifle. He saw smoke from the alder bushes upstream.

"Jaysus, Mary and Joseph, I've been shot!" The pain made him throw up as he began to sink into a beaver den. Luckily, Brian McCaffrey grabbed him by the arm before he went in. They floundered on the bank as Brian half-dragged him toward his rifle.

"You can't kill a squirrel with that thing, let alone the bastard who's trying to kill us," gasped Ned.

"What do you mean, 'us'? He shot you, didn't he?" retorted Brian. "By the way, where is he?"

"Over by that alder bush," groaned Ned. God, his leg hurt, and here he was, being covered by a seventeen-year-old greenhorn from St. Louis. He had to admit that the kid was a good shot with a great sense of humor as well as being eager to learn.

"Do you think it's an Indian?" asked Brian.

"Dunno, could be a Blackfoot or one of them Tory bastards from the British Fur Company. Probably a Brit, since he was using a Hawken." A second ball struck a rock next to Brian's head.

"Looks like he wants a piece of you too, lad. I guess it's us

1

rather than me after all."

Brian fired at the alder bush where he had seen smoke from the last shot. To his surprise, he heard a grunt and saw a dark figure scramble up the bank and into the woods across the river. "Damnation," Ned muttered. "He's a Blackfoot, all right." The words sent chills up Brian's spine. Captain Clark had warned him about the Blackfoot Indians. "Well, lad, you hit him. I think you got him good. Too bad you're using that squirrel rifle. All right lad, hunt him down like a dog, and watch your topknot."

"What's a topknot?"

"Jaysus, it's your scalp! Didn't they teach you anything in school in St. Louis?"

"I probably wasn't paying attention—or more likely I skipped school to go hunting."

"Be careful."

"I'll try."

Brian swallowed hard as he forded the river and headed into the woods. He picked up a blood trail. "Please, God," he prayed silently, "not a Blackfoot. What am I doing here in Montana in the first place?"

Brian heard him before he saw him. He was singing a song between his raspy breathing. He was propped against a tree, his moccasins touching and his hands clenched in a prayer. The Hawken lay at his feet. The Indian watched him warily, resigned to the fact that he was dying. Brian was shocked at the amount of blood pouring out of the Blackfoot's chest, and the sucking sound of the Indian's breathing through his chest wound disgusted him. He had heard that sound not long ago when he had recently killed an elk. But this was a human being. "Why, he's blue! I thought Indians were supposed to be red," thought Brian. The Indian suddenly stopped breathing and his eyes glazed over. Brian shuddered, and grabbed the Indian's rifle, leather bag, powder, and knife. He should be proud, thought Brian, that he had shot the Indian, but the idea of killing another man made him nauseous. He thought about burying him, but remembered Ned's wounds and bolted back to camp.

2

Luckily the horses had been hobbled before Ned was shot. The last thing Brian needed was to be horseless in Indian country with a one-legged trapper. He found Ned shivering by a fire. There was quite a bit of blood on the ground where he lay and his buckskins were soaked. He added wood to the fire and put his Hudson Bay blanket and a buffalo robe over Ned's upper body.

"All right, let's get those buckskins off."

"What for? Your father's a doctor, not you."

"Well, I've seen him take care of gunshot wounds before."

"Where did he get his training?"

"University of Dublin."

"Fine school. You sure he didn't get his degree from some mail-order mill in London?"

"My Da's a good doctor! Why is it every time I talk to you I sound like I just got off the boat myself?"

"Ahh, I guess you've been blessed to have an Irish father and to meet me, a man of letters, from the auld sod itself."

"Man of letters? The way you cuss? If you're a man of letters, I'm Pope Boniface the Second."

"Ah well, then have it your way. What do you intend to do, lad?"

"Stop the bleeding."

Ned then pulled his buckskins off. The entrance wound was black and blue and bleeding slightly.

"Hmm. . .lucky you got a small bean. Missed it by about two inches."

"Yeah, well, me left bollock must be singed."

"I'm afraid you're not that well-hung, Ned. Roll over." The exit wound was ugly and pumping blood.

Brian said, "Got any whiskey?"

"A little. I always save some for me tooth."

"Well, drink it all, you've got plenty. Here, put this stick in your mouth."

"Stick?"

"Yeah, that way you won't break your teeth if you bite down too hard."

"Lad, I don't like the sound of this. Are you sure you know what you're doing?"

"You probably won't like the smell of it either. Besides, I'm the only one here with one hole in his ass."

"I thought you didn't approve of cussing."

"Be still."

Poor Ned was shivering uncontrollably now. Brian applied pressure to stanch the flow of blood with one hand and stealthily poured powder from his horn into the wound. "I hope that damned Indian didn't put that ball in moose shit before he plugged me. I'll get the gangrene and you'll have to cut me leg off."

"Don't worry, that won't happen," Brian said soothingly.

"Really now, are you that good?"

"No, I just never got to see my Da amputate."

"Jaysus! Seriously, Brian. If I get the gangrene shoot me and get the hell out of here as fast as you can. The horses, pelts, and guns are all yours. Just promise me two things."

"What?"

"Bury me deep so the wolves won't eat me."

"And?"

"Pull me back teeth."

"Are you crazy? I guess the whiskey's working."

"No, Mr. Whiskey isn't speaking for me yet, lad. Those teeth are full of gold."

"Gold?"

"Yes. I got it in a poker game with a drunken dentist over in Fort Union. I cleaned him out. Nextday, when he was sober, he filled them for me. I got over five hundred dollars' worth of gold hidden in me choppers for safekeeping. It's for me Ma, if I pass on."

Brian made sure that Ned had the stick in his mouth and reached quietly for a burning stick, "Where's your Ma live?" he asked. The powder was getting wet with bright red blood, a bad sign.

"South Dakota," mumbled Ned.

He pushed the stick in as far as he could. The size of the flames and smoke surprised Brian and he fell over backwards, narrowly missing falling into the fire. "Waugh!" screamed Ned as he passed out. The stick came out easily. Brian got all of it and mercifully Ned stopped bleeding. He dressed the wound and turned Ned over. Ned awoke as he was pouring more powder into the entrance wound.

"Hold it, lad. You just set me arse on fire and you're going to blow up the crown jewels?" he asked incredulously.

"Stop calling me 'lad'. . .we're equals now."

"Equals? How so?"

"Now each of us has only one hole in our asses."

Ned cackled appreciatively. "Look, you really don't have to do that now, me being such a fine specimen and all."

"Hah, fine specimen indeed. I told you before, your being so small it won't get touched. Heck, you didn't even bite through the stick. It's still in your mouth. Besides, now that I have experimented on your behind, I'm sure I've got just the right amount of powder for this one. I'm making no guarantees about your left bollock, though."

"Fine kettle of fish," groused Ned as his eyes widened with amazement when Brian lit the charge in the entrance wound.

7

There was a small flash and smoke oozed from the wound. The bleeding had stopped. Ned stayed awake for this one. "Ahh, old Lucifer and the jewels are still intact. What a blessing! He might be small now, but when aroused he can be a massive organ indeed."

Brian smirked and expertly finished dressing the wound.

"Say, Brian. Can you get me some of me spirits? Me 'tooth', you know."

"I thought that dentist fixed your teeth."

"Ah, me teeth are fine. In Dublin, when a man has the 'tooth' it means he likes the taste of whiskey."

He covered Ned, checked the horses' hobbles, fed them, and got Ned his whiskey.

"Thanks, lad. . .er, Brian you're right, we're equals. You dress the wounds and I'll teach you how to get out of here still wearing your topknot."

Ned was soon snoring, Brian rolled up next to the fire. He was exhausted and all he could think of was Bridget's beautiful blue eyes. As he drifted off, he heard wolves howling and snarling across the Rosebud. He wondered vacantly if they had found the Indian.

3

It was just before dawn. Brian lay half asleep. He had to get up; his bladder felt like it was ready to burst. He lay there dozing, looking into Bridget's deep blue eyes when, to his horror, he found himself staring into the blazing green eyes of a she-wolf. The fetid odor from her maw permeated his nostrils. He felt an icy jolt of electricity in his spine as he levitated out of his robes. He grabbed a firebrand and launched it at the wolf. She yelped and loped off. As she looked back at him he noticed her fangs were bloody and some small turquoise beads were lodged between them. She had found the Blackfoot.

Ned calmly rolled over, appraising him and the wolf. "Looks like they found him."

"Do something!" Brian shrieked.

"Calm yourself. All those stories about wolves are malarkey. They only eat dead people. A word of advice, though."

"Should I have shot her?"

"Nah. Next time you take your morning leak, unbutton your longjohns. It becomes quite messy, you know."

Brian looked down and to his chagrin, he had wet himself.

"No problem. I've been meaning to tell you to wash them. You've been smelling pretty gamey for a greenhorn, you know."

Brian shuffled, crimson-faced, down to the river and jumped in. The jolt of cold water rejuvenated him. He took off his longjohns and washed the yellow stain and weeks of accumulated grime from them. The sun had peaked over the mountains and warmed him as he sat on the bank of the river. The sky was so big out here. The clean smell of the mountains relaxed his fears. "God, I'm a mountain man in Montana. It's 1849, I'm young, strong, alive, and still wearing my scalp!"

He picked up his longjohns and strode back into camp. Ned was actually standing up. He hobbled around the campfire, and was chewing some jerked elk meat. Brian felt proud. He had saved Ned's life and the Irishman was chomping on elk meat that a greenhorn from St. Louis had killed two days ago. Brian made biscuits and brewed coffee while Ned tested his leg. "That old Blackfoot missed me hambone."

"Femur," Brian corrected.

"No difference. Main thing is, I can walk, and that old Blackfoot's dead and been chewed on by wolves and coyotes all night."

"I thought you liked Indians."

"I do. People back East call them savages. Hell, the real savages are those bastards back East and in Washington, D.C., feeding the masses and the press this pig-shit about "manifest destiny." Mark my words, some day there will be a war between the Indians and us Visigoths over this part of the country."

"Why?"

"Because white men, or Visigoths as I call them, don't respect the land. They want to buy the land from the Indians, who laugh at us and say, 'Why not let us sell you the sky and the waters too?' See, Indians have no concept of property. They worship the land, the animals, and everything around us. Hell, as soon as the Visigoths buy land, they burn down the trees, plant corn, and raise cows and pigs...lousy meat. The Indians are free. They love to hunt buffalo, elk, and deer, and range over this beautiful land. They use every part of the buffalo—the hide for teepees and robes, the horns for powder, the sinews for bow strings, the hooves to glue arrow feathers, the bladder for pouches, the bones for tools, and the brains to tan the hides. They leave no mark on the land. But the Visigoths save nothing. They eat pig meat, belch, fart—and a couple of days later they crap in the river and spread dysentery and cholera among themselves. Hell, the very people who saved Lewis and Clark's asses are dead from smallpox brought by white men. So I ask you now, who are the real savages?...By the way, do you know why we're here?"

"No."

"The Louisiana Purchase. Old Thomas Jefferson sent James Madison over to France to talk to Robespierre about buying this land from Napoleon. Mr. Bonaparte was quite pissed at the limeys for firing at French Island in the Indies while fighting in Louisiana in 1812. Good old Saint Andrew Jackson kicked their asses down there and drove them out. Jefferson was wily enough to figure out that Napoleon needed money to fight the Brits, and he bought all this land for a song. Then, while negotiating peace with the limeys, he sent Meriwether Lewis and Bill Clark out to explore the land. He couched the whole thing in beautiful prose about compiling flora and fauna and meeting the Indians, et cetera. But his real purpose was to find an inland waterway to the Pacific Coast."

"What would that do?" Brian asked.

"Simple. If we claimed all the land up to the forty-eighth parallel, or the Canadian border, we could simultaneously keep the limeys in Canada and destroy the English fur trade. The man was a saint and a bloody genius."

Brian was amazed. He had learned more history from this profane Irishman in one morning than he had in all his years of school back in St. Louis.

"Sad thing is, those bastards are still waging war against us from Canada."

"How?"

"Simple. They give the Indians guns, powder, whiskey for their pelts. The Indians can kill us and then the limeys drug them with whiskey for cheap trades. The Indians and Irish are alike, you know."

"How's that?"

"We can't handle whiskey."

"My Da hates the English too," said Brian.

"Ah, I knew he was a good man."

"Guess who my Da's favorite patient is?"

"Pope Boniface the Second?"

"No. Captain William Clark."

"You mean of Lewis and Clark?"

"The same."

"My God, you know him?"

"Yep. We used to have him over for dinner all the time. He loves the Indians too. If it weren't for him, they would have perished. He was tough with the Sioux along the Missouri and they respected him. He was kind to the Mandans, Assiniboines, and the Shoshones. He made peace with those Indians, gave them gifts, and Sacagawea got him over the Rockies. He said they would have perished save for those good Indians and their horses."

"Saints preserve us, you know him."

"He gave me my Kentucky rifle."

"That squirrel rifle? I was going to tell you to leave it here now that you've got the Hawken from that Blackfoot. Why, that's a religious icon. Don't lose it."

"I won't."

"By the way. Do you know why the Blackfeet hate us Visigoths, Brian?"

"No."

"Well, when Captain Clark came back this way, he went south along the Yellowstone and old Meriwether went north of the Marias river for one last stab at finding a way to the Columbia and the Pacific. The only mistake during the whole expedition was that Captain Lewis and his party ran into some Blackfoot Indians and camped with them. When they awoke, as Captain Lewis had fallen asleep on his watch, the Indians had their guns. Old Meriwether wrestled his gun from a Blackfoot and killed him as well as another Indian. Ever since, the Blackfeet have been our sworn enemies."

"You don't say."

"Captain Lewis was never the same. They never got the praise they deserved. Poor Meriwether was found shot in his cabin in Kentucky. Some say that road agents did it, but Captain Clark said he was subject to fits of depression after killing those Indians. He was also hounded by Congress over a measly two-hundred dollar difference between his accounting of the expedition and theirs. Captain Clark thinks he blew his own brainpan out."

"Jaysus, I'll bet my golden hind teeth those Congressmen were Tories in sheep's clothing hounding him to his grave. The bastards!"

Brian put out the fire. Ned exclaimed, "Well, we got to get to the Rendezvous down in Jackson Hole. I want you to meet some real mountain men—Jim Bridger, Kit Carson, and the Liver-Eater."

"Liver-Eater?"

"I don't want to spoil the surprise. You'll meet him soon enough," smirked Ned.

They broke camp. He helped Ned up on his horse, old Hell Bastard. He put his Hawken in the scabbard and got up on his own horse, Sweet Nell, cradled his squirrel rifle, and forded the Rosebud. Brian wasn't looking forward to what he'd see on the other side.

4

The wolves had torn the Blackfoot to pieces. Ned blasted a coyote into oblivion and they dismounted. The dead man's remains were unspeakable. The ravens had plucked his eyes and his entrails hung out, savaged by coyotes. Brian threw up. Ned smiled and said, "Welcome to Montana." Brian glared at him.

"Shall we bury him?"

"Nah, they'll just dig him up and eat the rest of him."

They hoisted him up into a tree with his few possessions and put him to rest Indian-style.

"Shall we say a prayer?" Brian asked.

"Sure," said Ned thoughtfully. "Ashes to ashes, dust to dust, glad you're here 'cause it's Rendezvous or bust."

They mounted up. Brian wondered, How could a land so beautiful be so treacherous? They headed south towards Jackson Hole.

"Have you ever seen a grizz?" asked Brian.

"Oh yes," said Ned reverently. "You don't want to mess with them. They're God's smartest and most fearsome creatures. Let me tell you about grizz. If you're downwind of them and get between a mother and her cub, you're a dead man. She'll charge you. Cover up your vitals and neck, roll up in a ball and pray. They'll usually take a couple swipes at you but they don't like the taste of our meat, so play dead. If it's a male, it will probably stand up and roar at you with his arms in the air. Do the same thing back. Look him in the eyes and calmly say, 'I mean you no harm, brother.' Stand your ground. You can't outrun him. They can catch a horse, so what chance would you have now, Brian? If a bear sees you are afraid, he'll probably charge, so ball up or shoot. I prefer to shoot and ball up—or if you're lucky, climb a tree. But remember, they can reach about twelve feet up in the air."

"Have you ever killed one?"

"A few, actually. I've also been treed, charged, and swiped at. I hate them almost as much as the Brits."

"Where should I aim?"

"Well, now. If you have the Kentucky rifle, I'd go for the brainpan. Shoot through the mouth and aim upward."

"But that's impossible if he's down on all fours charging at you."

"Exactly. You aim at your brainpan 'cause that rifle of Captain Clark's will only piss him off. You might try practicing getting the toe of your moccasins through the trigger guard."

"Very funny, Ned. What about the Hawken?"

"Now that's a different kettle of fish. Hit the beast in the chest with the first shot, aim slightly to the left of the middle but nobody is ever calm enough to do it. Then reload. The Hawken can actually put him down for a while. Next, if there's a tree, get up in it and aim down at his braincase. Then reload and put another in his brain and upper spine, if you can get it from the side. No sense shooting him in the back of the neck because his hump will absorb the ball."

"Then what?"

"Reload and wait. If it doesn't move for twenty minutes, you're probably safe. Get out of the tree, walk over, put the Hawken barrel in its mouth, and if it twitches, pull the trigger and run. If not, you got your meat."

"Good God, they're that dangerous?"

"Aye. And the meat doesn't taste that well. The hide's pretty warm but not as warm as a buffer's."

"You mean buffalo?"

16

"Of course. You weren't in the Dull Learner's Class in St. Louis now, were you? Oh, by the way. The claws are good as ornaments. The Indians are impressed by them. Even other trappers know you're not a man to be trifled with."

"Hope I *never* tangle with a grizz."

"You will—and when it happens it will be over very quickly, one way or the other," said Ned in his most earnest tone. Then he added, "Brian, I've got a question for you. I thought doctors poured saltpeter into wounds?"

"They do, but powder is about the same thing with a little mercury added in. Besides, I figured the mercury might poison the gangrene bacillus."

"What about poisoning me?"

"Not a chance. To be honest, I figured the saltpeter might dampen the spirits of Lucifer, that mighty organ, for a while."

Ned looked even more pale.

"I'm just kidding. It blew up before it could have any lasting effect."

"Thank the Lord! You know, there will be some whores at the Rendezvous and I've been looking forward to it so. Have you ever been with a woman yet, Brian?"

"Not quite. I love a girl, Bridget O'Brien, back in St. Louis. I'm saving it for her."

"Ah, noble intention. A word of advice with your purse around the whores at Rendezvous. Watch it as closely as you do your topknot out here."

"I intend to. I'm going to make as much profit from the pelts as I can and propose to Bridget as soon as I get back."

"You're not going to make a career out of this?"

"No, I think I'll study medicine and learn from my Da. I don't think I'm cut out for killing Indians and the like."

"I see. I've been lucky. Never had to kill a man. I doubt I would like it either."

"You sure wanted that Blackfoot dead."

"Yeah, but you'd be doing the killing. Besides, I don't think he meant to kill us."

"What?"

"Sure. The Hawken's so accurate he could have hit me in the chest or head easily from that distance. I think he was just giving us a warning to stay out of their hunting grounds."

Brian felt even more morose.

"Cheer up, lad. You're becoming a mountain man and getting an education from a man of letters."

"Don't call me 'lad'. How old are you, anyhow?"

"Thirty."

"That's not much older than me. How come your beard's gray and those red locks of yours have a touch of gray already?"

"When you worry about keeping your scalp on, it seems to turn gray quicker than being in the city. As you can already see, this is a hard life."

"Indeed it is."

"Cheer up, old Brian. Few men get to see God's country. The sun's at our backs, the air is sweet and the water is pure. The land is covered with wildflowers, elk, and buffers, and the mountains are covered with snow. Most importantly, we have our freedom. We are blessed. I have always loved history; and in this country of yours, we're making history."

They smiled as they crossed over into Wyoming. Brian wondered what could possibly happen in Jackson Hole.

5

They rode for two more days, camping but not trapping. The third night, they lay next to the campfire.

"Ned, you know everything about me yet I know very little about you."

"Ah. What would you like to know?"

"Where'd you grow up?"

"Dooblin."

"When did you come over?"

"Three years ago, with me Ma and Da. Me Da died within three months in a railroad explosion. You know, they gave all the dangerous work to the Chinese and the Irish, and then made them sleep and eat in different quarters. They even had separate bars for the Irish and opium dens for the Chinese. Fockin' railroads are probably owned by the bloody bastard limeys too."

"Where's your Ma?"

"South Dakota, on the south side of the Platte River, away from the Sioux. I miss her so. I write to her, but one can't mail the letters very often. Another reason I'm looking forward to Rendezvous."

"What's her name?"

"Eileen Katherine O'Grady. Me Da's name was Ned, too."

"Do you have any other friends or relatives over here?"

"No other relatives. My friends are mountain men also."

"You haven't been doing this long, then."

"Two and a half years. Believe me, I've got plenty of

experience. I just don't talk about it much. We Irish act a little bit dumber than we are."

"So I've noticed. You've taught me so much in these past six months. Not all of it is about trapping. Most of it has been about mankind, freedom, history, and the beauty and danger around us."

"Thank you, Brian. You've become a good man. Whatever happens, as I'm sure we'll part ways soon, you will always be my brother."

"And you will be mine."

"You once told me that you have no brothers or sisters. Is your Ma alive?"

"No. She died when I was twelve. She got the cholera and was dead in forty-eight hours. My poor Da was crushed, him being a physician and all. There was nothing he could do to save her."

"Aye, a tragedy. I have a favor to ask you again. If something happens to me before we part ways, please make sure me Ma gets me gold."

"You have my solemn pledge." They shook hands. "How's your leg? I see you're walking around on it, but riding for two days must be tough."

"Ah, it's only a minor pain in the arse. You done me a great job. I will be eternally grateful. Good night, brother, for tomorrow you will Rendezvous."

"Good night, brother."

The campfire flickered as they both fell into a deep sleep.

6

They rode into Jackson Hole in the late afternoon. It was an amazing sight. There were tents erected in a circle, while dogs and pigs scampered about in the dirt. There were wagons advertising whiskey, guns, powder, shot, buckskins, moccasins, coffee, flour and tobacco. There were booths for the American and British fur trading companies where men were arguing over the price of beaver pelts. Ned made a ceremony of contemptuously spitting in front of the British fur booth. There was a makeshift saloon and a large series of tents behind it advertising "Fifty Cents a Poke."

"What's a poke?", asked Brian.

Ned smiled and said, "You'll find out soon enough."

They arrived at a corral and paid to have their horses lodged and fed. "Take care of Nell, as she is the best friend I have—present company excluded," winked Brian.

"Well thanks, brother. Sir, feed the Bastard and watch out—he bites!"

They trudged back toward the center of the crowd and after depositing their pelts for safekeeping, headed straight for the saloon.

There was smoke everywhere in the dimly lit saloon. Card games abounded. Fur traders, gamblers, and prostitutes mingled with the trappers, all with the same intention: separating them from their money, their furs, or both.

"Lad, can you serve me and me friend some whiskey? I've

got the 'tooth' real bad." Ned gave Brian a conspiratorial wink.

"Sure sorry to hear it. That'll be fifty cents."

"Fifty cents! That's twice what it was last year. That's highway robbery, man!" Ned clanged a fifty-cent piece on the bar.

The bartender said, "Where have you been? Haven't you heard? The price of beaver has gone down since last year. People are starting to wear silk hats now. A man's got to make a living, you know."

Ned glared into his drink and downed it and rasped, "Another, please."

Brian, having never tasted whiskey before, almost spit it out on the man nearest him but managed to let it burn down his throat while keeping a straight face. The man had cold, steely eyes but they lit up when he spotted Ned.

"O'Grady! You're still wearing your scalp. Good to see you."

"Why, Kit! You still look as mean as hell. Glad to see you made it through another year. Meet me partner, Brian. Brian, say hello to Mr. Carson."

"It's an honor to meet you, sir."

"Don't call me 'sir,' greenhorn. I ain't that old."

"Yes, sir. . .I mean Mr. Carson, er, Kit."

"That's better," grumbled Carson.

Brian was in awe of Kit Carson, who had a wide reputation as a fierce fighter with legendary guiding and hunting skills.

"Brian here saved me life the other day. Got shot by a Blackfoot and was bleeding to death. He stopped the bleeding by setting me arse and crotch on fire with gunpowder."

"You don't say?" Carson was amused. "Pretty spectacular way of saving old Ned's ass, Har Har."

"He also killed a Blackfoot."

"Good boy. Unlike the others around here, I don't much like Indians."

Brian fought wave after wave of dizziness after managing to finish his first glass of whiskey. He said nothing and stared dumbly into space.

"Strange boy, Ned," Carson whispered.

"Aye. Is Jim here yet?" asked Ned.

"No, Bridger will be a little late. He's up on the Yellowstone, probably still looking for Colter's Hell."

"What's Colter's Hell?" slurred Brian as Ned handed him another drink.

"You know who Jim Colter is?"

"Sure. He went with Lewis and Clark but stayed in the mountains and never came back to St. Louis. He's famous for escaping the Blackfeet and running two hundred miles naked to safety. Wouldn't that be hell enough?" asked Brian.

Carson said, "No, son. Colter describes a place in the mountains above the Yellowstone River where there's steam shooting up into the air like clockwork and the air smells like rotten eggs. Supposedly, there are pools of hot water where you can cook a fish after catching it out of a cold stream only yards away. I know it sounds crazy, but Bridger thinks he can find it. He claims the reason why nobody can find it is the Indians won't go near the place because they think it's haunted."

"Sounds scary to me," Brian slurred, and worked his way through his second whiskey. Ned led him to a table and Brian sat down unsteadily.

"Brian, this is my buddy, Del. Why don't you tell him the story about your partner, John Johnston?"

"Glad to, Ned. See, John's pretty quiet so I tell all of his stories. He has a hobby of killing Crows. They killed his squaw wife and unborn baby and John aims to get even. Anyway, he was trapping up north last winter when some Blackfeet pounced on him. They knew the Crow would pay handsomely for him. He had a drum of whiskey on his horse and they started drinking it. Their second mistake was to tie his hands in front of him. And their third mistake was to leave him in a teepee with only one brave to watch him.

"The brave kept looking out to see all the fun outside. Meanwhile old Johnny gnawed through the rawhide holding his wrists. He steps up behind the brave and breaks his neck. Then he takes the Indian's scalping knife and cuts his leg off."

"Why?" mumbled Brian, as Ned brought him his third drink.

"Why, to eat, of course. He was two hundred miles from our cabin, couldn't build a fire or hunt because the Indians would find him. Anyway, he cuts his way out of the back of the teepee and hightails it home. One night he crawls into a cave and feels a tuggin' on his Indian's leg. Turns out it's a mountain lion trying to steal his meal ticket. Old Johnny beats the cat senseless with the leg and then he hears a roarin' behind him and makes a quick exit. Seems he'd picked a hibernatin' bear's cave to sleep in."

"Jaysus, Mary and Joseph!"

"That's not the end of the story. One night I'm sitting in our cabin—I had figured old Johnny was history—and there's a knock on the door. I opened the door and old John's standing there with no shirt on, buckskins and leggings all tore up, icicles on his beard and a bizzard blowin' in behind him. In sails this Indian's half-eaten leg and, cool as a cucumber he says, 'How're you fixed for meat, Del? I brung you some.'"

Brian sat slack-jawed. Ned howled with laughter.

"Wanna smoke?" asked Del.

"No, thanks, but I'll try a chew of your tobacco, Ned."

"I thought you didn't touch the stuff."

"Well, I never had whiskey before, either. I'm going to try a chaw."

"Suit yourself," smiled Ned.

The tobacco tasted like fire and burned his tongue and throat worse than the whiskey. He sneezed and almost swallowed the chaw. He spit it out on the boots of the largest man he had ever seen. Ned said reverently, "Brian, meet Liver-Eater Johnston."

The man lifted Brian by his neck with one hand and held

him four feet off the ground. "Pleased to meet you, son. Did you do that on purpose?"

"No, sir," stammered the suddenly sober Brian.

"I didn't think so. You ought to lay off that stuff. It'll stunt your growth." He sat Brian down gently.

"So you're the Liver-Eater?" asked Brian incredulously.

"My name's John Johnston and don't believe all the stories you hear."

"How 'bout a drink, John?" asked Ned.

"Sure." Ned brought over four whiskies and they downed them, except for Brian, who was drinking much slower than the others.

"Well, lad. It's time to visit the ladies. See you tomorrow."

Ned put Brian's arm around him and they staggered out the back.

"Brian, give me your purse. Here's fifty cents."

"What's that for?"

"You're about to be poked."

Brian was expertly guided to the loss of his virginity by a woman named Tess. All he could remember was fumbling around and slipping out a few times, as he had a hard time keeping an erection because of his drunkenness. He did distinctly remember Ned chortling loudly next to him. "Ah, yes, ah yes. Old Lucifer's as good as ever. Thanks, brother."

When Brian awoke the next morning his head was pounding and they were laying on cots in a strange tent. He looked over and saw Ned squinting at him through one half-opened, bloodshot eye. "Brian, you saved me life, but why didn't you chase off that mountain lion that must have taken a shit in me open slumbering mouth last night?"

He rolled over, smiling, and fell back to sleep. His head hurt too much to laugh at Ned.

7

They awoke about noon and left the tent and washed in the nearby stream. They put on clean clothes. Ned gave Brian back his purse. "Well, now. Guess I'll need some powder and balls. Me traps are still good." Ned also bought some Castoreum. "Do you remember you thought that Castoreum was for your bowels?"

Brian smiled. He remembered Ned's consternation at Brian's not knowing that the scent was used to bait beaver traps. Brian bought paper, a stamp and an envelope, then he bought another of each so that he could write his father as well as Bridget.

"Ah, love," chortled Ned.

"Well, we've put it off long enough, brother Brian."

"What?"

"We've got to reclaim our pelts and do some trading. Watch me and don't say anything. Those bastards wind up with your pelts as well as the buckskins on your back and they want you to pay them for the privilege of dealing with them."

They paid the man guarding the pelts. He told them gravely that they would be disappointed with the price. Ned glowered.

Brian was surprised at the number of Indians at the Rendezvous. "Well, Brian, everybody's welcome; it's Rendezvous. Few of us have hard feelings towards the Indians and vice versa. This is why they call it the fur trade. You see, everybody is bartering something, from that man over there selling snake oil to

27

the lovely dears who sold us their bodies last night." Brian groaned at the thought. So much for saving himself for Bridget.

They approached the American Fur Trader's booth, though rumor had it that the British Fur Trading Company was paying higher prices than the Americans. The trader looked over the pelts and said, "They're good quality. I'll give you two hundred dollars for the lot of them."

"Jaysus H. Christ! You're nothing but bloody highwaymen."

"Sorry, but the price is going down. Those fancy dandies back East are buying silk hats instead of fur. You might try and get a better price from Sir Reginald of the British Fur Company."

"If he's a knight, I'm the bloody Christmas Fairy."

As Ned approached Sir Reginald's booth, Brian feared the worst. Their last six months' work was in the hands of a badly hung over, profane Irishman who hated the English. To Brian's astonishment, Ned bowed reverently and said softly, "Why Sir Reginald, how good to see you. Ned O'Grady's the name."

The Englishman eyed him warily and said, "Well, what have you for me this year, Paddy?"

"Ah, I've got many fine pelts. I beg of you to be generous— not for me but for my partner here, young Brian McCaffrey from St. Louis. You see, he needs the money to get married."

"Indeed!" snorted the Englishman. "O'Grady has a familiar ring to it. They and the Meaghers were being hunted for sedition against Great Britain."

"Aye, but they are distant cousins and traitors, and that was long ago in the old country."

Brian was disappointed at Ned's obsequiousness towards the Englishman. To his disgust, Ned got down on one knee and begged, "Sir, I beg of you to give us a fair price. Perhaps I can find something down here to help you find it in your heart to treat us fairly." Brian saw that Ned's charade was ending. Ned had slyly fingered a tobacco spittoon.

"I'll give you and your friend from St. Louis a hundred and ninety dollars," said the Englishman.

"And I, sir, will give you a lesson in negotiations with the Irish." He flung the contents of the spittoon into Sir Reginald's eyes. He then sprung up and purposely hit Reginald's chin with the top of his head. The tip of Sir Reginald's tongue flopped uselessly into the dust. Ned began beating him with the spittoon.

"Thoo fifthy," bleated the Englishman.

"More!" shouted the Irishman. Even the other trappers were amazed at Ned's violence.

Brian cried, "You'll kill him!"

"I intend to," said Ned quietly, as he winked at Brian.

"Thwee hunded."

"Ahh, that's getting closer," said Ned as he straddled the prostrate Englishman and began to strangle him. "How about three fifty and we'll settle the deal?"

Sir Reginald's eyes bulged and his face grew violet. He nodded and choked, "Yeth."

"It's a deal, Reginald. Pleasure doing business with you. By the way, me mother is a Meagher."

The Englishman rapidly paid Ned and Brian and hurriedly closed his booth, announcing that the British Fur Company would no longer deal with the bahbahian American fur tradeths." The staff of the American Fur Trader's booth nearby clapped loudly and the trappers hooted derisively at the Englishman while Ned nonchalantly ground the severed tip of the Englishman's tongue into the dust with his moccasin. He then folded his arms and looked sideways at Brian. "Aye, Brian. Not only have you learned trapping and hunting from me, but now I've taught you the fine art of negotiation."

Brian realized, belatedly, that his kindly, humorous mentor was not a man to be trifled with.

That night they ended up in the saloon with Johnston The Liver-Eater, Del, and Kit Carson. They were deep in conversation about Indians when Jim Bridger walked in.

"Well, did you find Colter's Hell?" quipped Carson.

"No," Bridger replied tersely.

"I told you it's all hogwash," said Carson.

Bridger looked down at him disdainfully and said nothing. Brian reflected that Carson should know better than to rile a man who had been riding all day.

"How about a drink, old Jim?" asked Ned.

"I'd love one, thank you," said Bridger.

"Yeah. Ned and Brian here have come into a lot of money thanks to the British Fur Company," shouted Del.

"And by the way, meet me partner, Brian—Jim," said Ned. Brian shook Bridger's extended hand and said, "It's an honor to meet you, sir."

"Nice to meet you, son."

Brian noticed the man's clear blue eyes, and the prominent goiter which caused the Indians to name Bridger "Big Neck." Ned brought over a round of drinks and graciously served them all. Brian was consistently amazed by Ned. He was surrounded by the most legendary mountain men in America, who not only liked Ned but treated him with respect. Of course, this afternoon's display of violence had done nothing to detract from Ned's reputation amongst the trappers. Brian noticed that even the Liver-Eater was deferential to Ned. Johnston had taken a liking to Brian ever since he had spit the tobacco on his boots. It was hard to imagine that this huge quiet man was capable of violence. He guessed that having twenty Crow warriors trailing him at one time with the intention of killing him would wear on you.

"How many Crow livers have you eaten this year, John?" asked Bridger.

"Three."

"I guess that makes twelve then," said Jim.

"Yep. Only eight to go," said Johnston.

"Guess you hate Indians as much as I do," said Carson.

The Liver-Eater eyed him gravely and said, "I don't hate Indians. I just took an oath to get even with the Crows for killing my squaw and the baby in her belly. When I kill the last one, I'll make peace with them."

"Why, The Crow have been the most helpful tribe towards us since the Snake Indians and old Sacagawea rescued Lewis and Clark," said Ned. "Say, Jim, did you know Brian here is good friends with William Clark himself? Old Bill gave him a Kentucky rifle, he did."

"You don't say. Clark's a fine man. He likes the Indians too."

"What about you, Bridger ? Are you an Indian-lover too?" snorted Carson.

"I married a beautiful Ute girl this winter," said Bridger coolly.

Carson avoided provoking Bridger further. What about you, Brian?" he queried.

"I honestly don't know. I've never really met one, except for a Blackfoot."

"And you killed him. Good boy. The only good Indian is a dead Indian," said Carson. Brian squirmed uncomfortably, nursing his whiskey and hangover.

"Leave the boy alone, Kit," said Ned quietly.

"So you love those horse thieves too," said Carson angrily.

"You don't understand. It's a difference between our cultures. You see, in Ireland, if a man steals a horse, he is whipped in public. In the States, it's a capital offense. For the Indians, it's a way of proving their manhood. You see, when white men do battle, they try to kill as many of their enemies as much as possible. The Indians charge and touch each other with a lance, like the old medieval knights, and they call that 'counting coupe'. It carries the same honor as killing an enemy, but it preserves their race. Likewise, taking a horse tests a brave's ability to track prey, to move stealthily among his enemies. Moving among those high-strung

31

ponies without spooking them, he jumps on and hopes he doesn't get bucked off. He then hightails it through the camp, touching as many braves as he can with his coupe stick while they shoot arrows at him. Each horse he takes is a 'coupe' and when he returns to camp it raises his rank in the tribe. So in one culture a man would be hanged; in the other he is revered.

"Another big difference is that Indians are extremely honest. We're the ones that write treaties and insist that both parties sign them—even though we usually break them. What white men don't understand is that the chiefs may sign a treaty but they are powerless; they are leaders in name only. The warriors, who conduct raids and warfare, are responsible only to themselves. To a man, when a chief signs a treaty he will always say, 'I will sign this for the Great White Father but it means nothing.' The white man doesn't care. As long as he can show his superiors or some politician an Indian's X on a piece of paper, he's happy. The problem is, four years later a different Great White Father has been elected to power, all the agreements are out the window, and we take more of their land. I tell you, we're the thieves, and the Indians are not savages. Some day they will rise up—and when they do, there will be a lot of dead white men."

Carson glared at Ned and said, "Nice speech, Indian-lover."

The only sound then was chairs simultaneously scraping on the floor as the men moved away from the table.

Ned, smiling at Kit, cagily fingered a spittoon under the table away from Carson's view.

"I'm only stating an opinion—'freedom of speech' is a principle of your great country, you know."

Johnston, who was sitting between them, stood up, glaring, and said, "I'm tired of listening to idle chatter." He then grabbed Carson and Ned by the backs of their necks and lifted them high off the floor.

Carson reached for his revolver. Ned splashed the contents of the spittoon into Carson's eyes. The Liver-Eater dropped Ned, then casually took Kit's pistol from him and hit him between the eyes with it. Carson crumpled to the floor, unconscious. The Liver-Eater said "Good—night, Ned, boys. Del, you ready to turn in?"

"Yep," said Del as he turned and winked at Brian. "Ain't he somethin'? You know how he kills those Crows? He lifts them above his head and drop-kicks them across his thigh. Snaps their spines in two. I never saw a stronger man." Brian just stared in amazement.

"Come on, Del. Quit feeding the boy those stories of yours. Good night, Brian."

"Believe me, it's true," whispered Del adamantly.

They went out into the darkness. Bridger said, "Brian, you're a lucky boy—he's taken a liking to you. Well, I'm going to turn in."

"Me too," said Brian. "I've had enough excitement for one day."

"Think I'll take care of me tooth," said Ned. "Besides, somebody's got to stay with old Kit till he wakes up. If he's still nasty, I'll rap his pate with me trusty spittoon."

Brian just shook his head and trudged toward their tent. He lit a lamp and began a letter to Bridget.

"My Dearest, I miss you so much. I am in Jackson Hole. My partner and I have made a profit of a hundred and seventy-five dollars apiece. I plan on selling the gun that Captain Clark gave me for even more money. When I reach Fort Union I will sell Sweet Nell (she's my horse). You'd love her. She's the greatest animal I have ever owned and is almost as sweet as you. I will take a steamer from Fort Union on September 25th and will be back in your arms in a short time. With the money I've made I can buy a proper house and land for us to raise a family. I will ask your father for your hand, as we discussed before. I think he will give his permission, as I have given up wanting to be a mountain man. I plan on studying medicine and providing for you and our family. Love, Brian."

The next morning he woke and saw Ned snoring comfortably on his cot. He went outside and washed and noticed it felt painful to urinate. Dismissing it, he sought out Joe Hanks, an agreeable gambler who was leaving directly for St. Louis and would deliver Brian's letter to Bridget long before Brian would arrive there. He thanked Hanks profusely and Hanks said, "Glad to help you out, lad. Getting quite an education hanging around old Ned?"

"I most certainly am," smiled Brian as they shook hands and parted ways.

Unfortunately, Brian's letter was never to be delivered, for Hanks was shot in a gambling dispute aboard the steamer bound for St. Louis. Ironically, he had kept the letter in his vest pocket. When his assailant shot him, the bullets tore through the letter and into Hanks' breast. Blood left it unreadable and it remained undisturbed in his pocket as he was hoisted overboard to rest in peace at the bottom of the Missouri River.

8

The next day Brian went up to a tent with a cross in front of it. It was the "church" of Father De Smet, the Jesuit missionary who preached Christianity among the Indians throughout the West. He was hearing confessions. Brian got in line. When his turn came he went in, knelt, and began, "Bless me, Father, for I have sinned. It has been six months since my last confession."

"Have you been in the woods all that time?"

"Yes, Father. I committed the sin of drunkenness once; I had relations with a prostitute once, and chewed tobacco once."

"My son, chewing tobacco is not a sin, but I wouldn't recommend it for your health."

"I know, Father," said Brian, thinking of the Liver-Eater's moccasins.

"Anything else?"

"Yes, Father, I killed a man."

"You what?"

Brian then told Father De Smet how he had come to kill the Blackfoot. When he finished, Father De Smet said, "My son, you killed in self-defense. I know you are very sorry for this, but you should not hold yourself guilty of the sin of murder. I ask you to pray for the Indian's soul, and for your penance say three Our Fathers and three Hail Marys. Now make a good Act of Contrition."

"Yes, Father. Thank you."

"Good luck and watch your topknot out there, my son."

After saying his penance, Brian walked out into the so-called streets. He was greeted with friendly "hallos". He was one of them—a mountain man. It was a great feeling. But Brian knew that all their days as hunters and traders were numbered; the fur trade was coming to an end. Still, there was nothing else on earth like Rendezvous.

Ned was just getting up, rather bleary-eyed, when Brian came in. "Well, how did Kit do?" Brian asked.

"He behaved himself, especially when he saw that I had his gun and was armed with a spittoon. He was a little riled up but I got him laughing with my favorite Indian joke."

"What's that?"

"This Indian boy asked his father how he had gotten his name. The father said, 'When a child is born, the father goes outside and looks for a creature, and gives the newborn babe the name of the first animal that he sees. When your brother was born, I saw a deer, so we called him Little Deer. Likewise, on the morning your sister Little Sparrow was born, I had seen a sparrow. Why do you ask me this, Two Dogs Focking?'"

Brian howled.

"Kit liked it, too. Cooled his temper right down. We're friends again."

"Ned, I've got a problem."

"What's that?"

"Well, it seems when I pass water it burns, and I think my bean's got a cold."

"A cold?"

"Yes. You know how your nose runs when you have a cold? Well, my bean's doing the same thing."

"Jaysus. It's either the clap or Hong Kong Dong," said Ned worriedly.

"Hong Kong Dong?"

"Mind you, I've never seen it, but me Da told me about a

36

lad who got it from a whore back when they worked together blowin' up tunnels."

"What happened?"

"Well, the lad had a discharge much like yourself and went to the railroad doctor and he tells him, 'Son, I'm sorry, but you got Hong Kong Dong.' The lad asks the doctor what that meant. The doctor says, 'I'll have to amputate.'"

Brian went white.

"The doctor told him that if he would like a second opinion, there was a Chinese doctor who cared for the coolies. The lad goes to the Chinese doctor who examines him and says, 'What American doctor tell you?' 'He said I have Hong Kong Dong,' said the kid. 'He right,' answers the Chinese doctor.

"Do you have to amputate?' 'No, no. No amputation.' 'Oh thank God,' said the boy. The Chinese doctor says, 'No problem. Two days bean turn black; third day fall off by itself. No need surgery.'"

Brian nearly fainted on the cot while Ned howled.

"Why, Brian—I just told you my second-favorite joke and you didn't even laugh! Don't worry, brother. There's no such thing as Hong Kong Dong; you've got the clap. There's a pharmacist's wagon around the corner. We'll get you some arsphenamine and in two days you'll be as good as new."

As it turned out, Ned was right. Two days later Brian's symptoms were gone.

9

The remainder of the Rendezvous went quickly for Brian. He enjoyed meeting and trading stories with these men—men who would become legends. He knew that his own life would be different from theirs: more civilized, more regimented. He wondered if he would miss the freedom. They were the freest men on earth and in some ways the most honest, law-abiding people he had ever met. Even the Liver-Eater had a strict code of ethics, save for killing Crows. They were in some ways like "civilized" men—except when they got up to go to work. They might wake up in a blizzard. They could be mauled by a grizzly bear or a mountain lion, bitten by a rattler, or scalped by an Indian. Their only means of transportation could go lame or be stolen in the night. They endured blinding snow storms, searing sun, raging rivers, dysentery, mosquitoes, animals still alive in their traps that could fatally injure them, and other dangers of the wilderness. Yet for all the dangers they faced, they were the happiest, most serene men he had ever met. All of them knew that they were survivors, the most self-sufficient men on earth. They could feed and clothe themselves and live off the land, obtaining necessities with their bare hands if they had to. Of course, a good horse, rifle, and knife made things a lot easier for them; because of this, they were like highly-trained cavalry soldiers— meticulous about caring for their livestock, rifles, and ammunition. Some things suffered: personal hygiene, contacts with relatives and friends back East, their love lives. Many would break their ties to marry Indians and live with various tribes. Yet not one of them would trade places with a man back East for they only felt alive when they were five thousand feet above sea level, downwind of their prey, with the sun at their backs and a trusty Hawken cradled in their arms.

As Rendezvous came to an end, they were like any other men ending their vacations. They sobered up, stopped gambling, wrote letters back home, and started making plans to go back to work. They bought provisions, ammunition, traps, castoreum, new blankets, moccasins and buckskins, flints and powder to get them through the next winter. It was a time of contemplation and some sadness, but mostly it was exhilarating, for there would always be adventure waiting for them when they departed into the wilderness.

Brian wondered if he would miss this life. The past six months had been his happiest so far. It was the most terrifying yet exciting period in his eighteen years, and never had he learned so much.

Ned had taught him to survive, hunt, and avoid war parties. Brian had learned sign language from him so that he could communicate with all Indian tribes. He had even learned how to "negotiate" with Englishmen. But mostly he learned to laugh—and had learned to love his country because of its freedom. He now believed, like Ned, that all men were indeed created equal, whether red, white, black, or yellow. They all needed each other out here to survive.

Brian knew now, however, that he was different from the mountain men. He needed to get back to Bridget. He realized more than ever that he loved her, wanted to spend the rest of his life with her, and father her children. He had great misgivings about saying goodbye to Ned, a man whom he had come to love as his own brother.

When the time came, Brian could hardly express himself. "Ned, I don't know how to say goodbye. I. . ."

"Then don't, brother. I know our paths will cross again

some day. Maybe I'll come back and get some dentist in St. Louis to pull me Ma's fortune for me. That'll get you off the hook."

"I promise I'll get the gold to your mother."

"I know you will."

"Tell me one more time—how do I get to Fort Union?"

"Cross over the Rosebud and head west. I know you're going east, but you need to head up to Henry's Lake. Go due north over the pass. You'll see a big river. It's beautiful, blue and wide. That's the Madison. Follow it for fifty miles. About three-quarters of the way through the valley, look to your right and behind you and you'll see a mountain that looks like a Sphinx. Head north twenty miles. You'll reach a canyon. It's called the Bear Trap. Head west three miles and then go north; you'll go over a pass and find the Madison again. Just before the end of the river, you'll see a buffalo jump. The Crows'll find you and guide you. Watch out, because Blackfeet come there to hunt this time of year. Just follow the Madison; it's joined by the Jefferson to the left and the Gallatin to the right. These rivers form the Missouri. It then heads north and then turns east. You will come to the Great Falls that Lewis and Clark discovered. Don't try and go through this, you'll find the bypass around it. Then just follow the Missouri down to Fort Union, get on that boat of old Mike Fink's, and go to lovely Bridget's waiting arms."

"Thanks, brother."

He wanted to say more but they both knew that they would break down in front of the other men. They shook hands. He was about to go when the Liver-Eater, Del, Kit Carson, and Jim Bridger strode up. Johnston said, "Well, are you going to sell me Captain Clark's gun or not?"

"No, you can have it."

Johnston said, "Here's a hundred dollars. Consider it a wedding present."

He knew better than to argue and said, "Thanks, Liver-Eater. I mean Mr. Johnston."

"Just call me John. If you come back, I'll teach you how to survive on a diet of Crow liver."

Del howled. Ned and Bridger laughed. Even Kit Carson laughed.

"Thanks, John. I'll try if I come back."

Johnston said, "Don't let the savages get you!"

"Blackfeet?"

"No, them pig-eatin' savages in St. Louis."

"Don't worry, I can handle them."

"Watch your topknot, son," said the Liver-Eater.

"You too, boys," said Brian as he mounted Nell. He headed north and never looked back, for he didn't want them to see that he had tears in his eyes.

10

The rattlesnake lay under an outcropping of rock. It had just eaten a mouse and was languidly digesting it when it felt a repetitive, rhythmic sound heading its way: clop, clop, clop, clop, clop. When the sound was directly overhead the snake struck, driving its fangs into the big brown thing's leg, its venom spreading quickly into the horse's foreleg. Nell screamed and bucked Brian over her shoulder. She came down directly on the rattler's head, crushing it. She stomped it several times. The serpent died as his rattles slowly stopped shaking.

Nell stopped prancing and her agitation gradually wore off. She saw Brian lying unconscious on the ground. She felt pain, nausea, and something like shame at having thrown her master. She nuzzled him with her nose but was becoming increasingly weak. Her breathing grew labored as the venom's toxins reached her brain. She sensed that she was dying. She tried to get up and kick the thing again, but saw that it was dead. Her breathing was becoming more difficult. She cast a baleful eye at Brian. She couldn't move her legs and her head was becoming heavy. She draped her head across Brian's chest and listened to his slow breathing, his steady heartbeat.

Brian woke and to feel the pressure of Nell's head on his chest. He rolled out from under her, ordering, "Get up, Nell!" But Nell wouldn't move. Then he remembered the rattler striking Nell just before she reared. Out of the corner of his eye he saw the snake. Enraged, he grabbed it by its tail. The dead snake's reflexes caused its tail to buzz in his hand; Brian snapped it like a bullwhip until its head came off. He stabbed it into small pieces. Then he went back to Nell. Her flanks were heaving and he noticed that her hind leg was broken, the bone protruding through the skin. He cradled her head in his arms, hugging her and stroking her mane. He said softly, "Ah, sweet Nell, please don't die." But it was no use. She was dying, neighing softly in pain. He couldn't stand to watch her suffer but he couldn't bring himself to put her out of her misery. She looked up at him with one eye open and he saw her big soft brown eye had filled with tears. Cradling her head, he reached down and pulled out his Colt pistol so that she wouldn't see it. He soothingly stroked her head, hugged it, closed his eyes and pulled the trigger.

Nell convulsed once and she was gone. He held her for an hour, sobbing uncontrollably. He took off the packs and saddle, the scabbard with the Hawken, and the traps that he would no longer need. He found a shovel in his pack. His sorrow turned into maniacal fury as he dug a large hole for her. He buried Nell, covering her grave with dirt and large boulders so that wolves wouldn't get to her. He put a cross on top. He didn't build a fire but sat shivering on the boulders all night. Whenever a wolf ventured near he shot it. Brian killed six wolves that night. The remainder left at dawn. Next, a coyote came too close; he shot it, but it didn't die. He leaped to his feet, ran it down, and slit its throat. He had become an animal, killing for the sake of killing. He cut out the coyote's liver and ate it. He threw the carcass on Nell's grave, knowing that it would keep other coyotes away. Only then did he leave her grave.

He found a stream where he washed the blood from his hands and buckskins. Slowly Brian regained his sanity. He knew he was in serious trouble. He was just above Bear Trap Canyon with no horse or food and suddenly realized that he would never reach Fort Union by the 25th of September.

He put the traps on Nell's grave and set them, so that any

predators would be caught if they tried to dig her up. He cut a long piece of lodgepole and tied the pack to it. He took the Hawken out of its scabbard again, reloaded it, and threw the scabbard away. Slinging the pole over one shoulder, he checked his compass and headed west toward the pass with his Hawken in his other hand. He turned back and looked at the grave and said, "Good-bye, old Nell."

He made it to the pass and found the Madison as it came out of the Bear Trap. He camped next to the Madison that night. He built a fire, washed down some elk jerky with whiskey and fell into a much-needed but fitful sleep. He kept having a recurring nightmare where all he could see was Nell's soft, dark eye with a tear flowing from it.

Brian awoke when the sun came up over the Madison Range. It was cold. He got up and placed some more wood on the fire. The fire caught, warming him, and he began to feel better. He shot a deer that had come down to the river to drink, as he was ravenously hungry. He dressed it and had venison, biscuits and coffee for breakfast. He had seen several large rainbow trout rising in the river, so he set up trout lines using strips of venison as bait, as Ned had taught him. He aired out his blanket and buffalo robes, and began to take stock of how much powder, shot, and percussion caps he had left. He realized that he no longer had the luxury of shooting wolves and coyotes for the sake of killing them. He needed to hoard his ammunition, using it only to shoot edible game and protect himself against grizzlies and Indians. He then repacked his possessions, hauled in the trout lines, and cooked the three fat trout he had caught. He planned to take a nap, then head north along the Madison in the afternoon and night so that the darkness would hide him from Indians.

Brian was awakened from his nap by a blood-curdling scream. A Blackfoot had his arm around his neck. He couldn't breathe and he felt a searing pain in his scalp as the Blackfoot's knife tore through it. Somehow he managed to get free and wrested

45

the knife from the Indian's grip. Brian stabbed him in the chest several times and the Indian's eyes finally glazed over. Brian could barely see; blood kept streaming into his eyes. He tried to wipe the blood away but hair kept getting in his way. To his horror, he realized that a piece of his own scalp was dangling in front of his eyes. He felt his head. Part of his scalp was hanging over his forehead from a thin piece of flesh. He pulled his scalp back and, drawing the Blackfoot's knife from his breast, Brian cut through the thin piece of flesh that still held the piece of scalp to his head. He was bleeding profusely and growing increasingly dizzy. He dunked his head in the ice-cold river, and slowly the bleeding stopped. Then he threw the Blackfoot's body into the river. It rapidly disappeared downstream in the rapids.

He went back to his gun just as a second Blackfoot attacked. The Hawken roared and the ball ripped open the Indian's naked chest. The brave died instantly. Brian shuddered. He knew if the Indians' bodies were found, they would hunt him down like a dog. Quickly he took off his own clothes, undressed the Indian, and changed clothes with him. Fighting his nausea, Brian cut off the brave's nose, hands and feet, disfiguring the face so it would be unrecognizable. He cut off the Indian's entire scalp and threw all of the body parts into the river. He made sure that the Indian's blood soaked his buckskins. He took his own scalp, drove his knife through it and into the Indian's chest, and dragged the Indian next to the bank. He then pulled his pack next to the Indian. He got a pine bough and brushed away all the evidence of their skirmish as well as of his camp, all the way to the corpse. Next, he picked up his pack and rifle and forded the river, throwing the pine bough downstream. Whoever found the corpse, Brian hoped, would think it was him. He walked downstream on the opposite bank of the river for about a mile and got out. He checked his compass bearings, put on his remaining buckskin shirt and buffalo robe, and trudged along the lower Madison toward the buffalo jump. At dawn he found an uninhabited cave. He pulled out his blanket, made sure his Hawken was loaded, and placed it inside his blanket and robe. As he drifted off to sleep, Brian still could not believe that he had killed two Indians and mutilated one beyond recognition. Just as he was about to fall asleep, he remembered the deer—and also the fact that the Indian's eyes were brown while his own were blue. Then, to his relief, he realized that the wolves and coyotes would take care of the deer and the predatory ravens would make sure no one ever saw the color of the Indian's eyes. He fell into a deep, dreamless sleep.

At that same moment, Ned and Jim Bridger dismounted and saw two snarling wolves caught in the traps Brian had set over Nell's grave. They shot them both. They saw his scabbard. Ned was concerned that Brian might be buried under the rocks. But Bridger said, "No, here's his tracks heading toward the pass." Then they surveyed the carnage around them. There were six dead wolves, one dead rattlesnake cut to pieces, a dead coyote with its liver missing, and one buried horse.

"Looks like poor Brian had himself a hell of a night," said Ned.

"I think he picked up one of Johnny Johnston's bad habits."

"What?"

"Did you notice that coyote's liver was gone?"

"Brian wouldn't do that...he's such a kind kid."

"Looks like to me he went on a rampage and killed everything in sight. Must have went crazy after Nell died. I think the snake got Nell and then Brian killed it, as well as the wolves and coyotes. He couldn't carry out the traps so he left them to protect Nell's grave."

"Well, let's go find him before he gets scalped. We can find Colter's Hell after that," said Ned worriedly.

"Well, it's not too bad around here; the Crows are pretty friendly. Sometimes the Shoshones and the Sioux come here to hunt, but they're pretty hospitable too." Bridger was certain they were within fifteen miles of Colter's Hell.

"Aye, but you've forgotten one thing, Jim—the Blackfeet come down here to hunt too. The lad won't last a day out here amongst them without a horse."

"All right. Let's track him, get him on his way back to Fort Union and then, by God, we're going to come back here and find it once and for all."

They rode off quickly and made it over the pass. They followed his tracks and found the remains of a deer.

"Strange, no campfire. It looks as if this area has been swept clean," said Bridger. Ned was elated. He had taught Brian to do that. Maybe the boy would survive till they found him. He reminded himself that Brian was no longer a boy. He had turned eighteen last week; he was large and powerful and could stay cool under fire. Ned's hopes were dashed when he saw the body next to the river. He recognized Brian's buckskins, his hair and knife protruding from its chest. "Bastards! They scalped him and killed him with his own knife. Jim, could you do me a favor and just go over and see if he might be alive? I can't bring myself to look at him."

Jim went over. The boy was dead, all right. They had mutilated him beyond recognition. It didn't add up, as there were no tracks to the river. Maybe he had come up upstream and was attacked as he got out. Who knows, thought Bridger. They could be next. He wanted to get out of there. He pulled out Brian's knife, cleaned it in the river and gave it to Ned. They buried him and headed back to the Bear Trap. Brian's grave had overwhelmed him. Finally, as they reached the summit he said, "Poor lad, he never had a chance. He was so sweet and loved the Indians so."

"Yeah, it's a shame. You taught him well and he learned all he needed to know. It's not your fault. Besides, you can't blame all Indians for Brian's death. Only the Blackfeet hate us."

"For now," said Ned sullenly.

"Look down there," said Bridger. "I know we're close. See

the Sphinx? Well, just south of it there's a break in the mountains above Henry's Lake. The Madison comes out of there. All we have to do is follow it up and we'll find Colter's Hell."

Ned said, "All right. Once we find it, I've got to get a letter to his Da and Bridget. I can't believe he's dead, poor kid. Just felt so bad for killing that Indian—and now they've got him."

Little did they know that Brian was sleeping in a cave ten miles away and had killed three more Indians than the two of them combined.

11

Brian awoke in the cave at about seven in the evening. The sun wouldn't be down for another few hours. He was already cold and hungry. He ate some jerky and knew that he had to get back on a regular schedule of sleeping at night. He had acted completely insane, eating the coyote's liver, mutilating Indians and the like. Yet he marveled at his own quick thinking, which had kept the other Blackfeet off his trail. If he could make it to the Buffalo Jump, the Crow would help him. He peered out the cave and looked for any sign of Indians. He hurried down to the river, drank some water, and rushed back to the cave. He castigated himself for not taking his rifle with him. He knew that he wasn't thinking rationally. He had to get more food.

At dusk he crept back down to the river and set trout lines. He gathered some firewood and brought it into the cave. He shaved some kindling and set the wood so that when he got back he could light a fire in the cave where no one could see it. He set his flint next to the wood, packed his meager belongings, and tied the pack to the pole. He cleaned the Hawken and reloaded it. Fortunately his powder had remained dry in crossing the river. When it was dark he checked his lines and pulled in a fat rainbow, a cutthroat trout, and a small salmon. He returned to the cave, cleaned them, and cooked them. He ate quickly, doused the fire and broke camp.

He walked north all night along the Madison. At dawn he saw a promontory above the river. That had to be the

Buffalo Jump. He backtracked up the bank to the plateau above the river. He headed toward the precipice, noticing that all around him were large boulders that formed a V with its apex pointed to the cliff. Everything was quiet: No birds were singing, no wildlife was visible. Just then the earth began to shake and a muffled roar came from the ground. "Earthquake!" he thought, as he saw dust rising. Suddenly an Indian wearing a buffalo head and robes ran straight toward him. Close behind him were hundreds of stampeding buffalo. The Indian ran past him and disappeared over the Jump. From behind the boulders Crow Indians suddenly appeared, shooting their rifles in the air. He started to run towards the nearest boulder. A huge bull was charging him, its horns lowered. Just as Brian was about to be gored, strong arms pulled him over the boulder. He somersaulted over and landed flat on his back, his rifle out of reach. He tried to reach for it but was momentarily stunned— the wind had been knocked out of him. His rescuer looked at him and laughed, then turned his back and began shooting again toward the buffalo. Brian was saved. He had found the Crow. Slowly, he got up and watched in amazement as the buffalo, one by one, stampeded over the cliff.

The Indians whooped merrily and Brian too was soon caught up in the excitement. Finally, the herd stopped and reversed directions and the Jump was cleared. To his astonishment, the Indian wearing the buffalo head pulled himself back up over the cliff; he had perched on a ledge below the stampeding buffalo. The other Crows lifted him on their shoulders and whooped in victory. His rescuer approached him and they offered each other the sign of peace. Brian gave him some turquoise beads. The Indian smiled appreciatively and gave him his hunting bonnet of eagle feathers. They talked in sign language. Brian learned that the hunter was called "Many Coupes," but when he tried to explain that his own name was Brian, it was obvious that there was no translation. "Many Coupes" signed that Brian's name was to be

"Man-Who-Outjumps-Buffalo." They both laughed as they headed towards the Crow camp. Coming in the other direction were squaws with horses and travois which would carry the dressed remains of the buffalo. Brian was so happy to be among these jubilant Indians; these were the noble people that Captain Clark and Ned had told him about. The camp was in an uproar with hunters and warriors shouting, children laughing, and older squaws busily preparing a feast. Fires were built, pipes were smoked. They danced and sang hunting songs late into the night. Brian awkwardly tried to imitate their dances, much to the amusement of the Crows. The young squaws demurely approached him and tried to teach him the proper way to dance. Gradually, he learned some of the steps. One of the squaws was stunningly beautiful with deep brown, soulful eyes. She was Many Coupes' younger sister, White Fawn. Brian felt drawn to her but wisely kept his distance, for he had noticed a sinister-looking warrior watching them. His name was Spotted Owl and Brian could sense that he was hopelessly in love with the young squaw. Days passed and Brian became closer to Many Coupes. One morning he and Many Coupes, communicating in both sign language and some basic Crow that Brian had picked up, discussed Brian's quest. When Many Coupes learned that Brian needed to get to Fort Union, he offered Brian a horse.

Brian jumped at the offer. He gave Many Coupes the Blackfoot's knife, which was valuable to the Crows, and the bargain was sealed. The next day he departed with Many Coupes as his guide to the headwaters of the Missouri. As he left, he saw White Fawn gazing at him longingly and felt the piercing stare of Spotted Owl on his back as they departed the Crow camp. In two hours they reached the three forks of the Madison, Gallatin, and Jefferson Rivers. Brian and Many Coupes exchanged the sign of peace. Then Many Coupes turned back west and Brian started east along the Missouri, hoping to reach Fort Union before the last steamer for St. Louis departed on the twenty-fifth. He rode all day and into the night before finally setting up camp on the banks of the Missouri. He would get back to Bridget after all.

The next morning when he awoke, a chill was in the air and cold, howling winds were blowing in from the north. A storm was brewing, and it smelled like snow. He hastily broke camp and pushed the Indian pony into a gallop towards the Great Falls.

12

N ed and Jim Bridger rode back south along the Madison. It was barren country with few trees. There were low bluffs overlooking the river where nothing but prairie grass grew. Buffalo roamed the bluffs, and the winds howled incessantly. No wonder the Indians thought this place was haunted. The Bannock and Shoshone tribes would only venture here in the summer to hunt buffalo. It bothered them that the river ran south to north. The Crow who lived east of here along the Big Horn went far north to the Buffalo Jump. Bridger knew he was going to find Colter's Hell. The Crow thought that the place was especially haunted. He was sure that if he followed the Madison into the mountains, he'd find it. He could never find it coming up west from the Yellowstone. It had to be there!

"Hurry on, Ned. You look like you've lost your best friend." Bridger immediately regretted saying it, but it was too late.

"I just may have," said Ned morosely.

"Look, we all know the risks of this hunting life. You can die any number of ways—Indians, weather, wild animals—but he could just as easily have been shot in a saloon in St. Louis. At least he got to see God's country. Why, I'd rather die out here any day than live with them civilized dandies back East. Most of them couldn't skin a rabbit, let alone a grizzly bear, and they wouldn't last more than three days out here. So cheer up. We're going to make history!"

Ned smiled and said, "Aye, we are lucky. Let us explore and find it."

They rode up into the timber and looked down where the Madison cut through a deep canyon. Higher up, on a beautiful lush plateau, it split into two rivers. They bore right, along a river whose water was warmer and had a sulfurous taste. They named it the Firehole River. Herds of elk and buffalo were everywhere. The place was absolutely breathtaking. The higher up the Firehole, the warmer the water became. Soon they saw mud that bubbled out of the ground. The air began to smell like rotten eggs. They rode into a meadow and saw steam coming from the ground. Ned, who had been speechless, crossed himself and said, "Jaysus, it looks like we've found Lucifer's living room."

"This is it! It's just like John Colter said," exclaimed Bridger. "It's beautiful, and yet it's hell on earth." As he spoke, a stream of water began to shoot up into the air, accompanied by a low rumbling sound. The horses shied away as it rose higher and higher. Finally a plume of steam and water rose a hundred and twenty feet into the air. They were horrified, yet they couldn't keep their eyes off it. They got their horses under control and continued on by, Ned continuously rising up in his saddle and craning his neck to get a better look into the steamy ponds.

"Whatcha lookin' fer?"

"Devils," said Ned. "Hell's gotta be right below us."

"Nonsense. This country's too pretty to have hell nearby. You didn't see Satan sitting on top of that geyser, did ye?"

"No."

"Well then, quit acting like some superstitious Indian."

As they rode on, the geyser erupted again, sending its plume skyward at exactly the same height as before. They decided to hobble the horses and see if it happened again. Sure enough, it erupted about twenty minutes later. Bridger took out his timepiece, and so did Ned. Exactly twenty minutes later it rose again.

After clocking three more eruptions it was obvious that the geyser had a predictable timetable. Exclaimed Ned. "She's as faithful as me old timepiece," Bridger grinned and said, "Let's call her 'Old Faithful.'" They laughed, remounted, and headed further upward. Soon they escaped the smell of the geysers. They shot an elk and had a sumptuous dinner. They were able to boil the meat in one of the bubbling water holes. They slept uneasily, but when they awoke neither had seen any devils or ghosts. They finally began to relax and enjoy the incredible grandeur of the place.

"I wish Brian could have seen this," said Ned.

"It is indeed a special place," said Bridger. "Even the Liver-Eater and Kit would be in awe of it."

They rode on and saw a large blue lake filled with cutthroat trout. Eagles and ospreys circled endlessly, then dived to the surface, invariably rising up with a large fish in their talons. At the far end of the lake was an enormous waterfall.

"What grandeur! If this place is haunted, then I'm Pontius Pilate!" exclaimed Ned.

Bridger laughed. "I think we'd better head down the Yellowstone—a storm's brewing, and it smells like snow to me." They headed east down into Paradise Valley as the first flakes floated to the ground. They found a sheltered area with plenty of firewood. They feasted on more of the elk. The campfire was warm. The horses were hobbled nearby to share its warmth.

"Well, Jim. Where are you spending your winter?"

"I think I'm gonna head back to the Ute camp to see my wife. How about you?"

"I'm going up to Fort Union."

"What for?" asked Bridger. "You're welcome to winter with me. We got good huntin' and there are plenty of beautiful available squaws. You could use a good wife."

"Thanks just the same, but I need to send a letter to Brian's father to tell him of his son's demise. Besides, there's a dentist there who's a poor card player and likes to contribute to my gold supply."

"Be careful in them saloons—you can get killed there easier than you can out here. Civilization ain't good for your health."

"Aye. But those saloons are good for me 'tooth.'"

Jim Bridger gave Ned a quizzical look, decided not to ask about Ned's teeth, rolled over and went to sleep. Ned did the same. He entertained the thought of joining Bridger and frolicking with the squaws. He really dreaded writing Brian's dad. Then again, the saloons at Fort Union were nice and warm, the whiskey and gambling were good, and he missed some of the whores. He smiled and fell into a deep sleep as the snow settled around them. The next morning Bridger headed east and Ned headed north.

13

The snow squalls were blinding yet Brian doggedly drove the pony on. It was not uncommon to have snow this early in the year, but time was running out to get to Fort Union. Fortunately, the Indian pony seemed to go forever. It was far more spirited than Nell. The snow stopped after a few hours and not much had stuck to the ground. He noticed that the hills were no longer green; they were now golden brown. The aspen trees glowed in beautiful orange colors. The mountains were beginning to collect snow on their peaks. Geese were making their way south. Montana was beautiful in the spring and summer but after the fall and early snows, Brian knew that the winter would be treacherous. The wind howled incessantly, biting into his cheeks and hands. Fortunately he had gotten warm buckskin leggings from the Crows, and a new buffalo robe as well. It was much warmer than his old one, which had become infested with fleas. He had also traded for a beaver cap which not only was warm but hid his slowly healing forehead and scalp. He had felt some tufts of hair growing back. His scalp was itchy but had not become infected. He remembered feeling very self-conscious about his looks around White Fawn, but she seemed not to notice and did not comment about it. Many Coupes was in awe of his "medicine" at surviving a scalping. When Brian told him of dispatching the two Blackfeet, the Crow treated him with respect. He wondered vaguely if his hair would have grown back by the time he saw Bridget.

Even though the snow had stopped, the winds slowed his

progress. He remembered Ned telling him how the winds in the winter drove white men crazy. He pushed on for three days, sleeping only a few hours a night and surviving on jerky, pemmican, and water. The next day the sun came out but it was still bitterly cold.

Then he heard the roar of the falls. Captain Clark had told him that this was the most treacherous part of their journey; how they had portaged their canoes around the steep cliffs. He knew that he would have to go down the south side of the falls. When he got there, however, the mist from the falls had frozen on the surface of the rocks. The pony began to slip more often. Finally he dismounted and they picked their way down through the icy cliffs. He found a game trail and followed it. But the sun went behind the clouds and it started to snow again.

For the first time in his life Brian was certain that he was going to die. The cold was merciless and the wind picked up. Ice formed in his beard and eyelashes. When he could no longer see, he grabbed the pony's tail and followed him down the slippery trail.

At nightfall, they arrived below the falls. He found a stand of trees protected from their icy mist and hobbled the pony. He was too exhausted to eat or build a fire. He curled up in his robes, hoping that he would somehow stop shivering and survive the night. When he awoke the next morning it was still bitterly cold, but the sun was out and he guessed that it was close to noon. He had to get moving! It was three days' hard ride to Fort Union. He wasn't sure of the date but he thought that it was September twentieth or twenty-first. He *had* to make it. Onward they rode. Ice was beginning to form on the banks of the Missouri. If it iced up, the steamers would never make it down the Missouri—or worse, Mike Fink would leave before the twenty-fifth.

Brian rode all day and night, following the river. At noon Brian stopped to eat and let the pony graze. As he ate he heard a strange wailing song. He followed the sound into the woods and saw an Indian about his own age, sitting in a clearing, his eyes closed, singing softly. Brian pulled the trigger back on the Hawken. When it clicked, the Indian opened his eyes—then closed them and resumed his chant. Brian was flabbergasted, for the Indian showed no fear whatsoever. After another ten minutes the Indian stopped, then opened his eyes and stared at him, bemused. Brian smiled and they offered each other the sign of peace. Then Brian lowered his rifle and the Indian rose to his feet and strode fearlessly toward him. He seemed to be about Brian's weight but was much shorter and broader, bowlegged, with a slight limp. Brian sensed that he was very powerful, yet serene and good-natured. They talked in sign language. His name was Sitting Bull and he was a Hunkpapa Sioux. Brian tried to tell him his name in English but it was impossible. The Indian laughed and finally Brian gave him his Indian name: 'Man-Who-Outjumps-Buffalo.' Sitting Bull laughed and signed that since he was short and Brian was tall, he could indeed outjump him...especially since his name was Sitting Bull. They both laughed. The Indian said, "You look hungry. Stay here and I will get us some berries to eat." Brian lay down and promptly fell asleep.

The bear weighed perhaps eight hundred pounds, and her two cubs were thirty feet away. She smelled a man approaching the bushes between her and her cubs, her hackles rose and she snorted. The man stopped. One of her cubs started to run toward the man. She grunted and the man froze. She stood up and roared, but her cub kept coming. She got down on all fours and charged, bowling the man over and slashing at him with her claws. He rolled over, motionless. Before she could determine whether he was dead, she heard a second man crashing through the bushes behind her with a big black stick, yelling. She knocked him down and turned to close her jaws on his head. She saw him gag at the smell of her breath; she felt the fear in him. She would crush him! Then she sensed the first man coming behind her and felt a sharp pain as he stuck a sharp object into her side. She turned to attack him. Growling, she stood on her hind legs to frighten him off and warn

PADDIES

her cubs to stay away. As the bear dropped to all fours to try to kill the first man, she heard a sound like thunder behind her, followed by an intense pain in the back of her head. She was dizzy and could not see. Worse, she could not feel anything. She fell over backwards. Faintly sensing the second man coming around in front of her, she tried to slash at him with her claws—but her arms wouldn't move. She heard him cursing, then the sound of something being pushed down a tube. She growled but her breathing was becoming very rapid; the pain in her head was terrible. She could begin to see again out of her left eye and heard a loud click as he stood over her. He pointed the black stick at her; she felt an explosion in her chest. Fire and smoke came from the stick. Then she heard the loud thunder again. Everything went black.

Brian was shaking uncontrollably as he rammed another ball into the Hawken. The cubs were mewling loudly. He put the barrel into the grizzly's mouth when Sitting Bull motioned him to stop, saying, "she is dead." Brian's first shot had been the luckiest of his whole life. The ball had broken the bear's neck and entered her brain. He pointed the gun at one of the cubs, thinking it would not survive the winter without its mother. But Sitting Bull gently took the gun from him and signed, "Do not kill them; they are sacred. Besides, we have plenty of meat now." Brian noticed that the Indian was bleeding heavily from his left arm. Sitting Bull stared at him and smiled. He pointed at Brian's leggings and said, "Man cannot outjump me now his legs are too wet." Brian realized, to his great annoyance, that he had wet himself. "Do not be ashamed," Sitting Bull added encouragingly. "You are a brave man and a great hunter." Brian dressed Sitting Bull's arm and stopped the bleeding.

Sitting Bull placed herbs on Brian's chest where it had been slashed by the grizzly bear. They dressed the carcass, and Brian gave the bearskin to Sitting Bull, who would need it for warmth. In turn, Sitting Bull ceremoniously presented the bear's claws to Brian and promised to make a necklace of them for him. As they cooked the meat, the cubs howled piteously in the forest and Brian felt sad for them. He signed to Sitting Bull that he must leave immediately for Fort Union. Sitting Bull sadly signed that Brian's pony had bolted and that they would never find him. Sitting Bull was on foot and badly injured. Alone, Brian finally faced the prospect of spending the winter in Montana.

"Come," said Sitting Bull. "You will stay with us this winter. We will keep you warm and full of buffalo meat. You are my savior and brother. Let us depart to my camp."

They trudged east toward the Dakotas, missing Fort Union by fifty miles. The weather became even colder and snow squalls slowed their progress. En route, he learned that Sitting Bull was seventeen years old. He had been called "slow" by his family because of his methodical way of analyzing things. He had been named Sitting Bull at the age of fourteen when he had recklessly charged into battle with Crows and had counted his first coupe. He had acquired his limp that very year when he charged a Crow chieftain and was wounded by a rifle ball in his heel.

Sitting Bull casually killed the Crow and had become a leading warrior of the Hunkpapas at the age of seventeen. Brian told him of his friendship with Many Coupes. Sitting Bull darkly said that the Crows were his sworn enemies. He told them of their war parties against his people and how they had killed his relatives. Brian was silent, for he loved the Crows. Sitting Bull told him not to worry, that since he had saved his life, no Sioux would ever harm him, despite his friendship with the Crows.

The last two days of their journey were freezing torture. Sitting Bull's limp was getting worse and his arm was losing blood again. Brian half-carried Sitting Bull to his lodge one night during a blizzard. His father, Jumping Bull, hugged them and his mother cried at the sight of them. They lay down next to the fire and

PADDIES

Sitting Bull's mother gave them buffalo stew. She treated their wounds with herbs and covered them with robes. They slept for two days.

14

Brian awoke in a warm strange place and realized that he was in a lodge. He got up, made sure that his rifle and his bag were in the corner, then went outside and relieved himself. To his surprise, the weather was mild. The snow had melted. He went down to the stream nearby and washed his face. Several Indian women smiled demurely at him. Walking up the creek looking for Sitting Bull, he encountered three Sioux warriors whose faces showed neither hostility nor friendliness.

They walked past him. He then saw a familiar but older face, although he couldn't quite remember how he knew the man. Suddenly the Indian rushed to Brian and embraced him. "Thank you for saving my son," said the man.

"You know English?"

"A little. The missionaries taught us. What is your name?"

Brian quickly answered, "Oh, never mind. My name is Man-Who-Jumps-Over-Buffalo."

The Indian laughed. "My name is Jumping Bull. One day we will see who jumps the highest. Someday I will tell you how I and my son were named. I am proud of him. He will be a great leader of our people. He also has powers to see the future."

"I wish he could have foreseen that grizzly bear."

Jumping Bear did not quite catch the meaning of his quip but said, "Ah, the yellow bear—a ferocious spirit. My wife, Mixed Day, has made a necklace of the bear's claws for you.

Tonight we honor you for your bravery. You are a great hunter."

"Thank you," said Brian.

Just then Sitting Bull came down the path and smiled at Brian. He always seemed to be smiling. As they walked back to the camp, Brian noticed the way squaws were smiling at Sitting Bull. The little children adored him, and even the dogs loved him—he was constantly petting them and throwing sticks. Brian also noticed that the Sioux women were taller than other Indian women that he had seen. Their legs were not thick, but very shapely, and they had proud, beautiful faces. Brian caught himself musing that he might even enjoy the winter here with his new young friend.

That night around a big ceremonial fire, two Indian men and a warrior wearing a bear's pelt reenacted the battle that Brian and Sitting Bull had fought with the grizzly. Brian did not understand much of what was said, but the whole thing sent chills through him as he realized what he had done and how lucky they were to be alive. Finally, Jumping Bull asked him to stand and placed the bearclaw necklace around his neck. The men whooped and danced around Brian and Sitting Bull and his family. They stopped when an old medicine man began to sing and gesture toward Brian. They all nodded signs of approval, then passed a pipe and smoked it.

Brian coughed and several squaws giggled. After a feast of buffalo and elk meat the dancing resumed. Several beautiful young women taught Brian to dance like a Sioux brave. He caught on slowly. Yes, a winter with the Sioux might not be so bad. After all, Bridget would still be there when he got back.

15

Ned rode straight into the saloon at Fort Union the night of September 24th. The bartender shook his head as Ned's horse kicked the barstool out of its way. Several whores shrieked at the commotion as Ned exclaimed, "Well, lad, how about a whiskey for a poor thirsty Irishman?"

"Get that horse out of here, O'Grady, goddamnit!" swore the bartender.

"Can't I have a drink first?"

"Not until you tie that horse up outside."

"You're getting mighty testy in your old age," grumbled Ned as he backed the horse through the swinging doors. "By the way, Mr. Fink—please don't leave—I have a letter that desperately needs to reach St. Louis." Mike Fink grunted in his direction as Ned ducked to keep from hitting his back on the doorjamb.

Ned took his horse, Hell Bastard, down to the livery stable, and left his pelts and traps with Henry Jacobs, the livery master, for safekeeping. He took his Hawken with him back to the saloon. "Now can I have a whiskey? Me 'tooth' is quite severe, you know."

"Good to see you, Ned. I see you still got your scalp on," said Michael Boyd, the bartender, as he poured Ned a stiff drink.

"Where's Brian?"

"I'm afraid the boy lost his. Some Blackfoot got him on the Madison. I've got a letter to send to his Da in St. Louis to tell him."

"'Tis sad—he was a nice boy. Damn Blackfoot," said Boyd.

"Well, he was in their hunting grounds. You know they don't tolerate our presence there."

"Just the same, he was so young, so quiet. Did he ever open up to you very much?"

"No," answered Ned. "He didn't like to talk much about himself. I did find out his Da's a doctor, and he was going to marry a young lass in St. Louis. He was on his way back to catch tomorrow's steamer. I wish I'd gone with him—maybe I could have saved him."

"Not likely, the country's full of Indians. He probably would have died the same way." said Boyd. "Stop blaming yourself."

"Ah, you're right," sighed Ned. "How 'bout another whiskey, Michael me lad?" Ned carried his drink over to Mike Fink's table. "Mr. Fink? Good evening, sir. I have a favor to ask of you."

"What's that?" growled Fink.

Ned told Brian's story and explained how he himself had ridden all the way from the Yellowstone to deliver the letter.

"I remember him," said Fink. "Nice boy. Didn't say much, was never in any trouble on board."

"Yes, that was Brian. I'll miss him."

"Well, it would be an honor to deliver the letter," said Fink.

"Thank you. Could I get you a drink to repay your kindness?" asked Ned.

"Nah, I got a fight or two coming up in a few minutes. You could get me one after I beat a couple of 'em to a pulp, though."

"Ah, yes. I remember now. You like to establish who's boss before you set sail."

"It is very effective in keeping order on board," said Fink.

"Have you ever lost?"

"Nah."

"What would you do if you ever did?" asked Ned.

"Oh, I'd let him on board and when we were about ten minutes down the Missouri, then I'd keelhaul him."

Ned knew that Mike Fink was no one to mess with. This was proven in the next ten minutes when Ned saw him drop three challengers from among the crew and passengers under his barrage of furious punches. Afterwards, he drank a beer with Ned, and Fink promised that he would make sure that Dr. McCaffrey received Ned's letter. He then politely excused himself and headed out to his paddlewheeler.

"Has anyone seen the good Doctor Burch lately?" asked Ned.

"He probably won't be in tonight. He'll be here tomorrow for sure to play poker."

"Ah, delightful," sighed Ned. "Well, Louisa, what are me chances of a lovely poke tonight?" She was Ned's favorite woman. She was petite, with strong, beautiful legs, and nice but not large breasts. Most of all, he loved her face. She wasn't beautiful, but she was pretty, with curly black hair, dark eyes, and a beautiful smile. Ned couldn't quite figure out if it was her smile or her witty intelligence that he liked most about her. All he knew was that he loved to simply sit and talk with her. The sex wasn't bad either, but Ned just liked to be around her. She was the only thing that he missed about civilization. She liked him, too. Often she wouldn't charge him, but Ned would manage to sneak some change onto her dresser.

Louisa smiled and said, "Chances are poor unless you wash first. You smell rather gamey to me. I could give you a bath—free of charge, of course."

"Why Louisa, that would be most delightful. Would you mind if I smoked a cigar and had some whiskey to drink while you bathed me?"

"Not if you share, Ned," she smiled. He loved her soft little laugh. God, he had missed her, and hadn't even realized it until now. He excused himself, ordered a bottle of whiskey and a cigar, and returned to the table. She stood, gazing at him with her shining dark eyes. He offered her his arm and they marched proudly up the steps to her room.

"Ah, the lovely Louisa! I've missed your companionship, my dear."

She patted his hand and smiled. "I've missed you too, darling Ned."

He wondered if she said that to all her customers. Somehow he didn't think so, but he knew his pride was doing the talking here. At any rate, he didn't care. He couldn't wait to be inside her. He knew that afterward they would cuddle together, sharing their deepest thoughts and fears through the wee hours of the night. He loved that as much as the sex. Just being next to Louisa, listening to her voice, smelling her, sharing her warmth and laughter…She was his best friend.

16

The cold winds were unrelenting, permeating everything. It had been three weeks since Brian had seen the sun. The walls inside of the lodges were covered with frost. Only the fire inside and their robes kept them from freezing to death. The weather bothered Brian much more than the Sioux. They seemed impervious to the cold. When the children went out in the snow to play, they dressed lightly. The warriors often spent hours outside shirtless. Brian, in the meantime, wore all his clothes and robes when going out to relieve himself. He also noticed that he required more food than the Indians. He felt badly about this, but they seemed not to mind. Sitting Bull openly teased him about his appetite. "If Jumping Man continues to eat so much, he won't be able to jump over a stone, let alone a buffalo." The Sioux had shortened his name to "Jumping Man" and included him into their lives.

Brian marveled at how simple their lives were and yet how, in their customs and survival skills, they were much more sophisticated than white men. He was intrigued by the children and their play. Superficially the boys games looked violent: The boys would stalk each other, pounce upon their victim, and begin to wrestle or even punch him. They also played games with bows and blunt-tipped arrows, which rarely resulted in more than a bruise. Their parents never interfered with their fighting; it was the way the boys learned to survive. As the boys grew older, they would need these skills to survive attacks by grizzlies, mountain lions, stampeding buffalo, the Crow and Blackfoot tribes, and eventually their most dangerous predator—the U.S. Cavalry.

The girls were more docile, with sweet smiles and big brown expressive eyes. They followed their mothers and learned to gather wood, sew, clean game, and pack up the lodges and move them. Brian was amazed at how much work the women did. It seemed that all the men had to do was to find the game and kill it. The women did all the heavy work while the men celebrated and bragged about their skills at hunting, stealing horses, or counting coupes on their enemies. The women never showed any resentment and were very affectionate towards their husbands and children.

Yet for all their submissiveness, one disapproving look from their flashing black eyes and furrowed brows could reduce the bravest warrior to slinking about the lodge like a flea-bitten coyote. The women could be cruel to one another. There were definite cliques and hierarchies among the Sioux. Weakness and, worst of all, infidelity were not tolerated by them. If a woman tried to seduce another's husband, the wife would inflict disfiguring wounds upon the transgressor with knives, tomahawks, or rocks, whatever was available.

Brian was horrified one day when Running Dog's wife attacked a young squaw and cut off her nose and an ear before the braves stopped her from killing the young woman with a rock. Ironically, if a man wanted a second wife, the first wife could do nothing about it but accede to her husband's wishes, sometimes enduring the ignominy of having to listen to her husband and the new wife make love as she lay next to them in the darkness. Once the husband left for the day they would bicker and taunt one another, but to inflict physical harm was forbidden. Brian wondered why a man would want more than one wife(having one seemed complicated enough).

It grew colder each day. As far as he could tell, it was now mid-December. Food and wood were still plentiful, but he knew that sooner or later they would have to hunt to make it through the winter. The days were shorter this far north; they all slept a lot. He noticed that the Indians were more content than Whites to sit for hours and talk about their ancestors, or how the earth, sun, moon and stars were formed—stories that fascinated Brian. He also noted vague similarities between the Indians' religious beliefs and those of white Christians. Some of their minor deities seemed similar to those of the ancient Egyptians and Romans. As the winter progressed, Brian's interest in the Sioux stories spurred his interest in their language, and he became quite adept at speaking and understanding the Sioux dialect. Sitting Bull and he often listened to the elders when they spoke about ancient battles with the Crows and other tribes. He learned to play Indian games of chance, which resembled playing dice, but he never seemed to win very often. He and Sitting Bull would also talk for hours about hunting game, about women and their ways, and about the great similarities and differences between their races. One day Sitting Bull said, "I know there will be a time when we will be at war with your kind. We Hunkpapas are originally from further east, the place you call Minnesota. The white men drove us out by killing our game and planting crops in our hunting grounds. We finally left and came here. We have vowed we will never give up this land or our way of life. Already the great warrior, Red Cloud, is talking of uniting all the Sioux to keep the white men out." Brian looked crestfallen. "Don't worry, my brother. We do not hate all white men. No Sioux would lay a finger on you because you are my friend and have saved my life. With each day you become more like us and less like your white brothers."

It was true. Brian's hair had grown in and he was wearing it in braids. He had shaved off his beard, and wore beads along with the bear-claw necklace. He had become more fastidious about cleaning himself and his teeth. He found going into the sweat lodges to purify himself to be invigorating. Afterwards, they would jump into an ice-cold stream, wash, and quickly return to the lodge for dinner, having long talks and smoking pipes. All in all, it was a very peaceful life.

Yet somehow, Brian had a sense of foreboding that this peaceful existence could never last. If it weren't for Bridget he probably would never return to St. Louis. Maybe, he thought, he could talk her into coming here with him? But he knew it was useless. Some time in the spring he would have to decide how he would live the rest of his life. For now, he was going to enjoy every moment that he spent with the Sioux.

17

The card floated lazily across the table and landed in front of Ned. He tucked it into his hand: the ace of spades. Ned frowned, looked Dr. Burch in the eye and said, "Not only will I match your wager, good doctor, but I'll raise it to twenty dollars."

"Damnit, O'Grady, you're either the luckiest Irishman in the world or the best bluffer I know. Since you're Irish, I'll bet you're bluffing. Call."

"Hah! Read 'em and weep. Full house," laughed Ned. "How about another whiskey, Dr. Burch?"

"Don't mind if I do," said the dentist. Ned walked over to the bar. He saw Louisa engaged in an animated discussion about the cost of her services with a French Canadian named Pierre McKenzie. He hadn't liked the man from the moment he saw him, but he didn't want to interfere with her life. Business was business, after all; this was how Louisa made her living. Yet it was becoming harder and harder for him not to be jealous when another man took her upstairs. Louisa saw him looking at her and winked at him, smiling his way, as the trapper tried to get her to lower her price. Ned stared darkly at the back of the man's head as he returned from the bar.

"Your deal, good doctor," he said grumpily.

"Why Ned, do I detect a bit of jealousy over lovely Louisa's business?" smiled Burch. "You're winning lots of money tonight and drinking fine spirits. Why the long face?"

"Appearances can be deceiving, doctor. I care not what

75

that woman does. Deal me another fine hand, will you, kind sir?"
Ned sourly asked for two more cards as Louisa and McKenzie went
up the stairs. She glanced worriedly back at Ned. Ned stared back
with a dour expression and tried to bluff his way through a lousy
hand. Burch grinned knowingly at Ned.

"I don't know which is a bigger lie…that you don't care
about her, or that you've got a good hand. Call."

Ned threw down his meager hand and said, "Here's your
twenty back." Burch laughed. Barely perceptible over his laughter
came the sound of a slap, followed by a muffled shriek. Ned bolted
up the stairs and kicked open Louisa's door. McKenzie was
straddled over her in his longjohns, with a knifetip indenting her
neck.

"Leave her be, swine," snarled Ned.

"Mind your own business; she won't do what I want," said
McKenzie.

"Get off her now or I'll kill you!" Louisa's eyes grew wider.
She was speechless and hyperventilating. She didn't know which
looked deadlier, the knife or the look in Ned's eyes. She couldn't
believe the fury contorting his face. McKenzie turned and whirled
off the bed and slashed at Ned.

"You stupid Irish fool! How can you kill me? I've got a
knife."

"Ah, but not for long." At which point Ned kicked
McKenzie directly in the balls.

As the man bent over, O'Grady hit him with a vicious head
butt. The French Canadian dropped the knife and its point became
embedded in the top of Ned's foot. Ned saw the knife stick there
but felt nothing but rage. He grabbed the French Canadian and
said, "I hope you enjoy your trip before you get to hell!"

"What?" mumbled McKenzie.

O'Grady picked him up and threw him out the second-
story window. The noise of shattering glass, broken wood, and
McKenzie's screams pierced the Montana night air. Ned pulled the

knife out of his foot and grabbed Louisa. She sobbed and shivered. He could smell fear in her sweat mixed with her sweet perfume. She held onto him. He tried to dry her wet lashes with his finger. He stroked her hair.

"Everything's fine, my sweet. Nothing can harm you. Old Ned's got you in his arms."

"Thank you, sweet Ned. He would have killed me."

"That reminds me...I need to make sure Mr. McKenzie keeps his appointment with Satan tonight."

He slipped from her grasp and said, "I'll be right back."

"Ned, please don't kill him."

"Louisa, your only fault is you're too kind."

He took the knife and went down the stairs and out into the street. McKenzie was still alive. Amazingly, his only injury was a broken rib. He was trying to get up when O'Grady pushed him onto his back with his foot. He noticed that his foot hurt and was bleeding on Pierre's chest. He knelt on the trapper's chest, holding the knife to the owner's throat. "Do you want to know what's the last thing you'll see on earth before you go to hell?"

"Please don't kill me! I'll leave now and never come back to this country."

"The last thing you're going to witness is me standing over you eating your liver, you French piece of merde."

"No! I beg of you...I meant no harm."

"If I ever hear of you mistreating a woman again, I will track you down and present you with a slow, painful death, and I'll keep my promise about your last sight on earth. Leave now or die!"

Ned went back inside. The French Canadian quickly got his horse and supplies and left town. O'Grady went upstairs and sat down next to Louisa on her bed. He brushed her hair and he held her in his arms. She finally stopped shaking and fell asleep with her head on his chest. He said softly over and over, "Sleep tight, my sweet. Old Ned's got you. Nothing can harm you now."

77

18

The late January winds howled. The blizzard was relentless. Buffalo and elk huddled in the shelter of the trees, whose bark was their only food. The Sioux meat supply was getting dangerously low. Fortunately, there was still plenty of pemmican. This year, most of the tribe's babies had survived childbirth and the many infectious diseases that the white settlers had introduced into the country. This year, there has been no outbreak of smallpox, which would normally have killed off many of the youngest children. But this meant that more nursing mothers and small children needed meat. Brian had begun to cut down on his own intake of food so that the mothers and children would have more to eat. His leggings and buckskin shirt were beginning to hang loosely on him. Curiously enough, however, he felt as if he had more energy; he felt stronger than he ever had. The Sioux always seemed to be one step ahead of starvation.

He had been honored to accompany the hunters on their forays for game. He had always been an excellent shot, and soon became revered by the Sioux as a great hunter. From Sitting Bull and Black Elk he had learned how to get downwind of the herds of buffalo and elk. He knew how to conceal himself among the rocks, timber and sage.

Brian also learned the most dangerous game of hide-and-go-seek ever invented: an Indian would cover himself with a buffalo hide, crawl among the buffalo herd, then suddenly lance a prime bull in the chest. Death was never instantaneous and the bull would charge the hidden attacker, who might be gored or trampled by the bull as the herd stampeded around them. Others used a bow and arrow, more effective than a single-shot rifle, as they could fire arrows more quickly than Brian could reload. If he missed the bull's heart he would be dead before he could reload. Strangely, he felt no fear as he had with the grizzly or the Blackfeet. He craved the excitement of stalking among these huge beasts. It was a deadly game, and he felt an intoxicating sense of power when one of the red-eyed snorting beasts, steam coming from its nostrils, finally toppled in front of him. He loved to stand close, like a matador, as its horns grazed him. He screamed out war whoops as they charged by. Standing tall and feeling invincible, with death all around him. Brian never felt more alive and happy than at these moments, and his bravery became legendary to his Sioux tribe.

Early one morning Sitting Bull and Black Elk woke him up, exclaiming excitedly that there was a herd of buffalo not far from their camp. He dressed quickly and checked that the Hawken was loaded and primed. He double-checked the percussion cap, lowered the hammer gently on the cap, and strode out into the frosty air. The sky was blue and the sun was coming up over the snow-covered white Big Horn range. Mist rose from the Little Big Horn river. God, how he loved it! The tension among the men palpable as they donned their hides and approached downwind of the herd.

Brian was the point man. He stifled a laugh as Sitting Bull, intent on stalking a large bull, carelessly stepped in a steaming pile of fresh buffalo dung. Sitting Bull rolled his eyes upward in disgust. Black Elk mockingly grimaced and held his nose. Sitting Bull broke the silence with an uncontrollable laugh. The huge bull snorted, pawed the earth, and charged straight at Brian. His only chance was a shot directly to the brain. He quickly pulled the hammer back and depressed the first trigger. No time! He pulled the back trigger—and the cap failed. Nothing! Now the bull was on him, horns aimed straight at his groin.

At the last instant he vaulted over the three-thousand

pound beast's eviscerating horns, grabbed the mangy fur behind them, reversed himself in mid-air, and mounted him. He was riding a furious killing machine at a speed of nearly forty miles an hour. The bull was bellowing, snorting, bucking, and throwing great clods of dirt and snow everywhere. The livid beast turned and rumbled toward Black Elk, who quickly lanced him through the heart–but not before the buffalo gored poor Black Elk in the chest. The bull trampled Black Elk and simultaneously tried to buck Brian off his twitching back. Sitting Bull had grabbed Brian's Hawken and began to bludgeon the bull with the stock. Finally, the beast collapsed and rolled over on Brian's leg. It lay gasping, still trying to gore him with its dying efforts.

Sitting Bull pried Brian's leg from under the black hulk. His leg was covered with blood and his hands ached from their death grip on the killer's mane. The two men staggered over to Black Elk. Blood poured from his chest. He was coughing blood, and his eyes were filled with pain and despair. Slowly, he began to sing his death song. As he did so, his face was no longer contorted with agony; it filled with serenity and peaceful acceptance of his death. He plaintively croaked at Brian to shoot him, as he was in great pain. "Kill me now, brother. I do not want to die in camp with wailing squaws and my family. Do it quickly, for I want to meet the Great Spirit." Brian put another cap on the nipple of the gun and aimed at Black Elk's head, but he couldn't pull the trigger. Finally, Sitting Bull grabbed the gun and mercifully dispatched Black Elk, freeing him from his agony.

"Never, never hesitate to put one of your brothers out of misery," raged Sitting Bull, who by now had tears in his sad dark eyes. "Promise me now that you would do the same for me or any of my Sioux brothers if need be."

"I'm sorry, Sitting Bull, I just couldn't do it. But I will if I have to. I give you my solemn promise."

"Very well, you are forgiven. I will never tell anyone about this. I'm sure Black Elk's spirit has forgiven you already as he felt your compassion for him. But you must never be weak about death—never!"

Sitting Bull stalked away and kicked the dead buffalo. Then he sank to his knees near Black Elk's body and began to wail a plaintive death chant into the cold blue air. Brian covered Black Elk with his buffalo hide, knelt down beside Sitting Bull, and joined him in the haunting song.

19

When Ned awoke, he saw her looking at him. "Well, Ned O'Grady, what are we going to do about ourselves?" "What do you mean, Louisa?" He got up out of bed and limped across the room. His foot looked awful and his head throbbed from drinking too much whiskey and head-butting Pierre McKenzie. He needed to clean his teeth and get the taste of stale cigars and rotgut whiskey out of his mouth. He wasn't in the mood to discuss his deepest feelings or future plans with her.

"I mean, we can't go on like this," she protested.

"Ah, Louisa, not now. Me head feels like a bloody battering ram."

"Do you love me?" she asked.

"Well, of course…I'm at least hopelessly infatuated with you," replied Ned lamely. He knew that he loved her but just couldn't muster up the courage to say it—especially this morning.

"That's a pretty vague answer, isn't it?"

"Didn't I risk my life for you last night? What more can a man do for a woman?"

"Ned, I see the way you look at me when I go upstairs with another man. It makes me feel so cheap and it's not good for my business."

"I know," he sighed, "but what else can we do?"

"You could propose to me."

Ned gulped. "Now? In me underwear?"

"Why not?"

"I just can't do that. When the time comes I want to do it properly, like a gentleman."

"You? A gentleman?"

"Yes. I have many refined qualities hidden by a thin veneer of rowdiness that you could only guess at." he answered.

"How could you support us? You know I like fine clothes and perfume and the theater. Oh, Ned—why don't we go to San Francisco? They've discovered gold in California! We could live there and open a boarding house with fine rooms and a lovely bar. I could study drama and become an actress on the stage. We would become rich and see plays and go to the opera."

"You? An actress?"

"Why not? I'm pretty and talented," she said wistfully. Ned had to admit that she did look lovely, standing there with the morning sun silhouetting her face and beautiful body.

"How do you know you can act?"

"Oh, Ned! Every time I'm with a man it's one big grand act."

"What about me?" asked Ned.

"With you it's different. You excite me and make me feel like a woman."

"Thank God for small favors...now, I didn't mean that the way it sounded," he said defensively. She looked hurt.

"Ah, Louisa. Why can't we stay here? I could trap for one more year, come back, and with the money I make we could have a fine homestead. I can farm and even teach, or open a school."

"You? *Teach?* What would you teach, profanity?" she smiled.

"No. I can teach history, philosophy, English, many things. I am, after all, a man of letters." She laughed and tousled his hair playfully and hugged him. They made love— not hurriedly but slowly, rhythmically, gently, and then again—wildly and passionately. She had him under her spell. She knew it and he knew it.

"What about children? I love children and want lots of them," announced Ned.

"Well, maybe someday," she answered moodily. He decided to let that one go by for now. He washed his face and said, "Why don't we go on with your business as usual? You could save money, too. I'll come back next year and then we'll decide how and where we want to live."

"All right," she said. "Have it your way. I'll never be able to tie you down."

"Ah, but you have...more than you could ever know, my sweet."

Ned couldn't limp out of there fast enough. He loved her, but he felt trapped. "Jaysus! Women! They're such lovely, cunning creatures." He loved her–but the thought of running a boarding house in a big city was the last way he wanted to spend the rest of his life.

20

A month after Black Elk was buried, the weather began to turn warmer. The snow began to melt down in the valley. Game was becoming more plentiful. At night, Brian could hear the ice in the river groan and crack above the cries of the wolves in the distance. As the plains began to dry, the rivers became swollen. Trees, great ice floes, and an occasional dead buffalo were swept downstream in the foaming torrent. The children resumed their out door games. The men competed too, shooting arrows at smaller and smaller targets. Brian tried to match them. One day Red Dog, the tribe's best bowman, challenged him to try his luck. Red Dog's arrow hit the center of a one-inch mark in a tree. Brian shot next and missed the tree entirely. The Indians laughed at him. Brian calmly raised his Hawken and aimed at the arrow. The arrow exploded as the ball hit the shaft.

Then he reloaded the Hawken and handed it to Red Dog. But Brian had put in a double load of powder while the Indian was examining the disintegrated arrow. Red Dog aimed and fired—and an enormous flame shot out of the Hawken, knocking him off his feet. The ball hit a tree four feet to the right of the target. Everyone laughed, including Red Dog.

Brian said, "Guess we're even. That's called white man's archery."

A week later, all the men engaged in the tribe's annual wrestling contest. Brian was an exceptionally good wrestler; at the end of the week, only two contestants remained: Brian and Sitting

Bull. They faced off. Sitting Bull solemnly charged Brian who smiling, dodged to the right. Soon the match became dead serious. They battled for over an hour. Both men were near exhaustion. Finally Brian grabbed Sitting Bull in a hold that would easily have permitted him to break his adversary's neck, had he chosen to do so. Sitting Bull raged and thrashed, but couldn't break the hold. But, rather than pinning him to win, Brian surreptitiously loosened the hold so that Sitting Bull could roll over and pin him. The braves let out a mighty roar. Afterward, when they were alone, Sitting Bull demanded angrily, "Why did you let me win?"

"Because you will become their leader, 'Steps-In-Buffalo-Shit'—I mean Sitting Bull. Then all the braves would start calling you 'Shitting Bull'."

Sitting Bull rolled on the ground, doubled over with mirth. "Please don't let the others hear you call me that," he laughed.

"Don't worry, brother, I know my place."

That night there was a grand celebration around the campfire in which Sitting Bull was named the champion wrestler and given an ornate headdress of eagle feathers. He gave a speech to his fellow Sioux. He told them that they must love each other and protect their sacred land; that they should never trade it away, and must be prepared to fight to their death should anyone try to take it from them.

They erupted in frenzied war whoops and danced in celebration. When they had quieted down, he grimly told them of Brian's jumping on the back of the buffalo that had killed Black Elk. The Indians were in awe of him and said that Brian had powerful medicine.

"No longer will you be known as 'Jumping Man' among your Sioux brothers. Your Sioux name will forever be 'Man-Who-Rides-Buffalo'." He then gave Brian a brightly painted war vest and said, "As long as you wear this in our country, no Sioux will ever harm you."

Brian put on the vest as the Sioux cheered. "I will always remember this time I have spent with you," he said. "It has been the happiest time of my life. Soon I must leave and marry the woman I love. Someday I hope to return to your camp with her so that she can meet my Sioux brothers and sisters." Saddened by his imminent departure, one by one they hugged him and offered him a sign of peace. When it was over, Sitting Bull shouted, "You and your bride and your children will always be welcome in our camp." The celebration lasted far into the night.

As the weeks passed, the weather turned warmer. The prairie grass turned green and began to shimmer in the wind. The birds returned to Montana's valleys. A week before his departure, Jumping Bull gave Brian a beautiful unbroken Palomino. Brian and Sitting Bull spent hours being thrown from the spirited horse until it was finally broken. He was a magnificent animal, and by the time Brian departed, he could ride him with ease.

Sitting Bull accompanied him for half a day's ride towards Fort Union. At the end, they dismounted and talked of peace between the Sioux and the white man. Finally, they hugged and remounted, and facing each other they raised their hands in the sign of peace. Then they simultaneously wheeled their horses around and galloped off towards their loved ones.

Brian's journey to Fort Union was uneventful. He rode into town, left his horse and belongings at Mr. Jacobs' livery stable, went to the saloon, and ordered a drink. Mike Boyd, the bartender, dropped a whiskey glass when he saw Brian's face. "You're supposed to be dead!"

Owen Burch came over and said, "Ned O'Grady said he saw your body scalped and mutilated on the Madison!"

Brian told him the whole lurid story and they stared at him with wide eyes then he asked, "Where's Ned?"

"You missed him by two days. He headed south to the Rosebud to do some trapping," said a beautiful black-haired woman with shiny brown eyes. "I'm Louisa Barnes, a dear friend of Ned's."

She had been sitting with an expensively dressed gentleman. Brian had heard him asking her to go with him to San Francisco where they could open a boarding-house. She introduced him as "Sir Percy Gainsworth the Third."

"Nice to meet you, sir. Brian McCaffrey's my name."

The Englishman diffidently shook Brian's hand, murmuring, "Likewise." He escorted Louisa away. She turned back to Brian and smiled gaily.

"Ned says you're quite a brave young man."

Brian blushed. "Well, not quite as brave as Ned."

"Yes, he's something. If only a woman could pin him down…"

Louisa returned back to the Englishman's table and began to speak quietly to him about their upcoming business venture.

Brian asked when the first steamer for St. Louis departed. Mike Fink said, "Tomorrow, if you have the money."

"I do, sir, but I have only one request."

"What's that?"

"I'm not going to fight you."

Fink laughed. "It's a deal. Be at the ferry at seven o'clock."

Brian spent the rest of the day preparing to leave. He packed his meager belongings, sold the Palomino, bought his ticket, and spent the evening in the bar drinking and playing cards with Doctor Burch. Toward the end of the evening, Burch quietly told him not to tell Ned anything about Louisa's plans to leave with the Englishman.

"Why?" asked Brian.

"It would break his heart. Whether he will admit it or not, he is deeply in love with her."

"Don't worry, I won't. Chances are I'll never see him again. I'm going to St. Louis to get married and raise a family."

"Good for you, lad," said Burch.

"If you see him, tell him I'm alive and happy. After I get married, I'll write to him care of you and thank him properly for all that he's done for me. Tell him to come visit us in St. Louis—if he'll ever leave these mountains."

"That I will, son. Best of luck to you."

Brian went up to his room but couldn't sleep. He was too keyed up and the sound of Louisa making love with Sir Stick-in-the-Mud next door were very distracting. The next morning he was the first passenger on board. He spent most of the trip nervously pacing the deck, thinking of Bridget and where to buy her wedding ring.

21

The riverboat made its last turn on the Missouri and St. Louis finally came into view. Brian wondered vaguely if anyone would meet him at the gangplank. He doubted it, since the last letter he sent would have arrived in September. Never the less he looked vainly for Bridget and his father at the gangplank. He wondered nervously if somehow the news of his "death" had preceded him. Oh, well…he would surprise them.

He carried his bags and rifle down the gangplank and shouldered his way through the crowd. God, St. Louis had grown in the past eighteen months! He hurried up his own street. The house with his father's shingle looked exactly the same. He opened the front door and walked into his father's den. His father was busily writing on a patient's chart. He looked up distractedly and his face turned white. He was speechless.

"Aren't you going to say hello, Da?"

Brian's father burst into tears and rushed up and hugged him. "It's you! It's really you!" he cried.

"Well, of course it's me. Who did you expect, St. Patrick?"

Brian was puzzled at his father's uncharacteristically emotional display.

"I received a letter in late September from Ned saying that you had been killed by Blackfeet in Montana."

"From Ned?" What had made Ned believe Brian was dead—unless he had stumbled upon Nell's grave? Then to his sorrow, Brian realized that he must have found the body of the

Indian, mistaken it for Brian's, and sent his father a letter on the last steamer out of Fort Union.

"Oh, thank God, boy! I've grieved over you so much! To lose first your mother, then you....I didn't think I could go on. Quick! We must go tell Captain Clark the good news. He was so distraught when I told him that you were dead."

"Not so hastily, Da. Did you tell Bridget?"

"Yes, of course. She took it badly. She's moved from her parents' house and is running a home for destitute Indians, trying to get them to assimilate into our culture."

"Where is it? I must see her. I'm going to ask her to marry me."

His father looked as if he were about to say something but thought better of it. Brian thought that the shock of seeing him alive must have numbed his father to the idea of Brian marrying and settling down.

"She lives over on Spring Street in the large house on the corner."

"Da, I'm sorry to do this, but I must see her now."

"I understand. Go quickly to her."

He hurriedly washed and put on his finest suit and a gentleman's Stetson hat. He looked in the mirror and liked what he saw. He adjusted the Stetson to a jaunty angle. As he rushed out of his room, his father asked him how Ned could have thought he was dead. "It's a long, unbelievable story. I'll tell you tonight. Captain Clark will love it. It's so good to see you, Da. I love you, but I've missed her so."

"Ay, yes. Young love. Hurry to her, my son."

It was dark outside. The house seemed deserted, with a single lamp burning in the back. He knocked on the door. She came to him down the hallway. His face was hidden in the shadows of the porch. She seemed more beautiful—a woman now, exquisitely dressed and self-confident. She said, "May I help you, sir?"

"You could help me by giving me a kiss," said Brian.

"Who are you?"

He stepped inside into the light. Bridget turned ashen, frightened as if by a ghost. "You're dead! How."

"Later," he said, as he took her in his arms.

"You're alive! I've got to tell you something, Brian." She couldn't say another word—his mouth enveloped hers and they kissed. She moaned, they swayed backwards into the room, leaving a trail of corsets, hoops, petticoats, and the many other cumbersome undergarments of the Victorian era. Their passion consumed them. They turned red, sweating, panting and undulating as one. The room was spinning. He couldn't believe how good she felt. He explored her with his hands, kissing her everywhere.

"Brian, I'm so happy to see that you're alive, but life has gotten so complicated."

"There, there, Bridge…I'll take care of you. We're going to be married."

"But—" He smothered her mouth with his again and inhaled her breath. He entered her and exploded inside. He couldn't believe how quickly it had happened. She smiled up at him and teased, "Brian, my rabbits take longer than that, you know."

"I'm sorry. I guess that was for me. This time is for you."

He slowly, gently made love to her, satisfying her every need. This time she climaxed before him. She desperately wanted to tell him something but before she had a chance, they began again. This time it was perfect and they peaked together. It was exquisite. He had never felt such pleasure nor sweet release before. They nestled in each other's arms and kissed. He kissed her eyes, her nose, her ears, the dimples in her cheeks. He gazed into her deep blue eyes and said, "I love you so much, Bridget. You kept me alive through some very hard times. I can't believe that some day soon we can do this every night, and even have all those lovely children we talked about."

She looked at him sadly. Then she demurely covered herself, got up, and closed the door. She sat down next to him on the edge of the bed, tears rolling down her cheeks.

95

"Ah, Bridge, you can't be that happy to see me. Tell me about life's complications."

"Brian, I tried to tell you but you wouldn't let me."

"What could be so awful? I told you I'll take care of you."

"Brian, I'm engaged to be married."

"So? Break the engagement! You told me you wanted to marry me before I left, and I said we would be married as soon as I got back. That's an engagement as far as I'm concerned. If you remember, I couldn't afford a ring then; now I have enough money to buy you a fine ring, as well as a home for us and our children."

"You don't understand," she sobbed. "I thought you were dead. I wore black for two months, and then I met a kind and gentle man. He's a lawyer and will be a good provider."

"A lawyer! Jesus, Bridge."

"Brian, I never heard you swear before. He is a good lawyer."

"That's a grand contradiction," he groused.

"No, he's very concerned about the poor, especially the Indians. He helped me set up this home for them. He has interceded for them in the courts. Captain Clark uses him all the time at his Indian Affairs office."

"Very well, so he's the Sir Galahad of the Indians. Do you love him as much as me?"

"In a way. Our love is physical and spiritual; I love him in an intellectual way."

"Does he make you happy?"

"Yes, he does."

Brian was stung. "Well, do I have time to win you back?"

"No, I'm sorry, Brian, but we're getting married on Saturday."

"That's two days from now. I'd better get busy."

"Brian, please don't. The invitations are sent; the church is reserved. You're too late."

"Bridge, please give me a chance. You can't fathom how much I love you!"

"Brian, I can't. I'm going to marry him. I grieved for you, and I had finally written you out of my life when I fell in love with him."

Brian was devastated. He put on his clothes and said, "Well, if you'll be happy with him then I wish you two the best, but I'll never stop loving you. Goodbye, my sweet Bridget. I guess my letter meant nothing to you."

"What letter?" she sobbed.

"I sent you a letter last September saying that I would marry you. Don't tell me you didn't get it?"

"I swear upon God's breast, I never received a letter from you since the day you left. All I knew of you was that you had been murdered on the Madison River, September 12, 1849."

Brian cursed Hanks and his promise to deliver the letter last fall.

"Am I invited to the wedding?"

"Of course."

"I wouldn't miss it for the world."

"Thank you, lovely Brian...It would mean a lot to me."

He already was planning a speech for the moment when the priest would ask, "Does anyone here assembled know why this couple should not be joined together in Holy Matrimony?" He kissed her on the forehead and walked out of the room, saying sadly, "Goodbye, Bridget."

He walked outside, fuming at the injustice of it all. Soon he found himself outside a saloon. The sound of the honky-tonk piano enticed him inside. He ordered a whiskey. As he stooped over to sip it, a huge man, a stevedore from the docks, made fun of his "fancy outfit." "You look overdressed for this part of town, honey," he guffawed.

"Leave me alone. I don't want any trouble," answered Brian. But the bully persisted and shoved Brian as he turned back to his drink. The glass clattered to the floor. "Mister, please—I don't want any trouble. I lost my one and only love tonight. Just leave me alone." Brian bent over to pick up the glass he had dropped.

The man snarled, "I'll bet he was as pretty as you are."

Brian knew then he was about to get into his first bar fight. Instead of picking up the glass, he grabbed a heavy spittoon and introduced the stevedore to Ned O'Grady's style of fighting. Blinded by tobacco and spit as Brian head-butted him in the chin, the man was already unconscious when he hit the floor. Then Brian leapt on him and pummeled him with his fists. By the time they pulled Brian off the stevedore, he was banging the man's head against the barroom floor. Luckily they stopped Brian before he killed the man. He ordered another drink, slugged it down, and pushed his way out through the swinging doors.

His father was asleep when he got home. Rather than sleep in his own bed, he took his buffalo robe out to the porch, where he stretched out and fell into a fitful sleep.

That night, far away, Ned dozed by a campfire on the Rosebud River. His traplines were set. He was going to work extra hard to make enough money to pay for Louisa's clothes, perfumes, a fine house and, some day, acting lessons.

22

Saturday morning was a beautiful clear day. St. Louis gleamed in the warm spring air. Brian and his father tended to a few patients and set out for the church, riding in his father's exquisite buggy. It was his only extravagance. Brian drove the horses while his father took in the sights of downtown St. Louis. In the distance they could hear the church bells. "You're taking this surprisingly well, young man," said his father. Brian said nothing, causing his father to worry what he might do next.

Brian gave the horses and carriage to the liveryman in front of the church. Several people stared at Brian. Not only was he supposed to be dead, but here he was—a tall, handsome Indian fighter attending Bridget's wedding. Several of St. Louis's loveliest and most eligible young women stared at him, trying to catch his eye. Brian, as usual, was oblivious to the women who almost fell over themselves to get his attention. He was painfully shy around them, for he considered himself average-looking, and had always used his love for Bridget as an excuse for ignoring them.

In the church they were seated halfway down the aisle on the bride's side. For all his height and imposing presence, Brian looked like a lost child. When Bridget walked down the aisle he almost cried. He tried to catch her eye as she walked past, to give her a look that said, "Don't do it, Bridge! I love you!" She didn't see him but stared straight ahead, smiling at her waiting groom. When the priest asked the assembled congregation why the couple should not be joined together in holy matrimony, Brian adjusted his tie, about to stand up and pronounce his undying love for Bridget, to proclaim before everyone that they had been engaged and had just made love the other night. But Brian faltered momentarily, and his father pressed his elbow against Brian's chest. Brian sighed and did nothing. His father looked over at him approvingly and smiled.

When Bridget and her lawyer exchanged vows, Brian hung his head, unable even to watch. He let the sounds of buffalo hooves in a stampede drown out their words. They marched out afterwards, Brian dourly looking straight ahead with a blank expression on his face.

At the reception Brian began to drink heavily. He shook Bridget's hand and sat down in a corner of the lawyer's garden. Soon he was surrounded by a group of people including Captain Clark and some of the most beautiful young women in St. Louis. As the liquor took effect, he became a confident raconteur and enthralled his listeners with tales of escaping death on the Madison, killing a grizzly bear, and living with the Sioux.

By the time his father said it was time to go Brian was quite drunk. His father called for the liveryman to bring around the carriage. Brian slurred, "Juss a moment, Da...I must congratulate the groom." He went over to the unsuspecting lawyer who was standing alone in the rose garden. He quietly said to the groom, "Hello, I'm Brian McCaffrey. I wish to congratulate you. You are the luckiest man in the world." He shook his hand and as he smiled, everyone watched him. He squeezed the lawyer's hand in a death grip. The groom, to his credit, didn't let on that he was in pain and smiled back. "Uh, one more thing. If I ever hear that you have hurt her in any way, I'll come back and cut your liver out, put it on ice, and personally deliver it to Liver-Eating Johnston and drink a toast to him as he devours it."

John Ryan blanched but continued the charade with a smile and said, "Thank you, sir. I'll keep that in mind."

Brian walked off towards the carriage. Out of the corner of

his eye he saw Bridget watching him, but avoided looking at her as he ambled off with a drunken smile on his face. He plopped down in the carriage and announced, "Home, James...the butler is waiting." His father squelched a guffaw and they trotted off.

"You handled that well, my son. I'm proud of you."

"Da, she tore my heart out. I'll never love anyone else."

"That's what you say tonight. You should have seen how the women looked at you. You're a legendary Indian fighter."

"We'll see, Da. Forgive me if I'm somewhat moody."

"You have every right to be, but believe me, you'll be over her before you know it."

Brian didn't answer, and dozed off on the way home. He went to his room, took another drink of whiskey, took off his silk hat, and collapsed onto the bed fully clothed. His father blew out the candle and left. Brian's empty glass clattered to the floor, awakening him, and he silently cried himself to sleep.

23

Early the next day Ned awoke and checked his trap line. He had already caught nine beavers. Even if the price of pelts went down, he was sure that he would make enough money to buy Louisa more clothes than she would ever need. He kept thinking of her black, curly hair, her shiny brown eyes, that girlish voice, her throaty laugh, and her body, which made him weak with excitement. Jaysus, he missed her already!

Suddenly Ned's fantasies were interrupted by a glint of metal seen out of the corner of his eye. He instinctively ducked just as a ball whacked a tree behind him. An instant later, the sound of the gun registered in his brain. God damnit, O'Grady, he scolded himself, this is when most of us get it—right after we've been in civilization for too long; it dulls a man's senses. He peeked around a log and saw Pierre McKenzie looking for him while he reloaded. He crawled along a log and then another, hoping he didn't come face to face with a rattler. McKenzie was looking in the wrong direction when Ned shot him in the arm. Now McKenzie could no longer hold onto his rifle. Ned calmly walked up, reloading, and said, "Why Pierre! Funny meeting you here on this fine day! You weren't trying to shoot a squirrel near my head now, were you?"

"You bastard, O'Grady! What are you going to do now, kill me?"

"Heavens no," Ned smiled as he pulled the trigger and shot the French-Canadian in the kneecap. McKenzie screamed and went down as if he had been struck by lightning, howling in agony.

Ned reloaded. "No, Pierre, I won't kill you. I'm just going to show you how the Irish hobble men. It's a little bit more savage than the way we hobble our horses." He pulled the trigger and blasted the man's other kneecap.

"Kill me, you Irish clod! I can't stand this pain! Kill me now and go back to your whore!"

The words stung Ned. He couldn't think of Louisa as a whore, for some reason. Ned pulled out his knife and pointed it at the Frenchman's liver. "Remember my promise, Frenchie?"

McKenzie began pleading with him. "You wouldn't do that! Please don't!"

"Actually, you're quite right. I'm not like Liver-Eatin' Johnston. I hate the taste of liver—especially frog liver, Frenchie," Ned said scornfully. "No, I suspect that within a few hours a coyote or a cougar or a grizzly bear will be feasting on your various organs. Well, I must be going for tea, Pierre. Have a lovely afternoon." The Frenchman cursed him.

Ned took the Frenchman's pistol and possibles bag, made sure his rifle was out of his reach, unhobbled his horse, and mounted. He fired the single-shot pistol in the air, then tossed it back to the Frenchman. He smiled down at him and said, "I'm going to throw your bag to you. By the time you can reload that pistol, I'll be about a mile away. You'll need that for protection."

"What? That won't stop a grizzly or a cougar."

"Of course not, but you can put the barrel in your mouth and pull the trigger. It's a damn sight better than being mauled, don't you think? Oh, by the way—make sure you aim up." Ned mimicked a man shooting himself by placing his finger in his open mouth, aiming it towards the roof of his mouth, and crossing his eyes.

"You Irish thug!" screamed McKenzie.

"Oh, by the way—I'm sure in a few hours you'll be with your friend Satan. Tell him I said, 'Piss off.'" I won't be seeing him for quite a while. Who knows, maybe I'll get lucky, make a

deathbed confession and never meet the bastard. Oh well, ta-ta—
I must be off. I'll give Louisa your warmest regards." He threw the
possibles bag containing the Frenchman's powder and lead onto his
chest and rode off.

24

She had married another man. She would never have his children. They would never make love again...Brian thought back to when he had first seen Bridget in grade school. She was eleven years old, and even then he had known that he loved her. He couldn't believe how empty he felt inside. He had no purpose in life anymore. He wanted so badly to see her, to just hear her voice or listen to her laugh. It was all gone.

He spent his days with his father, learning how to apply poultices and dispense medicines. He learned the proper way to set bones. He assisted his father with amputations. But while they worked his mind would wander back to her. Several times his father looked at him as if about to say something comforting, but never did. Instead he would say, "Press on, Brian. Keep your mind on your patients. You have a special gift for medicine and you have very skillful hands. I think that someday you can become a great surgeon."

When Brian was engrossed in dealing with the sick, he felt a certain relief from his overwhelming sadness. He felt some satisfaction in relieving other peoples' suffering. He was gentle with elderly ladies and children. He listened to the ladies' accounts of their aches and pains; somehow they felt better just knowing that he had listened and felt that he really cared. He loved the way children gazed up at him with wide eyes, fearful yet trusting. He could always make them laugh. Every time Brian and his father lost a child he died a little inside, but then he would steel himself, forming an icy resolve to do better next time. Somebody's got to do this, he told himself, and I'm good at it—so I'm going to press on. If only he could find someone to relieve him of his suffering!

After a long day he and his father would close the office and eat dinner, usually silently, while the clock in the kitchen ticked relentlessly on. Sometimes they talked about difficult cases, politics, or his mother. After dinner, his father would retire, leaving Brian alone. He would go out at night and invariably find himself walking down Bridget's street, hidden in the shadows across from her house, hoping to catch a glimpse of her washing dishes or reading. He felt embarrassed at his need to know that she was still there, safe and alive. He feared that someday she would see him watching her, but he couldn't let her go. It was always the same: he looked at the house, his mouth became dry, and he found it difficult to swallow. He would feel a deep ache in his chest–not in his heart, but in his very soul. He wanted to sob but couldn't. He felt so low and ashamed, slinking around in the shadows just to get a glimpse of her! Then anger would set in. He raged inside at himself, at God for taking his mother, at Bridget's husband for taking her from him, even at the dogs barking at him in the night.

His days were filled with compassion; his nights were filled with uncontrollable rage that would inevitably end with heavy drinking in the saloons. He picked fights with men older and larger than himself, but he didn't care; he wanted to die.

Usually Brian won his fights but one night he stumbled home with one eye swollen shut, his mouth bleeding, and went into his room. He looked into the mirror, disgusted. He was bruised, disheveled, and hopelessly drunk. The room spun. He fell into his bed but couldn't sleep. His heart was pounding, his breathing was rushed and he thrashed wildly in his bed. He was suffocating! He needed to sleep outside. He found his buffalo robe, went out to the porch, and lay down. He felt a little better. Then the tears came and he started sobbing quietly, unable to stop. He knew he couldn't stay here. He hated the stench of the city, the bars, the fights—but mostly he hated himself and his terrible need for Bridget. He had to get back to Montana. He knew if he stayed he would die here in a fight, or end up as a bloated, jaundiced, drunk with bleary eyes and shaking hands. Finally Brian passed out, hoping that he would never awaken.

Silently his father watched him and when he was certain that Brian was asleep, he gently wiped his face and covered him. He patted his head and whispered, "There, boy. You don't deserve this." He went inside, wondering how a mere woman had the power to break the spirit of a man who could survive Indian attacks and the claws and horns of the most fearsome beasts on the planet.

Brian awoke the next morning to the sounds of his father playing the piano. He shuffled inside and looked down at his dad. He was getting old and his hair was thinning and gray; he was developing a paunch. His dad looked up at him, raised an eyebrow, and said, "Now just look at you, son. Do you know your longjohns are open and your pecker is hanging out?"

Brian didn't look down but looked him straight in the eye and, stone-faced said, "No, but sing some of the lyrics and maybe I'll just sing it along with you."

They both burst into laughter and hugged one another. "You'll get over her, son. With that wit of yours, you'll be better soon. Mark my words, you'll find the right woman and have many beautiful children. You'll be a good father. I know, I've seen you work with the wee ones. Maybe you'll get lucky and have daughters. Sons can be such a worry."

"I know, Da. I'm sorry. I'll do better. I'm gonna lay off the sauce and quit fighting so much. But I've got to go back to the mountains. I love you, Da, but I can't stay in the city. I need to roam free in the clean mountain air."

"I know that, son. Learn as much as you can. Go find your friend, Ned, and get on with your life."

"That I will, for you are a fine teacher and friend. Thanks, Da."

"Go clean up and then I'll put a compress on that eye. It's turning black, you know."

Later that day he almost knocked Bridget over as she came out of the Mercantile store, her arms laden with packages. He helped her with her purchases.

Their eyes met…those beautiful blue eyes. He could feel the sorrow well up inside him. He simply said, "I'll always love you, Bridge."

"I know. You were my first love and I'll always have a place in my heart for you, Brian."

He wanted to kiss her, but lamely took her hand and gently shook it. "Best of luck to you both." He noticed his reflection in the window. He saw his stooped posture and pitiful expression. He straightened up and smiled at her. He croaked, "Goodbye, Bridge. I've got to see some patients." He turned quickly away and walked arrogantly away from her. His awkward smile was frozen on his face but his eyes were watering. Passersby looked at him oddly but he kept on going through the crowd of shoppers, he couldn't look back, for he knew it would start all over again. No, a man shouldn't cry in public over a woman who had abandoned him for another. Brian genuinely wanted Bridget to be happy, while a part of him wanted to despise her for what she had done to him. But he couldn't even bring himself to do that. He just knew he had to get back to Montana and forget her. Down deep he knew it would take a long, long time.

When he opened the door to his father's office, all of these thoughts disappeared when he heard the woman shrieking as his dad tried to take the little girl from her arms. The child was about seven, with curly red hair and blue eyes that were sunken and uncomprehending. Her face was beet-red, her joints swollen, and she was consumed with fever. Any minute, Brian knew, she would start convulsing and they would lose her. She had scarlet fever. He remembered the mother, Tessie O'Malley, for her other child, a six-year-old boy, had died in this very office the year before of cholera.

Her husband, Michael, had died two years ago in a mining accident. She couldn't pay them, but that didn't matter to him or his father. Brian gently pried the child's swollen hands from her mother's neck. The look in the mother's eyes reminded him of the look in Nell's eyes just before she had died. "Don't worry, we'll take good care of her," he murmured.

They put her on the examining table and undressed her. His father listened to her heaving chest. "Good. The lungs are clear and there's no heart murmur…yet." His father's brow was furrowed and covered with sweat. They were both drenched as they desperately tried to cool her down with cold towels. A rash covered her body. She shivered, but hadn't yet had seizures. Her temperature was 104! They gently applied poultices to her swollen joints while she stared at Brian with her big blue eyes. So young, so afraid…Those eyes haunted him and he found himself thinking of Bridget's eyes. Damn her eyes and that woman! Forget her. You've got to save this poor kid, he thought to himself.

They gave her laudanum for her painful joints and throat. They worked for hours, exhausted, at the same time trying to calm the hysterical Mrs. O'Malley. Gradually her temperature dropped to 99 degrees.

The child opened her eyes and looked up sadly at him. He smiled at her and crossed his eyes. She giggled and wrapped her tiny arms around his neck. He picked her up gently and she clung to him like a frightened puppy. He felt a shudder go through his body. He was so tired, but he felt a warmth gradually infusing his spirit. She would recover, he realized, and somehow Brian knew he would make it too. There's more to life than pining over a lost love, he realized.

He carried her to a crib in the next room, where she instantly fell asleep. He straightened up. His back ached. He made a cot for the child's mother next to the crib. The look in Mrs. O'Malley's eyes was all the payment they would ever get—or need.

Brian went to his father's den. Seamus O'Grady looked exhausted. He poured them both a drink of Scotch. Brian took a deep gulp and its warmth slid down his throat. His father smiled at him. "You were wonderful in there, son, and I'm so proud of you. You learned what medicine is all about tonight. You have the wonderful gift of healing others. Medicines and poultices are great for relieving suffering, but healing comes from touching and showing your concern for them. You can't save them all, but their knowing that you care about them is the strongest medicine on earth."

"That, and vigilance," said Brian as he poured the rest of his Scotch into his father's glass. "Drink that and go to bed. You look terrible."

"I know. The strain just saps your soul."

His father weakly squeezed his hand. Brian trudged back into the child's room. Her mother stirred but didn't waken. He pulled up a chair next to the child and took her hand. Her tiny fingers grasped his and she slept soundly as the moonlight bathed her face. He kept his vigil with her alone with his thoughts. When he awoke it was daylight, and he had a crick in his neck from falling asleep in an awkward position next to her. She opened her eyes and said, "Hi, doctor."

He said, "I'm not a doctor, I'm just my Da's helper. He's the doctor."

"Will you grow up to be one some day?"

"I might, but I would have to go to school for a long time."

"You don't like school either, do you?" she smiled.

"No, I don't."

"Well, you should go anyway. You would be a good doctor."

"I know, but first I have to go to Montana to make my heart better."

"Did you get scarlet fever too? What's wrong with your heart?"

"Ah, wee one, it's a bit broken."

"Will it get better?"

"In time."

"What broke it?"

"A woman."

"How? Did she kick you in the heart?"

"In a way she did."

"I didn't know women were so strong."

"They are, more than you'll ever know. They can hurt a man's heart sometimes just by the way they look at him."

"I would never hurt a man's heart."

"Good for you, my sweet."

"What's your name?"

"Brian."

"Mine's Bridget."

"What a beautiful name," he said huskily.

"I'm tired. I'm going back to sleep."

"Good. You need to get lots of rest, honey."

She hugged him and said, "I love you, Dr. Brian."

"I love you too, Brid...uh, wee one."

He got up and walked out of the room with a frozen grin on his face and with a tear running down his right cheek. This time he felt good, unlike yesterday, after leaving his other Bridget. He sighed, "Jesus, when will I ever get over that woman?"

"What?" asked his father.

"Oh, its nothing, Da. She's better. Check her in an hour. She needs more sleep."

"Would you like some potatoes and sausage?"

"No, thanks, I need to sleep."

He left his clothes on and, collapsing face down on his bed, slept more peacefully than he had since leaving the Sioux camp.

25

It was late July and Ned had a hundred and fifty beaver pelts, a grizzly fur, ten fox pelts, and two white bighorn sheep furs. He planned to buy Louisa some fancy clothes and perfumes. He decided to go back, propose to her, and return in four weeks for fall hunting. He might even skip the Rendezvous and marry her in October.

He arrived at Fort Union early in the afternoon, and stored his horse and the pelts with Mr. Jacobs. Then got his hair cut and his beard shaved before checking into the hotel. He bathed and went out and bought a fine suit of clothes with a matching derby. He tied the knot on his gambler's tie and marched into the saloon.

"I need some whiskey for me 'tooth', Boyd."

"Why Ned, you look absolutely regal! How's the trapping business?"

"Ah, mighty prosperous this year. I might just settle down and become one of Fort Union's outstanding citizens. I might become the mayor some day."

Boyd guffawed and said, "I guess I'll become a preacher, then." Ned drank his whiskey and furtively looked around to see if Louisa was sitting in the corner. Her chair was empty. "She's probably still in bed. Maybe I'll go upstairs and wake her up and propose to her. How could she resist such a handsome rake?" he mused to himself. Just as he was about to head for the stairs, Owen Burch ambled into the bar.

"Ned! How good to see you. You look very prosperous."

"Well, I must confess, I'm loaded with furs. I'm going to be rich and settle down."

Burch raised an eyebrow. "Why don't you share the wealth with me? I feel real lucky today."

"I wouldn't mind some more gold in my teeth, you pirate!" scoffed Ned. They shook hands. "Say, you haven't seen Louisa today, have you?"

Burch's face clouded and he said, "No, uh…let me buy you a drink, my friend."

They sat down. Ned was beaming and said, "I'm going to ask her to marry me."

Burch sighed and said, "My friend, I'm afraid you won't be marrying her."

"What?"

"She left town soon after you left with a rich Englishman for San Francisco."

"She wouldn't do that now, would she?" Ned was pale with shock.

"I'm afraid so," the dentist said gravely.

"Jaysus H. Christ! A bloody Englishman!" He pounded his fist on the table. "Boyd, give me a whole bottle of whiskey and a 'gar!"

"She left this for you." Burch handed him a letter and a scarf. He could smell her scent on the scarf. He opened the letter.

> Dearest Ned:
>
> I'm sorry to have left you. I have gone to San Francisco to be an actress. I knew that you would never settle down and marry me. Besides, I couldn't live here and be a mother. I want to be famous. I'll miss you, sweet Ned.

O'Grady began drinking straight from the bottle. He made a brave show of lighting his cigar with her letter, then threw it on the floor and stamped out the flames. "Damn her anyway! She didn't mean anything to me," he snorted defiantly. "Well, Owen, I'll be back later to take some of your money."

Before the dentist could tell him about Brian, Ned kicked his way through the swinging doors, bottle in hand, and shouting, "I'm going to get pissed as a newt." He marched out as a cloudburst began, heading towards the river. He was soon drenched. He sat on the shore, soaked, and drained the rest of the bottle, then threw it into the river. He pulled out her scarf and inhaled her scent. He sobbed once but didn't cry. He picked up a stone and tied the scarf around it. He smelled it once more—heaved it into the Missouri. "God damn you!" he screamed, throwing his hat into the river. He took off his boots and placed them on the shore. Lightning and thunder surrounded him. He threw his new tie in the river, then his shirt, then his suit. His underwear went in next. Ned stood in the rain hurling obscenities at the sky as lightning flashed all around him.

Suddenly the bank caved away beneath his feet and the Missouri swallowed him under. Drunk, he was helpless in the current. He reached up, hoping that perhaps Brian would pull him out just as he had done on the Rosebud. Luckily he clawed at the roots of a tree on the bank and held on. He came up for air and yelled, "God damn you, Louisa!" He managed to crawl ashore, found his boots, put them on and walked naked back to town, still fuming.

He walked into the livery stable. Jacobs stared at him goggle-eyed.

"Where's me horse?" demanded Ned.

"In the far corner," answered Jacobs.

Ned went over and patted the head of Hell Bastard. He wrapped his arms around the horse's neck and said, "You're all I have left, you nag." The horse, unaccustomed to such affection, shied away and bit his shoulder. "So that's the way you're going to be? All right, have it your way." He calmly walked behind the horse and kicked it in the gonads with his wet, soggy boot. The Bastard grunted. "Now you're a gelding. Maybe that'll teach you some manners." From then on, the horse was as docile as a lamb.

Ned staggered out again into the storm and headed for the bar. He pushed open the doors and yelled, "Boyd! Give me another bottle! Burch, your deal." He sat across from the dentist, wearing only his boots, and announced, "Deuces are wild."

The bartender said, "Haven't you had enough, Ned?"

"Not even close, my friend. Bring us some glasses."

Burch said, "Ned, don't let Louisa do this to you."

"Louisa who? The lass is dead, as far as I'm concerned."

In the next hour, Ned won four hundred dollars from Burch. The dentist finally had a chance to tell him of Brian's survival, and Ned was happy again. He was drunk, naked, and shivering when a buxom strawberry blonde named Renée came over and invited him to come upstairs, dry off, and enjoy her company.

"Not a bad night," he said. "By the way, lovely Rowena, how much is a poke these days?"

"My name's Renée. It's on the house," she smiled.

Ned offered her his arm and squelched up the stairs in his wet boots, naked as a newborn baby, with a big grin on his face.

26

It was the second week of August and the humidity in St. Louis was stifling. Brian and his dad had just finished a harrowing, bloody amputation on a febrile, delirious Irishman who had been shot two days before in a saloon. They almost lost him from blood loss. Brian showed his dad the method he had used on Ned to stop the bleeding. "I must say, it is a bit unconventional, but it works. I may publish it," said his father thoughtfully, "It makes sense. Not only does it stop bleeding but it probably also kills the gangrene bacillus in the stump of the amputation. Think I'll call it the McCaffrey Cauterization Technique. You will, of course, get full credit in the article."

"Thanks, Da."

Just then, there was a knock on the door. "Christ, not another patient at this hour," Dr. McCaffrey muttered. Brian opened the door. He almost didn't recognize Ned O'Grady without his beard and long hair, neatly dressed in a suit.

"Ned?"

"You bet your sweet arse! God, it's good to see you alive and well, lad!"

"Da, this is my dear friend, Ned O'Grady."

"Sir, it is a pleasure to meet you."

"Brian has told me many a hair-raising tale of your adventures in Montana! You're from Dooblin, correct?"

"Yes, sir."

"Call me Seamus, and please don't call me 'doctor', or especially 'sir'…the latter makes me feel quite old."

"Well, Seamus, you look fit to me. I see where Brian gets his good looks."

"Ah, I see you've got a touch of the blarney in you too. How about some Scotch to replenish the fluid you've lost in this damnable heat?"

"Ah, it would be a blessing, kind sir—I mean Seamus."

They toasted Ireland, Montana, and each other long into the night. Ned told them of the beauty and mysteries of Colter's Hell. Brian's eyes gleamed with enthusiasm. "Why are you in St. Louis?"

"Well, me Hawken's breech is pitted from killing so much game. I needed a new one, so I thought I'd get one at the original gun works here in St. Louis—maybe sample some of the saloons and ladies before going back for the fall hunt and the Rendezvous. It's on the Green River this year. I thought maybe I could talk you into going with me, Brian, if the lovely Bridget will let you. How was the wedding, anyway?"

"Well, I got quite drunk. It seems that the groom turned out to be some Indian-loving lawyer instead of yours truly."

"God damn women! You just can't trust them to do what they say, can you now? Jaysus! A bloody barrister. She would have been better off marrying a bleedin' pimp. Well, you're not alone, son. I too have been recently jilted."

"You? I didn't even know you were in love with someone."

"Ah, I didn't know meself until I holed up with her in Fort Union this past winter. I was going to propose to her, but she left me for the bright lights of the stage in San Francisco."

"Good riddance to her. She must be a fool," said Brian's father.

"Ah, it's her loss," grumped Ned as he finished another Scotch. "Well, are you interested in going back to God's country?"

Before Brian could answer, his father roared, "Heavens, yes!

He's been moping around here all summer like a lost, sad-eyed mongrel puppy. Get him out there where he can be free again. He's not cut out for so-called civilized St. Louis."

"What thinks you, old son? Want to track down some grizz?"

"No, thanks. I tangled with one of those last winter. It was like you said…it was all over very fast." Brian then recounted the story of the grizzly bear, meeting Sitting Bull and living with the Sioux.

"Jaysus, killing buffalo and Blackfeet and surviving a lost love in one year. Hell! Jumping a grizz would be a walk in the park for you."

"Just the same, I'll pass."

"So you won't join your old history mentor, will you now?"

"I didn't say that. I'll go with you but I'm not going to purposely hunt grizz."

"All right, it's settled. No grizz trapping. You don't have a problem with black bears, do you?"

"No, that would be fine."

"When can you leave?"

"Next Monday. I was planning on taking a steamer to Fort Union and tracking till I found you. I figured the easiest place to find you would be in the saloon or at the Rendezvous."

"Ah, you know me too well. Monday it is, and we'll continue your education on wildlife."

"Hah! The only wildlife I learned about from you was in the bar at Jackson Hole."

"Well, yes, and that too, my brother."

Brian's father guffawed and asked Ned, "Do you have a place to stay?"

"Actually not, kind sir."

"You'll sleep here," said Brian, "but let's sleep outside on our robes.…it's too hot to sleep inside."

All three went outside, taking their Scotch with them.

121

They lay there laughing and drinking far into the moonlit night. Brian finally fell asleep with a smile on his face. "I'm finally going back," he thought, and slept peacefully.

27

The next few days passed quickly as they bought supplies and had their rifles refurbished. The nights were even more of a blur, for Brian somehow had to keep Ned from getting into fights with St. Louis' rowdies. However Ned did manage to insult several of them in his drunken rampages. Their closest brush with trouble occurred when a large man bumped into Ned and called him a 'mick'. Ned responded by telling him that he smelled like a freshly minted pile of steaming buffalo dung. To emphasize the point, he extinguished his cigar on the bully's forehead and said, "Oh, I'm sorry, you probably don't understand that term. That's 'shit' to you, you bloody cretin." Fortunately, both of them were so drunk that their first punches missed; then they were held back by their companions. Brian pulled Ned outside and said, "Time to go home, old friend."

"Ahh, he's nothin' but a stupid St. Louis pussy! Speaking of which, we have yet to frequent the local houses of prostitution."

"All right, I'll take you…but I'm not going in. I'll meet you at home. Just promise me you won't go back into the saloons and get into a fight."

"Ah, I guess I can refrain from fisticuffs for one more night. After all, it is love I seek among the finest of St. Louis' tarts." He then stumbled up the stairs of the bordello and waved Brian on.

Brian had remained sober and it was only eight o'clock. He somehow found himself standing in the shadows across from Bridget's house. This time he crossed the street and knocked on the door. John Ryan, her husband, answered the door with a surprised look on his face.

"Mr. Ryan," said Brian, "I came to apologize for my rude behavior at your wedding. I was quite drunk…"

"I understand. I know you went through a lot to get back to her. I'm sorry."

"Well, may you both have a good life and the best of luck to you, sir."

"Do come in. Bridget, please come out and say hello to Brian McCaffrey."

She had gained weight and her face glowed. She looked even more beautiful than he had remembered. "So good to see you, Brian. I understand you're going to be a doctor."

"Not yet. I'm going back to Montana with my buddy, Ned. I just don't seem to feel alive until I'm up about five thousand feet into the mountains. I guess someday I'll come back and study medicine, but for now I need to get back to her."

"Her?"

"Montana. Strange—I refer to it as 'she', but in a way she is much like a woman. She's very beautiful but quite unpredictable."

After an awkward silence she said, "Guess what? I'm expecting!"

"Oh, how wonderful. Congratulations to you both. Well, I must be leaving…we sail on Monday. Again, I wish you both well."

They all shook hands. As he stepped off the porch, Brian realized that he was over her completely. The thought that the unborn child might be his never crossed his mind.

28

The next day Brian introduced a badly hung-over Ned to Captain Clark, who still stood tall and commanded respect. "William Clark. Pleased to make your acquaintance, Mr. O'Grady."

"Sir, it is an honor to shake your hand. I've read of your adventures with Mr. Lewis since I was a boy. It must have taken great courage to cross the plains and mountains to the Pacific Ocean."

"Actually, we were well prepared, but I doubt we would have survived the first winter had it not been for the Mandans. The Shoshones guided us over the mountains. As you know, our biggest help came from an Indian woman, Sacagawea. She managed to interpret for us through many sticky situations with various Indian tribes. What do you think of Indians, Mr. O'Grady?"

Ned remembered Brian's comments about Clark's love for the Indians, but truthfully answered, "I haven't formed an opinion yet. A few that I have met have been friendly and honest. Yet one of them also shot me in the leg. Of course I was in his huntin' grounds so I can't really be too cross with him now, can I?"

"They are in general a proud, mysterious, kind people. Be good to them and they will treat you well; but take care not to offend them or you'll suffer an ignominious end. I've found that the best way to deal with hostile Indians is to be firm and never show fear. Look them in the eye and speak to them gently but with strength in your voice. Trade with them, give them trinkets, and they will smoke with you and feed you and treat you with the utmost kindness."

They talked for nearly an hour. Ned offered to write to the great explorer whenever he discovered a new species of plant or animal, as Clark was still interested in cataloguing discoveries made in the West. Clark thanked him and asked to be kept informed of the latest news regarding Indians, especially the Shoshones, Crows, Sioux, and the Blackfeet. Ned and Brian promised Clark to keep him up to date. Finally, the Captain gave them turquoise beads and coins bearing a likeness of Thomas Jefferson to give to the Indians as gifts. Even after over forty years they were held in high regard by the Indians. Finally it was time to leave. The great man hugged Brian and asked, "Do you still have my gun?"

"No, sir. A man named Johnston is using it now. I foolishly thought I wouldn't need it again."

"Don't worry, Brian. It's not worth much compared to today's guns, but if you could get it back for me I'd appreciate it. It saved my life several times during our expedition."

"I didn't know that, sir. That gun should be displayed in Washington."

"Aye," said Ned. "Don't worry, we'll get it back from the Liver-Eater."

"What?"

"Er, it's just a nickname…he likes the taste of liver for some strange reason."

"I prefer elk meat," said Clark.

"Me too," mumbled Brian, wondering how he was going to talk Johnston out of his rifle.

They shook hands. Clark gave them the old admonition to watch their topknots and they went to spend their last night with Brian's father.

"Looks like you'll need the charm of Demosthenes, plus a lot of money, to get Clark's gun back. Johnston can be a real skinflint."

"Shit," muttered Brian. How could I have been so stupid?"

"Why Brian, you're swearing again! I'm bloody shocked."

"It's your profound influence on me. Somehow your presence makes me a much more colorful speaker," grumbled Brian.

"Hah, I just can't wait to see Johnston," cackled Ned.

"Lovely, just lovely," growled Brian as he kicked a cobblestone in the street.

They spent their last evening with Dr. McCaffrey. Finally he said, "Well, son, I wish you well. I know this is best for you. When you are ready, come back and go to school. Captain Clark has written you a wonderful letter of recommendation to medical school. I also have a lot of influence with the Dean at St. Louis University. I told him of your skills and he was very interested in your cauterization methods. We're publishing an article in the next *Journal of Medicine and Surgery* and giving you credit."

"Thanks, Da. I'm still very interested in medicine, but maybe in a few years. I still need a few more adventures with old Ned here before settling down."

"Aye, lad. I envy you. I wish I had traveled before starting to practice, but I've got my patients, you know. I just can't leave them."

"You're a fine man, Dr. McCaffrey," said Ned.

"You've raised a fine son and you're a credit to your profession. Not much better can be said of a man now, could it?"

"Thank you, Ned. You are most kind. Take care of me lad, and don't get eaten or scalped."

"Don't worry about us—we're charmed, you know. We have the luck of the Irish."

"You don't say. Well, with the luck of the Irish, your damn boat will sink just after it leaves the dock, it will."

They laughed into the night. At dawn they parted. Brian hugged his father.

"If something should happen to me," said Dr. McCaffrey, "I left the letters of recommendation with Captain Clark. Also, he has my will. You get all of this. It's worth quite a lot, you know. If something should happen to Captain Clark, his attorney has copies of it."

"Bridget's husband?"

"Yes, he's a good man and honest. I trust him."

"That's good enough for me, Da. Quit talking that way. I'll probably see you in October or next spring at the latest. I love you, Da."

"Me too, boy."

They released each other and Brian and Ned rushed to the docks. Brian turned back and waved at his father as he rounded the corner. His dad waved sadly back. Brian was never to see him again, for he would die a year later in a cholera epidemic.

29

The campfire crackled. The elk was delicious. A cool pine-scented breeze wafted over them.

"Ah, life is delightful," sighed Ned.

"Yes, it is," agreed Brian, then suddenly belched.

"Such behavior. You have the table manners of a bleedin' Hun."

"I didn't purposely do it."

"Hah! Bloody savage, that's what you are," chortled Ned.

"Oh sure. And here we have the great, refined man of letters who swears like a stevedore, drinks like a fish, and frolics with women more often than Henry the Eighth."

"Ahh, you've learned some history after all. You see, my tutelage has penetrated even your dense pate. But mind you, your ultimate test will be the Rendezvous. I'm sure you will be able to charm old Johnny Johnston out of his squirrel rifle."

"I'll bet I can."

"And pigs can fly."

"All right. I'll bet you three beaver pelts."

"Will you now? Hah! You're on, lad. Let's see…that should be worth at least a week's worth of whiskey and three or four good lays at the Rendezvous."

"You know, Ned, some day you're going to be a decrepit, ranting, syphylitic old man from all your whoring."

"Perhaps, but I doubt it. Luck of the Irish. I suspect that I'll die in bed at eighty, surrounded by me lovin' wife and children and just in the nick of time I'll make me deathbed confession to the priest. Then—straight to heaven! Ah, maybe a few weeks in purgatory for some of me lapses in chastity, but after all, what kind of heaven would it be without a charming rogue like meself being present?"

"God, Ned. Sometimes you just amaze me with your prattle."

"'Prattle' is right. See, even your vocabulary is improving! You're becoming a veritable Chaucer before me very eyes. Of course, you'll need all your verbal skills tomorrow to get that focking gun back." He roared and fell over backwards into his robes by the campfire, shaking with laughter.

"Very funny, just hilarious. By the way, where are we going after Rendezvous?"

"I don't rightly know. I thought perhaps you wanted to go back to St. Louis for the winter."

"Nah, it's too soon. I'll go back and see Da in the spring."

"Winter's harsh in Montana."

"I'll say," said Brian.

"That's right, you wintered here already. Are you sure you want to do it again?"

"Yes, I loved living with the Sioux."

"I was sort of hoping we'd hole up in Fort Union," said Ned.

"With all those whores, saloons, and a drunken dentist?"

"Sounds like paradise to me."

"No, you fool. It's safer and healthier to live with the Indians."

"I'm not going to spend one bloody night sleeping with any goddamn Sioux!"

"I thought you liked Indians. What have you got against the Sioux?"

"Nothing, personally. I've just heard stories. They're almost as bad as the Blackfeet when it comes to scalping white men."

"That's rubbish. I'll tell you what. We'll winter with the

Crows, if that will make you feel better. They have some pretty squaws in camp—but keep your hands off White Fawn. I've got an eye for her myself. Actually the Sioux squaws are much prettier, but we'll have it your way, if it'll make you sleep better."

"Christ Almighty, next year you'll be marryin' one of 'em. I can see it now.Brian, father of a half-breed."

"You wouldn't?"

"I doubt I'll ever marry. Women can't be trusted—white, red, it doesn't matter. I'd still rather spend the winter with some lovely whores, drinking and gambling, than freezing me bloody arse off in a teepee with the Crows," he snorted.

"We'll see. Give it a try. What happened to your sense of adventure?"

"Bollocks," grunted Ned. "This is the dumbest thing I've ever done in me life. Ah, well, me poor liver could stand a break, I guess. I hear Indians love to gamble. Are you sure those Crow squaws are pretty? Don't be feedin' me a long line of blarney, now, Brian. Winters in Montana can be awfully long."

"Ned, trust me. There are some beautiful women there," promised Brian.

"Well, I have very high standards, you know. Ah well, I'll do it—just for the sense of adventure." Ned rolled up in his robes and mused about how many different Indian maidens he might be lying next to this winter. He was smiling as he fell asleep.

The next morning they forded the Green River and headed for the Rendezvous.

30

The Rendezvous was as raucous as ever. The price of beaver, though lower than earlier years, had gone up slightly since the year before. Silk hats were still the fashion but importing silk from China had become more difficult, giving the fur trade a final reprieve. Most of the participants accepted that this was would be the last Rendezvous.

Some of them were getting into new ventures. Jim Bridger had decided to lead expeditions for the U.S. government. He would eventually guide the U.S. Cavalry into the territories of Wyoming and Utah, and help gold seekers and their families through the gold fields of Montana. Kit Carson announced that he was becoming a scout for the U.S. Army in New Mexico and Arizona. Later he would help them exterminate the renegade Apaches and Navajos in the territories, as well as helping John Fremont on his expeditions opening the original Oregon Trail to Oregon and California. Johnston and Del planned on trapping for a few more years. Ned and Brian had no long-term plans, but they too had accepted the inevitable end of the fur trade. They avoided telling the Liver-Eater that they would be spending the winter with the Crows. Carson asked Johnston if he had killed any more of them. "Six," he answered nonchalantly as he munched on a piece of jerky.

"Jaysus," whistled Ned.

"I'm losing my taste for liver. When I get the last two that are tracking me, I'll make peace with them and maybe become a U.S. Marshal."

He did that and also distinguished himself later as a soldier in the Union Army for the Colorado Regulars. When Brian finally broached the subject of William Clark's gun, the big man grinned and said, "I've been keeping it for him. Can't kill Crows with it anyway." When Brian told him it was the very gun Clark had used on the Lewis and Clark expedition, Johnston unhesitatingly sold it back to Brian for the same price that he'd paid for it. Ned was dumbstruck but didn't say anything.

"I'm sorry your marriage plans didn't work out," Johnston said. "Somehow I just knew you'd be back with us some day. You got that look of adventure in your eye, boy. Just make sure the Captain gets his gun back."

"I promise you, we will have his gun sent to him as soon as we get to Fort Union."

After the huge man departed, Brian winked at Ned and said, "That'll be three beaver pelts."

"You pirate. What are you going to do with the money?"

Well, I plan to use it the way you would—drinking and whoring."

"I thought you said you would never mess with another whore as long as you lived."

"A man can change his mind. I'm just following your sterling example. After all, you're my mentor. Besides, I learned how to treat the clap and syphilis from my Da."

"Just what the world needs, another drunken Irish cocksman," grumbled Ned. "Well, let's drink up. Time's awastin'. Old Lucifer's about ready to jump out of me britches."

Ned and Brian spent the next three days trading furs, buying supplies, and of course getting hopelessly drunk and sleeping with every available whore at the Rendezvous. Fortunately, they caught nothing more serious than headsplitting hangovers.

The last Rendezvous drew to an end. The men didn't know it, but their paths would cross again during a bloody civil war and the Indian wars. They sensed that a great era in American history was coming to a close, but Bridger, Carson, and Johnston never dreamed that their names would be famous someday as founders of the great American West. They parted sadly on the last day. Each went his separate way save Brian, Ned, Johnston, and Del, who forded the Green River and headed towards Fort Union. Brian and Ned somberly gave Captain Clark's gun to Mike Fink, who would make sure to return it personally to its rightful owner.

They gambled with Dr. Burch and broke even. Brian was becoming almost as good as Ned at poker. One morning Burch filled Ned's teeth with the four hundred dollars in gold that he owed him. Ned's face was puffy and discolored when he entered the saloon.

"Ah, Mr. Boyd, I've got a severe 'tooth.' How about a bottle of whiskey?" he croaked.

"Uh, oh! Just promise me you won't sit in here naked playing cards again."

"Aye, I promise to stay fully clothed—but nothing else. I feel a hellacious drunk coming on."

Brian, before beginning the inevitable last debauchery of the year, wisely wrote his father a letter telling him that they would be back next spring after wintering with the Crows. He gave the letter to Fink with his thanks, then joined Ned and "Mr. Whiskey." At midnight they staggered up the stairs, one on each side of the lovely Renée. In her bed they shared her talent for lovemaking throughout the night.

At noon, somewhat the worse for wear, they mounted their horses and headed toward the Big Horn River. Brian swore that he would never drink another drop of liquor as long as he lived. Ned, knowing his own proclivity for drink, made no such rash promises, but loudly groaned about his head and teeth with every step that his horse took. Even Ned's horse could sense his painful hangover and trod gently on the Montana soil to keep his master from groaning and cursing.

"God, I'd forgotten how beautiful it is here. The sky seems huge; it stretches forever. And look at those beautiful mountains! Just look at it, Ned! This is the most spectacular scenery in the world."

"Brian, would you mind too much if I told you to keep your goddamned voice down and spare me the poetry, please?"

"Ingrate."

"And keep that nag of yours from kicking up so much dust in my face."

"Go on, you lead. I'll just look at these beautiful clouds and sky while you wallow in your sorrows."

Ned took the lead for twenty yards, then dismounted and ducked his head in an ice-cold stream. He staggered toward his horse, mounted him, and plodded resolutely to the south, grumbling and cursing until they collapsed into their robes that night. Brian sighed and said, "Good night, Ned." He was answered only by Ned's guttural snoring.

31

It began innocently enough, with a tiny spark from a lightning bolt that set the prairie grass smoldering at the base of a Ponderosa pine. The wind fanned it into life. It consumed the dry prairie grass in the valley between the mountains which would be named after President Madison and Jim Bridger. Ahead of it ran rattlesnakes, mice, rats, and prairie dogs. The eagles and hawks soared in the thermals and singed their wings as they plummeted in for a quick kill on the fleeing rodents. Next came the coyotes and wolves. The elk and deer quickly headed for the mountains rather than attempting to outdistance it on the plains. Finally, the buffalo began to stampede away from its hot, explosive breath and raced upwards towards the Yellowstone. It roared along at a hundred miles per hour, indifferent to the flight of the creatures below.

When it came within twenty yards of a pine tree, the tree would bend toward it and then be blown back and then explode into a shower of sparks and flame. The pines exploded with such force that they were launched into the air like missiles—which ignited even more fires. The firestorm did not need to travel on the ground, for soaring through the treetops was quicker. The ground would ignite later.

It created its own weather, causing hurricane-like winds, and disintegrating cloud patterns and causing heat lightning. The lightning caused other little sibling fires nearby; finally all melded together as it consumed everything in its path.

Many of its victims died from suffocation before the heat

ionized them into charred skeletons. It took their oxygen and smothered them before searing their flesh and exploding their tissues into charred carbon on blackened skeletons.

Ned, hungover as he was, was the first to stir to it. He heard far-off thunder and fierce winds rushing to the north. He groaned in his robes and wondered why the wind was blowing from south to north. He felt a strange rumble. He wondered...stampede? Ah, it's only a bad dream, he thought, still hung over, and went back to sleep. Brian was reawakened by dancing light and shadows, sharp popping noises, and the shrieks of small animals. Hot winds rushed over him. Then the unmistakable thunderous noise surrounded him. Where had he heard that noise before? He rolled onto his stomach, turning to the source of the noise and dancing lights, and said, "What was that sound?" He sat bolt upright. "Buffalo stampede!" he yelled. Smoke and fire singed him and smothered him. The stench of burning carcasses made him sick.

The horses screamed as the flames came closer. He punched Ned, who jumped out of his robes and headed straight toward their horses. Ned and Brian vainly tried to unleash them and drag them into the river. They tried to get their robes, guns and belongings but to no avail; they couldn't outrun the fire. Finally they dove into the Big Horn and watched the flaming mushroom rise over them, listening to their poor horses scream horribly as they burned to death. Ned muttered, "Poor Bastard," as they ducked under the current to escape the fire's heat. They came up to breathe, but the air was only smoke and heat and it seared their lungs. They ducked back under again, hanging onto each other to keep from being swept away. They surfaced again together, sucking in hot air. At times they were nearly bowled over by the current. They held onto the roots of trees whose tops exploded in the firestorm surrounding them. Finally it passed and the prairie to the east ignited. They still could hardly breathe. Their eyebrows were singed, and they could only smell

138

burnt hair from their nostrils. Their hair and beards felt thin and curly and smoldered. All they could see around them was black death, highlighted by the dancing lights of the prairie burning up to the east. The hot winds slowly subsided. Finally they dragged themselves to shore.

They felt around in the darkness, only to find that their robes were charred into useless piles of smoking stench. Their gunpowder had exploded, their lead balls were molten masses of useless black metal. Amazingly, the Hawken rifles were only discolored and their wooden stocks had not caught fire. But without percussion caps, balls, or powder, they were defenseless against Indians that would scalp them or animals that would maul and eat them. They slowly gathered their charred pots and pans. Their traps, though blackened, still worked. They stripped and dried their only remaining clothes in the early morning sunlight. Ned smiled and said, "Damnation, it's cold out. It's a pity we can't light a fire to keep us warm."

"Oh that's rich! Just what we need is another fucking fire."

"Your language amazes me. You needn't worry. There's nothing flammable within a hundred miles of here to keep us warm." Finally the heat from the sun warmed them. They picked up their rifles and put on their smoky, sun-dried clothes. They gathered the melted lead, of their shot and headed southeast toward the Little Big Horn. Everywhere they looked they saw black, stinking, devastation. The air reeked of charred buffalo, elk and deer. Only the raptors, rodents, and snakes had survived. Brian and Ned began to feel indestructible. They had survived nature's worst catastrophe; they would make it to the Crow camp. Still, they felt very vulnerable without gunpowder. "Well, let's hope we make it to the Crow camp before the Sioux or Blackfeet get us," said Brian.

"I thought you were a veritable god among the Sioux."

"I forgot to bring my war vest for protection."

"What a stupid, focking, bloody blunder," exhaled Ned.

"I guess I didn't bring it because I knew the Crows would see it and would be angry, or something like that," mumbled Brian.

"Sounds like a serious case of 'White Fawn' to me," Ned quipped.

"It would have burnt up anyway," retorted Brian.

32

The journey to the Big Horn River was uneventful but quite long without horses. Since they had no powder to shoot game, they lived on berries and fish. When they reached the Crow village they were quickly surrounded by warriors. They recognized Brian, and soon Plenty Coupes came to greet them. He told them that they had just fought off a war party of Sioux. The Blackfeet had always been their enemy but now the Sioux were moving into their hunting grounds from the east and acting quite warlike. Since the Crow considered this area their sacred hunting grounds, any incursion by the Sioux was considered a serious offense. Spotted Owl had been killed in battle by a teenage Sioux named Crazy Horse. Another Sioux named Sitting Bull had been extremely fearless in battle, and had counted many coupes amongst the Crow during the battle.

Ned looked at Brian, who said nothing of his friendship with the Sioux to the Crow leader.

"White Fawn will be happy to see you, my friend.

She looked lonely after you departed." Brian blushed as Ned snorted and tried to hide an impish grin.

After properly introducing Ned to Plenty Coupes and the warriors that he remembered, they headed into camp.

As soon as his eyes met those of White Fawn, Brian knew that someday he would marry her. She rushed to him and then demurely lowered her head. She gave him a shy smile and he stood there, dumbfounded.

"Jaysus, say something!" Urged Ned. "You looked like a stunned ox."

"Oh, shut up, you Irish slob."

White Fawn seemed taken aback by their gruff sparring. In due time, however, Brian introduced Ned to her and to his surprise, Ned behaved quite graciously, becoming especially well-mannered in her presence. Later, when they were alone, Ned asked if she had any sisters.

"Why?"

"Because she is absolutely stunning. She has the loveliest brown eyes I have ever seen. I've always been partial to dark-eyed beauties with black hair."

"Well, you'll see plenty of them here. As far as having sisters, I'm not sure, but believe me, you'll enjoy your stay."

"Ah, I think you may be right about this for once, old Brian. Yes indeed, a man could sure enjoy himself among these lovely maidens." Two beautiful young squaws shyly smiled at Ned as they walked past.

"Obviously they have very low standards when it comes to judging men," observed Brian.

"On the contrary. Did you see how they looked at me, didja now?"

"Yes, I'm sure they were trying to figure out if your hair and beard always looked like a buffalo or if it had been singed in a campfire."

"Ungrateful whelp. How dare you slander me Celtic good looks?"

"Good God, Ned. You've only been in camp for ten minutes and you're acting like Don Juan already."

"Aye, you must watch your mentor and I'll teach you the fine art of wooing a woman."

"You better be careful, or some jealous brave may decide to make a necklace out of your bollocks."

"Not likely. Old Ned can take care of himself," he

muttered as he sauntered off in the direction of two more lovely looking squaws.

Brian began to wonder if he had made a serious mistake in bringing the wild Irishman to the Crow camp.

33

Ned never ceased to amaze Brian. He quickly learned the Crow sign language, and within a month could speak fluently with the Crow, who also knew some English through their dealings with the English fur traders and the missionaries who had tried to convert them. They had a mutual distrust of the English who had tried to trade whiskey and guns for their furs. Plenty Coupes wisely forbade them to drink the Englishmen's alcohol. Ned even learned to hunt with a bow and arrow. When Brian asked him why, he replied simply, "I only get one shot with me Hawken, but arrows are a replenishable source of ammunition. Besides, I want to go with them on the buffalo hunts."

"It's very dangerous," said Brian. "I'll take a Hawken any day."

"Choose your own poison," replied Ned with a smile.

One day the word spread that a herd of buffalo had been seen three miles from their camp in an area called the Greasy Grass near the Little Big Horn. At night the Indians celebrated, donning buffalo capes and dancing around the fire to ask the spirits for success in their hunt.

Ned had taken a liking to a quiet, beautiful woman named Laughing Bird. She had a great sense of humor and, as her name suggested, a melodious laugh. She had been in mourning since her husband was killed by the Sioux in their recent raid. Since then she had not smiled—until she met Ned, whose prattle caused her to smile and laugh again like a young girl. She was twenty-nine and

Ned was hopelessly smitten with her. She begged him not to go on the hunt, for she feared for his life. Ned naturally ignored her. He couldn't wait until the morning.

White Fawn was also especially attentive toward Brian that night as well. They sneaked away from the others around the fire, and he kissed her for the first time. Brian was enchanted with her. They held each other tightly as they listened to the chants in the distance. Finally it was time for bed. They walked hand in hand back to the campfire. Plenty Coupes smiled at them both. They parted and Brian went to his wickiup. Ned came in soon after and collapsed next to him. "A man could do well to spend his life like this," he said quietly.

"I thought you would rather be in Fort Union with your whores and whiskey."

"Perhaps not. I think I might be falling in love with dear Laughing Bird."

"Hogwash. You falling in love with an Indian? I nearly had to drag you here, bitching and moaning all the way."

"Well, just for once you may have been right, old Brian."

"Get some sleep. You'll need it tomorrow."

"Hah! I'm ready. Those buffalo haven't ever seen the likes of an Irishman on horseback with a bow and arrow."

"You're crazy. You better take a Hawken," Brian cautioned.

Ned answered with a snore.

It was dark and cold. Ned was shaking him.

"Get up! You'll miss all the action."

Brian grumbled and exclaimed, "What the hell?" as he noticed that Ned had painted his face. "You look like a fucking red-haired raccoon."

"Watch your language, pale face."

Brian dressed quickly, and checked and rechecked his Hawken. His hands were shaking with excitement. He was getting that feeling of invincibility again.

"Jaysus! I haven't seen you so excited in your life."

"Wait and see. It's something you'll never forget."

Ned and Brian joined the other hunters who were strangely somber. This was no game to them; men could die today, and their families depended on their safe return with meat to get them through the winter. The hunt was a struggle for their very existence.

They rode quietly downwind of the buffalo. When they were within twenty yards, the sun peeked over the snow-capped Big Horn Mountains. Plenty Coupes burst into a screaming chant and led them into the unsuspecting herd. The ground began to shake and an unmistakable rumble began to echo throughout the valley. A huge cloud of dust rose. The buffalo bellowed, the Indians whooped, and Brian's heart exploded with joy. His horse charged into their midst. He whirled, turned, and began to chase the biggest bull in the herd. "You're mine, you miserable beast!" He was riding beside him. The buffalo's eyes showed no fear but looked at him sideways with a baleful stare. Brian fired the Hawken and hit the bull in the chest. The bull grunted but didn't go down; if anything, it sped up, and turned its horns toward his horse. Brian had an incredible urge to jump on him and ride, but his horse suddenly stopped and Brian went over the top. He hit the ground running. There were buffalo everywhere running at him. He laughed and played his game, deftly dancing away from them. Some of the Indians stopped and shook their heads in amazement. The bull heard Brian's laughter before he saw him, and charged. Before he could sidestep the bull, its horns had sliced into his thigh and thrown him in the air. He landed hard; pain was instantaneous. He tried to get up, but the wind was knocked out of him, and his right leg was useless. He tried to crawl, looking vainly for a weapon or a tree to climb. There were none. He rolled onto his back, choking in the dust. The sun blinded him. He could barely see the bull ten feet from him. The bull languidly pawed the earth and lowered his horns. "I'm going to die," thought Brian. "Ah, well, I'd rather go this way than in some saloon..." he thought. The bull was coming at him as if in slow motion, it seemed. Blood was coming out of the bull's nostrils. "You'll die too," Brian mumbled. Out of the corner of his eye he saw a blur of movement and heard Ned yell to the bull, "Leave him alone, you bloody bastard!" Somehow Ned had spurred his horse between the buffalo and Brian. The bull toppled Ned and the horse like a willow stick, gored the horse, and whirled in Brian's direction. He lowered his horns and grunted.

"Now I'm really pissed...first my friend, now my horse. Die, you bloody thug!" Ned calmly raised his bow and loosed an arrow straight into the bull's chest. The bull roared, lowered its head, and charged Ned. "Come on, I'll kill you with my bare hands!" Ned raged. The buffalo's horns dug into the ground five feet from Ned and it somersaulted onto its back, flanks heaving. Ned shot another arrow into its chest and the bull was finally still. Ned ran over and kicked it and jumped on its head yelling, "That'll teach you to mess with the Irish and my horse."

Brian moaned, "You're completely insane."

"I know, but Jaysus, I love this. I've never felt so alive before. Are you all right, lad?"

"Don't call me 'lad'."

"What gratitude! I save the bloody sod's life and he says don't call me lad. Silence, before I tell you to do something anatomically impossible."

"Whuzzat that mean?" Brian was becoming incoherent from blood loss and pain.

"The literal English translation for the uneducated man is, go fock yourself."

"Oh, I get it," said Brian, who proceeded to pass out. He found himself being gently lifted over Ned's shoulders. There were still buffalo careening around them but Ned carried him through the maelstrom of hooves, horns, grunts and dust. He faintly heard Ned grumbling and swearing something about Brian's needing to lose some weight, but for once he couldn't think of some smart retort. Besides, he felt weightless. He was shivering and he knew that he was going into shock. Got to stop the bleeding...

They put him on a travois and pulled him back to camp. He somehow managed to put pressure on the wound, which was gushing blood. He retched with pain and floated in and out of consciousness. When he awoke, he was in Plenty Coupes lodge. He felt the medicine man applying an herb poultice to the wound. Amazingly, the pain subsided. He became aware that his head was cradled in a warm soft place that was gently moving, and realized it was White Fawn's breast. He could smell her sweet breath. She stroked his hair and murmured plaintively, "Please don't leave me. I love you with all my heart." He was vaguely aware that his face was wet from her tears. She gently wiped his face. He thought, God, I love this woman.

"Ah, you needn't worry. He's too stubborn to die," Ned announced.

"Quiet, you crazy fool," said Laughing Bird. "She needs words of compassion. Be tenderhearted to her."

"I was just trying to help. I did save his life, you know."

"So I heard. They said you were fearless but I think you were crazy to attack that huge bull. I could have lost you," she glared.

For the first time in his life, Brian actually saw Ned back down from someone else. He didn't cower but was respectful of her.

"I'm sorry," he grumbled.

"You're forgiven," she said. "Come over to me and hold me, for I feared for your life, crazy one."

"Why, it would be an honor." He held her tightly and she began to sob. Brian saw Ned look at him slyly and wink out of the corner of his eye.

"There, there, sweet lass. Old Ned's got you in his arms. Nothing to fear. Perhaps we could go outside for a while and console one another." He took her hand and they stepped outside

149

together. Suddenly Ned's head peeked back inside and he said, "You're quite lucky, you know."

"How's that?"

"Well, the medicine man wouldn't let me light some powder on your crotch to stop the bleeding."

"Thank God for that."

"Oh, by the way…the bull missed your jewels and you aren't so well endowed yourself, old son."

"Ned, go do something anatomically impossible."

"To the contrary—I have something quite anatomically feasible in mind."

With that, Laughing Bird yanked him from behind and Ned's head disappeared. "You white men converse in strange ways. What are you talking about?"

"Oh, I think it's time to meet old Lucifer."

"Lucifer…isn't that the white man's devil?"

"Hush, hush, my sweet bird. You have nothing to fear from this Lucifer. Trust me."

"'Trust me,'" The man is completely impossible," groaned Brian. He had a smile on his face and he nestled between White Fawn's soft breasts and fell asleep. He dreamt of dancing among the buffalo. He heard the lovely rumble of their hooves and distinct from that sound, the rhythmic calm beat of her heart.

34

When Brian awoke, White Fawn was sleeping next to her brother, Many Coupes. Her father and mother were up already. The camp was awake with excitement. The herd was now five miles away. Their hunt had not been successful, partly because of the efforts to rescue Brian. Ned came in to check on him. Once again he had painted his face. "This time I'm going to get more than one of those buffalo."

"I take it you didn't learn anything yesterday," said Brian.

"Ah, I did. When in Rome, do as the Romans do."

"What's that supposed to mean?"

"Use a bow and arrow and leave your Hawken at home," laughed Ned.

"I guess I didn't use enough powder."

"No, the ball was wedged in the bull's skin but it did break a rib and rile him up."

"Next time I'll use eighty grains of powder."

"That could help. I take it you didn't learn anything yesterday either," Ned said.

"Next time I'll stay on my horse."

"So you'll do it again?"

"As soon as I can run again. It gets in your blood, doesn't it, Ned?"

"Ah, yes it does. There's nothing better than riding free in the wind chasing those beasts. I love it too, you know. Instead of being the mayor of Fort Union, maybe I'll become a great chief."

Brian laughed. "Go on and get a few for me. Be careful, Ned."

"As always, I'll look out for meself." He got up and walked out of the lodge. He could hear Laughing Bird's entreaties for Ned to stay. Typically, Ned told her to mind her own business. "I'll listen to you about compassion towards grieving women but hunting's another thing. It's my life and I'll be back with you tonight."

"You crazy fool," scolded, Laughing Bird.

"Ah, that I am, and I'm crazy for you, you lovely woman." She said nothing in reply. Brian heard him mount his horse and let out a yell. "Wait up, lads. We've got some fun ahead of us." They thundered off in the direction of the herd. Brian desperately wanted to be with them.

"I'll be back some day," he muttered.

"How could you?" she said.

"Because I love it."

"Do you love it more than me?"

"No."

"Well, give it up for me, I don't want to lose you."

"Don't worry. I'll be more careful in the future."

"Men...You're all alike, white men, our men. You're never happy unless you're killing something."

Brian couldn't think of an answer quickly. He wanted to tell her he was happy when he was with her or taking care of the sick, especially children, but she had stormed out to look for her best friend, Laughing Bird. Undoubtedly the two would denounce them as hopeless, immature savages. He was too weak to follow her and tell her his answer, so he rolled over and went back to sleep.

He woke up to the sounds of triumphant cries. They were all back safe and they had enough meat to last the tribe through the winter. He hobbled outside to greet them. Ned was the happiest of them all. Soon the whole camp was empty, as much work had to be done: the meat had to be prepared, hides stripped and stretched over the fires. The men were busy boasting about their bravery while the women quietly and effectively went about their work ensuring that all would survive another Montana winter.

Meanwhile, Brian had important business. He sought out White Fawn's father and asked his permission to marry her. Great Bear looked at him solemnly and said, "Plenty Coupes has said that you are a good man and a brave hunter, but I have one concern. I have seen white men like you before. You live with us and enjoy our way of life and customs. Then you marry one of our daughters. After a while, the white man misses his family and what he calls 'civilization.' He says he will go back to visit his family—and never returns. I do not want this for my daughter. Promise me you will never abandon her."

"Sir, you have my word that I will never leave her or hurt her in any way, and that I will be a good husband and father as long as we both shall live."

"Then you have my permission."

Brian gave him one of Captain Clark's coins, which deeply impressed Great Bear.

"I will give you a horse who will not falter during a buffalo chase, so that you will always come back to us. When will the marriage take place?"

"In the spring, when the missionaries come."

"So she will have to be a Catholic and my grandchildren baptized?"

"I would hope so, but I would also like to be married by your holy man and our children taught your spiritual beliefs."

"That is good, but we have already been baptized by Father DeSmet...Religions are irrelevant. Ours and yours are very similar. It is how one lives one's life that matters. Good, it is settled." They embraced.

"Does she know this?"

"No, but I will ask her soon."

153

"It is good that you asked me first. I am sure she will marry you."

"Thank you."

Brian was so excited that he nearly fell over as he limped too quickly towards the campfire. He sat down next to her, but she ignored him. Finally he said, "White Fawn, there's something I have been afraid to tell you."

"What?"

"I love you. I thought I was in love once before but this is different. I want to be with you the rest of my life. Just don't ask me not to hunt again, please."

She said nothing but had a puzzled look on her face. "What are you saying to me?"

"Will you marry me?"

She looked utterly dumbfounded. Finally she smiled and said, "Yes. I have loved you since the first time I saw you."

He kissed her. Plenty Coupes suddenly came over to them with a grim look on his face and said, "We do not kiss a woman in front of the others unless you are to be married. Please do not kiss my sister in front of the others again."

White Fawn laughed and said, "We are going to be married."

"Have you talked to Great Bear?"

"This afternoon he gave his permission," said Brian.

"This is good. I know you will be good to her. I am glad to be your brother." They embraced. He strode to the campfire and announced, "Silence! I have great news. Since Man-Who-Outjumps-Buffalo can no longer jump, we will call him 'Buffalo Dancer.' I am also proud that he will soon be my brother, as he is going to marry my sister." A great shout of joy ran through the Crows and they began to dance. White Fawn's mother and father began to dance with the rest of the Indians. Ned and Laughing Bird joined them. Ned said quietly to Brian, "Maybe we'll have a double wedding."

154

"You? Get married? You can't be serious."

"Aye, but I'll have to woo the woman quite a bit. She's quite headstrong, you know."

"Sounds like someone else I know," said Brian.

"We'll see."

"When will this take place?" asked Ned.

"In the spring when the first missionary arrives."

"Ah, just enough time. I'll have her licking out of me hand by then."

"Ned, you're impossible."

"That I am, lad."

"What are you two planning?" asked Laughing Bird.

"Ah, a trivial thing, my sweet. Come, let us dance sweet Bird." With that he grabbed her and began doing the Irish jig. The Crow stopped dancing and howled with laughter. She quickly caught on and her musical laugh drowned out the others. Plenty Coupes did a caricature of the Irish jig that caused Brian to fall backwards over the log they had been sitting on. White Fawn fell over with him and he kissed her gently and said, "I will be a good husband and take care of you and our children forever."

"I know you will, Buffalo Dancer."

"Well, at least it's shorter than 'Man-Who-Rides-Buffaloes'."

"What kind of name is that?"

"Well, it's a long story. I'll tell you some day after we're married."

They got up and went to their separate beds.

35

The winter was uncharacteristically mild. Brian and Ned spent their nights with White Fawn and Laughing Bird, listening to the elders tell of their customs, religious beliefs, and their wars with the Sioux and Blackfeet. Ned was enthralled with their history. He became a favorite of the elders, teaching them in turn the history of the white man from the Egyptians to the Romans, the Greeks, and the middle ages on up to the present. He spent an hour every day with the children, teaching them history. This is what finally won over Laughing Bird. Ned was a great teacher and he was so kind to the children. They soon announced that they would be married in the spring.

The missionary came and married them. Within a month, Laughing Bird told Ned that she was pregnant. He cried tears of joy the first time he felt the baby kicking inside her. They would lie together and he would place his hand over her round belly, giggling when the baby kicked. Ned often rode off on war parties and helped the Crows steal back horses from the Sioux and Cheyenne. He never killed, but he took great pride in counting coupes on their enemy. He was revered by the Crow as a hunter and as a warrior, but most of all as their teacher. Brian never went on war parties at his wife's insistence, but never missed a buffalo hunt. He was decidedly more cautious now that he was a father. Their daughter, whom they had named Sweet Child, was the light of his life. She adored him. When he returned from the hunt she would crawl on his lap. He would take her in his arms and tickle her belly with his beard and they laughed at her squeals of delight.

Brian had gone to Fort Union and sent his father a letter telling him of his marriage and that he was now a grandfather. He went back but there was no answering letter. Laughing Bird was two months pregnant when Brian told them that he was going to St. Louis to see if his father was all right. Brian had become deeply troubled because his father hadn't written. Surely his father wasn't angry with him for marrying an Indian; he had great respect for them and treated many indigent Indians for nothing. Ned decided to stay, not wanting to tempt himself with saloons and whores. Brian promised he would be back in a month.

"Promise you will return, because I am pregnant again. This time I think it will be a son," his wife said.

He told her not to worry; he would be back.

But when Brian turned the corner of his old street, he noticed that his father's house was shuttered and his sign was gone. With a lump in his throat, he ran to Bridget's house. She told him that his father had died in a cholera epidemic; he had contracted the disease from one of his patients. Brian barely noticed the little boy who looked strangely familiar to him. Bridget was pregnant again. He talked to her husband, who informed him that his estate was worth quite a bit of money.

"Put the house up for sale—sell it all. Do you still have my letters of recommendation for medical school?" he asked tersely.

"Yes," he answered.

"Well, maybe I'll be back some day and study medicine. Forgive me for being rude…but can you show me his grave?"

They went to the cemetery. Brian placed a flower on his mother's and father's graves and wept silently. Bridget and her husband consoled him. Brian never went back to the house. He slept on the docks, and the following morning boarded the same steamer that had brought him from Fort Union. He couldn't wait to get back to his wife and child.

36

When he arrived at the camp it was in a shambles. Women and children were crying. Ned and Plenty Coupes were nowhere to be found. He ran to his lodge; White Fawn wasn't there. He ran to Great Bear's lodge and found him weeping. "What happened?"

"The Sioux raided our camp. "

"Where are White Fawn and Sweet Child?"

"Murdered by Running Dog. They were down at the river washing clothes with Laughing Bird. She was killed by a *wickte* named Black Coyote. " He knew them both. They were not Sioux; they were Cheyenne's who had been shunned by their own people, hangers-on with Sitting Bull's camp. Great Bear took Brian to White Fawn and Laughing Bird. They lay in their burial robes. Both women had been scalped. His unborn child was dead inside her. He was too numb to be enraged. Shortly, Ned and Plenty Coupes and the other warriors rode into camp. Brian told Ned the news and he went inside with him. Ned trembled and sobbed when he saw Laughing Bird's mutilated body. He held her and vowed immediate revenge. But, Brian said, "First we must bury them; then we'll kill their murderers."

Plenty Coupes said, "We will not bury them, but place them above the ground in the sky in Crow fashion." They tried to console each other. Plenty Coupes asked to go along with them.

Great Bear said, "No, you are to be our chief some day. This

159

is a matter between the husbands and their Cheyenne murderers, not between Crow and Sioux." Plenty Coupes unwillingly relented. Ned said coldly, "I've never killed a man before, but tomorrow I will kill Black Coyote. "

"I thought you killed Pierre MacKenzie. "

"Nah, I wounded him and let the varmints do the dirty work. "

"Well, you must know that Black Coyote is a very skilled fighter with both tomahawk and knife; if you challenge him, you will have to fight him with the weapons of his choice. "

Ned coldly asked Plenty Coupes for his tomahawk and began to sharpen his Bowie knife. "What about you? How will you fight the man named Running Dog?"

"He is big and likes to wrestle. I beat him once already. Tomorrow I will just break his neck," Brian said quietly. Ned had never seen Brian act so calmly, and it worried him. Brian was keeping his rage inside. He now knew the demon inside Liver-Eating Johnston's soul and why it possessed him.

37

The next morning they rode out. Ned left his bow and arrow, but took the Hawken and a pistol as well as his knife and the borrowed tomahawk. Brian had his knife, pistol, and Hawken rifle. They quickly found the trail and rode grimly for hours, not speaking to one another. Brian had never seen such a murderous look in Ned's eyes. Finally Brian said, "Black Coyote is a *wickte*, that's why he was shunned by the Cheyenne. The Sioux are more tolerant of them. "

"What in Christ's name is a *wickte*?"

"Well, they don't like women...they prefer men. "

"You mean to say that the man who killed my wife is a bleedin' fairy?"

"In a sense, yes. "

"Goddammit! Now I really hate him. This is an abomination. "

"Actually, I kind of feel sorry for them. "

"Jaysus H. Christ! Sorry for them? You never cease to amaze me. That's completely against God's will. How could you defend someone who killed Laughing Bird?"

"I didn't say that. Just don't be fooled because he doesn't act like a man—he is very dangerous. "

"He'll also be very focking dead in a few hours," swore Ned, who kicked his horse savagely and raced him across the plains toward the Sioux camp. Brian shook his head. He had never seen Ned in such a murderous rage. That was the last thing that was

161

needed against a skilled killer like the *wickte*. He kicked his horse into a gallop and followed the mad Irishman toward the Sioux Camp.

38

Sitting Bull was playing with his children when two white men rode into camp, surrounded by sentries, one of whom was talking to the taller man as if he knew him. The other man was very quiet and wore a grim expression which his red beard failed to hide. Suddenly Sitting Bull recognized Brian. He jumped to his feet and said, "Man-Who-Rides-Buffalo, it is good to see you."

The red-haired man said, "Christ, you have a penchant for strange monikers."

Brian ignored him and said, "Sitting Bull! They tell me you are now the chief of the Hunkpapas. It is good to see you, my brother."

The men dismounted. Brian and Sitting Bull embraced.

"This is my friend, Ned O'Grady."

Sitting Bull greeted him and said, "Why do you look so angry?"

"'Tis an honor to meet you, Chief, but we are looking for two men who murdered our wives and his daughter."

"Why do you come here? The Lakota do not kill women and children. We always return white women unharmed if we should capture them in a battle."

"They weren't white women…they were Crow," said Brian softly.

"You married our enemies' women?" said Sitting Bull slowly.

"Love does strange things, and white men are not concerned with your ancient wars," said Brian.

"It is true. We do not concern ourselves with your wars with the English and as you say, love has remarkable powers over men's souls. But enough talk. How can I help you? My men raided their camp and came back with some of their horses, but there was no talk of killing."

"My wife's father saw them—one of them is the *wickte*, the other is Running Dog."

"They are not Lakota...I should have thrown them out long ago. Bring them to me now!" thundered Sitting Bull.

"I know they are not Lakota...you were kind to take them in. Since they are not Sioux, then you and the elders will not have to question them or punish them," said Brian.

"I will still question them, then you can challenge them."

The two were brought before Sitting Bull. They denied killing the women, but it was obvious they were lying. Neither would look Sitting Bull in the eye. Brian noticed that Running Dog had grown into a large, powerful man since he had last wrestled him. He wished that he had the choice of how to do battle.

"Man-Who-Rides-Buffalo says you killed his wife and child. He challenges you to fight to the death."

"Gladly," smiled Running Dog, who had always hated Brian since losing to him. "We will fight with our bare hands."

Suddenly a boy named Crazy Horse produced a scalp. "I found this in Running Dog's wikiup."

When Brian saw his wife's beautiful hair, he trembled with grief. Any fear of Running Dog was replaced with rage.

"You will fight in one hour."

"What about Black Coyote?" asked Ned.

"Has anyone found Ned's wife's scalp among his possessions?" asked Sitting Bull. No one came forward." I do not believe Black Coyote's answer. If you can get him to fight you, he is yours. He is a coward," intoned Sitting Bull scornfully.

164

Ned walked over and slapped the *wickte's* face. Black Coyote looked at Ned, and made a kissing motion with his lips, and licked his lips provocatively. Ned spit on him, yet the Indian did nothing.

"I will fight you with a tomahawk," said Ned.

A frightening grin crossed the Coyote's face.

"Prepare to die, Red Beard," said the *wickte*. Running Dog handed Black Coyote's tomahawk to him, and Brian gave Many Coupes' tomahawk to Ned. A circle formed. Ned, typically, went on the attack, charging the Indian and clumsily trying to bludgeon him. The *wickte* pirouetted and danced around the charges while smiling and laughing; he was toying with Ned. Ned's eyes stung with sweat and he was becoming short of breath. Eventually he could barely lift his weapon. Casually the Coyote twirled his tomahawk around his fingers and began stalking Ned. He smiled and struck Ned in the arm. Ned dropped the tomahawk and fell to his knees, clutching his arm. The Indian danced and whirled around him, smiling while making a great show of twirling his tomahawk around Ned's head. Ned almost seemed resigned to his death; he was exhausted.

"Stand up and die like a man," snarled the Coyote.

Ned got up and the Indian made a great show of spinning his tomahawk in the air and catching it easily. The crowd had seen this before. Death was always swift when Black Coyote made his final charge. In the midst of one of the fake charges Ned said, "Ah, bollocks, I'm tired of this little game." He pulled out his pistol and shot the Indian in the kneecap. The Sioux were outraged at first, but they also disliked the *wickte's* arrogance. Ned stalked over to the writhing Indian, stepped on his wrist, and wrenched the tomahawk from his grasp. Instead of bludgeoning him, he threw it away, then kicked the Indian in the groin.

"First you'll feel pain, then you'll feel no pain. Then you will feel pain again before you die."

He ground his heel into the Indian's face. Black Coyote screamed in pain.

"Enough pain." He pulled the Indian's head up and wrenched it suddenly. There was a loud cracking of broken vertebrae, then the Indian slumped to the ground and soiled himself.

Ned said, "I can't stand the smell of dung," and walked over to his horse, where he got his rifle and knife. Young Crazy Horse could take it no longer and charged toward Ned. Ned whirled and pointed the rifle at Crazy Horse. Brian jumped between the two and shielded Crazy Horse, holding him in his arms.

Sitting Bull said, "This is between the two men only. Stand back, Crazy Horse."

Ned dropped the Hawken and took his knife and said, "Ah, so you like to kill women and unborn babies? It's pain time again, faggot." He began to scalp the screaming Indian. "This is for my wife, you piece of dung!" He put down the scalp next to his Hawken and picked up the rifle. Walking over to the paralyzed Indian, Ned placed the rifle barrel against his eye socket and said, "Have a nice day in hell!" Then he pulled the trigger. He dropped his gun, dragged the dead Indian to the riverbank, and threw him in. The Coyote was sucked into the current and disappeared. Ned washed his bloodied hands and face and said, "I believe you're next, Brian."

The circle of Indians formed again and the next two adversaries faced off. As exciting as Ned's battle had been, Brian's was anticlimactic. Running Dog had indeed grown bigger and stronger than Brian—but also slower. In less than a minute Brian had pinned him down and snapped Running Dog's neck. Brian went to his horse, and took his knife, and scalped him; as Running Dog cried out in pain. Unlike Ned, Brian went about his mutilation silently. He considered throwing the paralyzed Indian into the river and letting him drown, but hesitated, remembering his promise to Sitting Bull not to ever let his brother suffer. Still, this man was not his brother. Finally he picked up Black Coyote's tomahawk and said, "This is for White Fawn, Sweet Child, and my unborn child," with that Brian raised the ax and crushed Running Dog's skull. He too dispatched his foe's body into the whirling river. This time the Sioux cheered, for it had been an honorable fight to the death.

Afterward, Sitting Bull asked, "Will you return to the Crow, or would you like to stay with us?"

"Neither," said Brian. "I'm tired of all the fighting and killing and dangerous animals. I'm going to go back home and become a doctor."

"That is wise. Red Cloud has already declared war on the white people. It is no longer safe for your people to hunt here. And what of you, Red Beard?"

Sitting Bull, like everyone else, had taken a liking to the Irishman after talking to him for a while—though he still disapproved of Ned's fighting tactics.

"I think I may try civilization myself. I might teach school and maybe get into politics. Would it be possible to join you on occasion to help with your buffalo hunts? I'm quite good with a bow and arrow, you know. I won't eat much and you can have the furs and horns and all."

Sitting Bull laughed and said, "Yes, you are welcome for a while. I will let you know when it is too dangerous to come back."

"Thank you," said Ned solemnly, aware of the honor.

They spent the night with the Sioux, got up early and headed back to the Crow. Before they left, Sitting Bull and Brian embraced.

"Have a safe journey, my brother."

"Thank you. I'm so glad you are a chief. You will be a great leader."

"I hope so, but I don't like being responsible for the safety of my people. It was much easier to be young and free and fighting grizzly bears."

"I'd rather be chief any day," said Brian. Then he grew melancholy." I probably will never see you again, my brother. May you have a good life." Neither guessed that their paths would cross again on a little river in the valley of the Greasy Grass.

Brian and Ned rode into the Crow camp, which was now back in order. They had decided to pass the rest of the summer there, then spend some time in the early fall trapping on their way toward Fort Union. Brian would then return to St. Louis and go to college and medical school. Ned was quite sincere about teaching school and dabbling in politics. Brian had told him seriously that he was quite an orator and had no doubt that he could win a public office. Ned felt strongly that his platform should be based on peace and mutual respect among whites and Indians. He knew that otherwise they would never be able to survive the upcoming influx of whites into the Montana territory.

39

Great Bear, his wife, and Plenty Coupes greeted Brian and Ned warmly. Brian presented Great Bear with Running Dog's scalp. Ned likewise handed the *wickte's* scalp to Laughing Bird's parents. A great celebration took place. That night, Brian told of Ned's epic battle with the *wickte*. The Crow were not bothered by the fact that Ned had resorted to his pistol to conquer the *wickte*. In turn, Ned embellished the tale of Brian's battle with Running Dog, making it into much more of a contest than it had actually been. Afterward Brian said, "Yes, Ned, you are quite an orator. "

"Aye, well, sometimes you must feed the masses what they want to hear. That's why the Irish are such gifted politicians, you know."

The remainder of their stay was peaceful enough, but neither man could enjoy his surroundings; they were constantly reminded of their lost wives and children. Finally it came time to leave. Ned promised to come back for the hunting seasons. Brian could promise nothing as he had several years of school ahead of him. Plenty Coupes promised him that because of their friendship, the Crow would always honor white people and help them settle in the area. For unlike the Sioux, Cheyenne, and Blackfeet, they realized that their futures would be intertwined—that both must cooperate to survive in the harsh Montana environment.

Ned and Brian left on August 20, 1853 for Fort Union. They hunted and trapped peacefully enough, encountering no

Cheyenne or Blackfeet. But when they reached the Dakotas they were suddenly surrounded by Sioux. Their knowledge of the Lakota language kept them safe, however, especially when they were recognized as Red Beard and Man-Who-Rides-Buffalo.

Fort Union had grown into a bustling port since they had last seen it. A church and school had been built. Ned quickly found a job teaching school and kept a low profile in the saloons. He had found that abstinence from alcohol made him a better person. Every now than then he would satisfy his whiskey 'tooth', but not like the raging excesses of his past.

One night they were sitting in the bar, talking with Mike Boyd, when a boisterous Irishman walked into the bar. Ned jumped up and yelled, "You pirate! I thought the Brits had exiled you to Tasmania for sedition! They said you were to be hung, drawn and quartered there."

"Ah, yes, but I managed to talk my way out of it. We Meaghers have the gift of blarney, you know."

"Brian, meet my cousin, a brigand of oratory, Thomas Meagher."

"Pleased to meet you," said Brian. "Any relative of Ned's is a friend of mine."

"Ah, the pleasure is all mine. Bartender, set the lads up with a few drinks. Beautiful country you have here, Ned. I wintered with your mother in the Dakotas. She looks quite fit, though she misses you. You should write her more often."

"Well, I think I might visit her next June after I'm done teaching school."

"Ah, the perpetual teacher. It's frightening to think that you're poisoning young minds with your skewed sense of history."

"Only the truth will they hear," said Ned, sanctimoniously.

They caught up on old times and drank into the night. Ned still refrained from getting completely out of hand and managed to resist the temptations of three lovely whores.

Two days later Brian sailed for St. Louis to begin years of

hard work at school. The two old friends swore to keep in touch. Ned promised to visit Brian every few years to make sure that he was becoming a proper man of letters and to keep him up to date on the turmoil of the Montana Territory.

40

When he arrived in St. Louis Brian didn't bother to stop at his old house, figuring that it had been sold. He went first to Captain Clark and told him of his decision to go back to school. Clark told him it was a wise decision, as he could foresee nothing but trouble in the Indian territories. He also told him that his father's house had still not been sold as of two days ago.

Heartened, Brian hurried over to Bridget's in hopes of catching her husband. He knocked on the door and a small boy answered. Brian suddenly realized the face looking up at him looked identical to the daguerreotype of himself that had sat for years on his father's desk. "Is your dad home?" asked Brian.

"No," replied the boy.

"How about your mother?"

The boy turned away from the door and called, "Mom, some trapper's here to see you."

Brian felt self-conscious. He hadn't bothered to buy any civilized clothes. Bridget came to the door and gasped, "Brian! Why are you back so soon?"

"I've decided to go back to school. I've had enough of the mountains…It's a very long story. "

"A wise decision. Liam, run along. Your mother needs to talk to Mr. McCaffrey."

The little boy dashed outside gleefully and began stalking the family dog before pouncing on it.

"He's quite a handful, isn't he?"

"Yes, he is. Does he remind you of someone?"

"Well…"

"He's your son, Brian. You can tell in one look at him. He's got your eyes, the dimple in your chin; he's got your disposition, too—it's all I can do keep him indoors."

"Does John know?"

"I don't think so, but every once in a while, he says, 'I can't believe he's our son. Did you behave that way as a child?'"

"What do you say?"

"I lie and say yes."

"Well, I'll never tell. I've told no one about our indiscretion."

"'Indiscretion'? It was much nicer than that." Bridget smiled and squeezed his hand. They looked away from each other, for they knew that their passion was ended, that they had given their hearts to others. Brian told her of his wife's death, and Bridget was extremely distraught at how White Fawn had died. Brian didn't tell her of his revenge. Instead he asked, "Is my dad's house still for sale?"

"Yes."

"Is your husband in his office?"

"Yes."

"Good. I want to cancel the sale."

Then Brian left abruptly. He didn't love her anymore. She was just a friend, and he felt uncomfortable around her. When he reached John's office he was relieved to hear the news confirmed that the house was still unsold. Brian told him of his plans for medical school, explaining that he would live in the house; it was close to St. Louis University. John informed Brian that he still had Captain Clark's letter of recommendation.

He said gravely, "Brian, I don't think you realize how substantial your father's estate is."

"Really? I've never had much interest in money."

"It's worth a hundred and twenty thousand dollars—in

addition to the house and one carriage. He didn't spend much money, did he?"

"No, he didn't," answered Brian.

"He put the money away in a trust. As long as the bank remains solvent, you'll be a rich man. He also gave the medical school twenty-five thousand dollars. In fact, if you hadn't returned within ten years of his death, all of the money would have gone to the medical school."

"Ah well, the school will be far wealthier by my presence than by the money." They both laughed. "How do I get some of this money? I'll need some clothes and so forth before I continue my studies."

"I'll arrange the paperwork with the bank."

He went home and looked around. He missed his parents—but it was his house now. He went back to the dock and got his buffalo robes and guns out of storage. He considered selling the weapons, but then he thought, Nah, maybe I'll go hunting some day.

Back at home, Brian burned his now flea-infested buffalo robe. He nearly threw his buckskins into the fire as well but reconsidered. Maybe he could use them some time at a costume party, or even wear them hunting again. He hung them in a back room of the house. Then he washed, put on one of his father's old suits—which was too short—went to the bank, and withdrew three hundred dollars from a fawning banker. Brian wasn't used to being rich. Next, he went to the barber; after a haircut and shave he looked ten years younger. Next he then went shopping for clothes. God, it felt good to wear nice clothes! Brian thought he looked rather elegant in his suit and top hat, and wondered idly if the hat had been made with one of his own pelts.

At the University Brian began the enrollment process. He felt a little out of place, for he was older than some of the upperclassmen. It was too late to start the fall semester so, he wouldn't be able to begin his studies until the second semester. He was relieved, for he felt he needed to acclimate to society before facing the rigors of academia.

He went to the book depository at the University and bought Homer's *Iliad* and *Odyssey*, Keenan's *English Literature*, and Dane's *History Of The World* (all recommended by Ned,) and devoured them over the next few months. There was so much to learn!

He rented out the office to a young physician named Welsh, but he usually stayed in the back of the house, figuring he had the rest of his life to spend in the office.

Brian steered clear of the saloons and soon had an active social life. He was constantly being invited to debutante balls and parties. After all, he was young, rich, and handsome. None of the women interested him, however. Compared to White Fawn and Bridget, they all seemed superficial and vain.

41

The holidays were quite depressing without a family. John and Bridget Ryan asked him to share Christmas with them, which helped. He had begun to take a real liking to John, who constantly pumped him for information about Indian ways and customs in order to help his Indian clients. Ryan was gradually becoming more of a rich white man's lawyer, but he still did a lot of pro bono work for the Indians on behalf of Captain Clark.

Brian bought Liam a present. As he opened it, the boy's eyes gleamed with excitement. Bridget rolled her eyes in mock despair and Ryan looked somewhat taken aback. It was a toy replica of a Hawken rifle. The boy immediately loved it and began aiming it at everything in sight, blazing away at imaginary animals.

"Sorry—perhaps I've created a monster for you," said Brian.

"No, I think it suits his nature," laughed Ryan.

"Men," grumbled Bridget.

Liam jumped on Brian's lap and hugged him and said, "Thank you, sir. Mom, can I call him Uncle Brian?"

"Ask him yourself."

"Sir, would you be my Uncle Brian?"

"Why, it would be an honor, Liam."

They began their friendship with a handshake. Brian secretly loved the child, but knew that no one was ever to discover who his biological father was. Every fall Brian took Liam to the woods and taught him how to hunt. If John Ryan ever suspected anything, he never let on. In fact, he encouraged Brian to spend time with Liam, as he himself had little spare time and knew nothing of hunting and the outdoors.

After the holidays, Brian finally began his studies at St. Louis University. He was surprised at how easily he made the dean's list. Ned's love of learning had rubbed off on him. He was accepted to the medical school just prior to his graduation from college. He had earned his undergraduate degree in only three and a half years, and was quite pleased with himself. He had a few friends now, but still hadn't met a woman who could hold his interest.

He started medical school in September of 1858. The courses were extremely demanding and left little time for dating. Ned kept his word and visited him in the summer of 1856, then came back for Brian's graduation exercises. Ned was overjoyed that Brian had finally become a man of letters. Meanwhile, Brian spent many nights alone in the library at the medical school, studying late into the night. Often he would find himself daydreaming about the mountains. He really missed Ned. "Maybe I'll go back to Montana and open an office," he mused. He knew that he would be very busy if he went there; they certainly needed physicians…"Enough daydreaming," he scolded himself. "First I've got to get through medical school."

The first two years were pure drudgery. The amount of material to be memorized was overwhelming. Brian hated the constant exams, the long hours, and the physical and mental toll that it placed upon him. But when he finally made it to his third year, he began to love it…now he had contact with patients. He caught fire again, and found studying much easier—it seemed now to have more of a purpose. He gradually rose to the top of his class.

He also had a little more time to read the newspaper. He read a lot about Red Cloud and the Fort Laramie Treaty. The Indians will get cheated again, he thought. He read that Sitting Bull had refused to sign the Treaty. And it seemed as if the whole country was being torn apart over the slavery issue. He respected

Mr. Lincoln, but being an Irishman he had voted Democratic in the last election. Besides, he liked Douglas' philosophy more than Lincoln's. Sometimes he wondered what would become of them all...the Indians, the blacks, and the whites. But it was too depressing to think about. He escaped back into the mysteries of surgery, childbirth, and physical diagnosis.

42

The day after his very last exam, he was startled by a loud knock at the door. He and his classmates had been out celebrating late the night before. "Who the hell would be knocking at this early hour?" He grumbled to himself, and opened the door. A clean-shaven man wearing the blue uniform of the U. S. Army stood on his porch.

"Well now, aren't you going to let the pride of the Union Army into your house?"

"*Ned?* Jesus, I didn't recognize you! You look so, so distinguished!"

"Ah, finally the clothes match the man."

"If that were the case, you'd be wearing a donkey suit."

"I see medical school hasn't dulled your wit. Best not enter battle with me half-armed. "

"Half-armed? "

"Half-wit," laughed Ned.

They hugged, laughed, and pounded each other's backs. "Come in, Ned. God, you really do look like a soldier. Say, how did this happen?"

"Me cousin, Thomas—you met him, Thomas Meagher is a very influential man now in Washington. He is almost Governor of the Montana Territories. Once it becomes a state, I know he'll be the Governor. Besides, he's now an officer in the Union Army. We've both become citizens of the United States." Ned's eyes sparkled; he was very proud of being a U. S. citizen.

"Congratulations, Ned, I'm so happy for you. But why the army?"

"An army record looks good on a politician's record. I did become mayor of Fort Union—and after this war I'll become a senator, just wait and see."

"Why risk your life in a stupid war? Haven't you seen enough killing and bloodshed?"

"You've killed four times as many men as I have."

"Nonsense," said Brian. "Pierre doesn't count; the coyotes got him. What does it matter, anyway? Why get mangled in a stupid war against your own adopted countrymen over slavery?"

"That's just it! Didn't I teach you anything? Don't they teach anything about freedom at St. Louis University?"

"Of course—but why risk your life, Ned?"

"Because freedom is *everything*. You Americans don't value your most precious gift! You haven't lived under the heel of British oppression."

"Oh, don't start with that anti-British crap. The Spaniards started the slave trade."

"The Brits were in it up to their eyeteeth. They profited from it. Political aspirations aside, that's why I'm in it. Every man should be free, regardless of his race or religion. Sound familiar? Are you familiar with the Bill of Rights?"

"All right. You win. I'll be sure to vote for you if I get the chance. So what brings you here to visit me?" asked Brian warily.

"I'm here to enlist your services for the Union Army."

"I knew it. Why is it when you come knocking on the door I know I'm in for some bloody adventure?"

"Admit it—life would be empty without sharing some of its fruits with old Ned. "

Brian laughed, then became serious. "Ned, this time I'm serious. I won't go. I won't fight. In a year I'll take an oath to save lives, not take them. I can't even practice medicine in the Union Army till I get my degree."

"Who said anything about the Hippocratic Oath or killing people? I'm asking you to be a scout for the Union Army! No killing, just a wee bit of danger. You could do it for the summer and resume your studies in the fall. I agree that you could do a lot more for your country as a doctor in the war, but what if we can beat these rebels in a few months due to good reconnaissance? Besides, wouldn't you like to fly like an eagle?"

"What are you talking about?"

"I'm talking about using hot gas balloons to spy on enemy movements."

"Why doesn't the enemy just shoot them down?"

"Their miniballs can't reach that high."

"Well, I'm not taking my balls any higher than a tree top," retorted Brian.

"Do I take this as a weakening of your original position?"

"Look, Ned. No killing. I'll do a short stint of scouting, but I'm not enlisting in the Union *or* Confederate Army."

"Which side do you think is right?"

"Oh, hell. I don't know. Each state has its rights. I tend to believe in state's rights over a federal bureaucracy but ultimately I know you're right. No man deserves to be a slave."

"Ah, that's the spirit. Now you're talking, old Brian. Keep an open mind about the balloons. None have been shot down yet. We could start a whole new reconnaissance unit for the Union Army."

"What's that?"

"I think we should call it the U. S. Gondoliers."

"Jesus, Ned. Sometimes your poetic imagination is a little too much. 'Gondoliers'—what a stupid name," he guffawed. "When do we leave?"

"As soon as you get your things packed."

He went to the back of the house and found his buckskins. Oddly, he found his Sioux war vest, too, and packed it as a good luck charm. He stared at his Hawken and Navy Colt pistols, then shook his head, and put them away.

183

"No more killing. Crazy Irishman. Gondoliers. What blarney," he muttered.

"Talking to yourself?" asked Ned.

"Nah, I was just thinking out loud. I'll bet the U. S. Army could save a lot of money by not using the gas generators for the balloon and letting you power them."

"Me?"

"Yes. You could simply talk and the balloon would be filled with enough hot air to reach the moon."

"Such pitiless humor."

"Where are we going, anyway?"

"Why, we board the train for Pennsylvania."

"What's there?"

"Ah, a little town called Gettysburg."

43

Brian marveled at the distances they were able to cover in one day riding the troop train. Ned, as usual, cursed the railroads as the 'Blight of the Union'. Brian had sent the dean of the medical school a telegram, informing him that he was volunteering as a Union Army scout but would be back for the fall semester. He had already informed Dr. Welsh, his tenant, of his plan, and the good doctor would inform Ryan and Bridget. He had avoided talking to Ryan personally about his departure, for Ryan had been after him for over a year to prepare a will; his estate had continued to grow even larger, and Ryan would have apoplexy if he knew Brian was going to enter a war zone without a will. When Ned asked him how much he was worth Brian said, "I really don't know—nor do I care."

"That's the spirit. Take care of the masses and don't worry about finances."

"What about you?" Brian asked.

"Me teeth, the clothes on me back, and me log house in Helena. Not worth much right now, unless they strike gold soon. There's not a pot of money to be made in teaching. I make more money in politics. 'Favors', you know."

Brian decided not to pursue this.

"Ah, cousin Tom Meagher's going to be the first Governor of Montana Territory. Virginia City is the capital now, but if they find gold in Helena, it'll be the capital. We'll be rich, me being Lieutenant Governor and all "

"I thought Bannock was the capital?"

185

"Nah, they moved it when they found gold in Virginia City. They'll do it again if they find it in Helena, simply because it's on the Missouri and would make a better place to run a goddamned railroad."

"Gold in Virginia City. I'll bet Red Cloud and Sitting Bull are just going to love having miners tramping all over their hunting grounds."

"War is inevitable," said Ned. "Some of the miners have already been found scalped just outside of Alder Gulch. If it weren't for this other war, we'd be at it. As it is, they're pulling troops out of Forts Phil Kearney, Union, and Smith to fight for the Union. The Sioux will overrun the settlers. They're madder than hell. Even Plenty Coupes is about to go on the warpath."

"Really?" asked Brian.

"Really. The Indians have had it. We've gone back on the Laramie Treaty too many, times and buffalo are getting scarcer. Your dear friend Sitting Bull will be in the middle of it. Remember that crazy kid— what's his name?"

"Crazy Horse."

"Ah yes. Aptly named. He's making a name for himself terrorizing settlers and miners out there."

"Hmm. It's a shame, isn't it? Such beautiful country, and we're killing each other over it."

Ned raised an eyebrow and said, "Well, all wars are usually fought over land or mineral wealth. Except this one. This civil war of yours is over a just principle."

"I'm sure the federal government is more concerned about the principle of losing taxation from all those textile mills in the south than it is about slavery," said Brian caustically.

"Some patriot you are," snorted Ned.

"Look, all I'm saying is that I believe Mr. Lincoln is right. I voted for Douglas anyway. I just don't buy all the justification of war because of this slavery crap."

"My, you've become a cynic since you've been at the University," observed Ned.

"I guess so, but you've always taught me to be somewhat skeptical too," Brian pointed out.

"Aye, I think it's just the nature of the Irish to be that way. I was never formally taught to be that way but I've always been wary of what the governments and politicians say—as well as what I read in the newspaper."

"By the way. I've been meaning to ask you, just how much education have you had?"

Just then a Sergeant Reno interrupted them and told Ned to report to Colonel Meagher's car. Brian asked if he should stay. Ned said, "No, you'll be needed to learn about our mission anyway.

"Civilians stay here," said Reno curtly.

"I beg your forgiveness, sir, but the man will be accompanying me," responded Ned.

"Oh shit," thought Brian." He's got that submissive look on his face again." He could just see sergeant Reno, tied upside-down to the back of the caboose.

"I outrank you, private, and what I say goes."

"Aye, that's correct, sir. But you're forgettin' four important things."

"What's that, soldier?" said Reno testily.

"Colonel Meagher's me cousin and I'm his best friend. Brian here is me best friend."

"So what's the fourth?" asked Reno tensely.

"Well, sir, it's extremely difficult to walk like an officer with your saber hangin' out of your arse."

With that, Ned smartly saluted the dumbfounded officer and ushered Brian quickly past him. It was all Brian could do to keep from laughing in his face.

"Pompous little twit," said Ned under his breath.

Brian finally burst out laughing as they entered the next

car. Colonel Thomas Meagher and General Meade stared at them.

"Sorry, sir," said Brian.

Ned stood at attention and saluted them both. "Sir, this is me cousin's friend, Brian McCaffrey. He's studying to be a doctor, but he is an excellent tracker and scout. He's killed his share of Blackfeet and Sioux in the past. Don't let his boyish looks fool you. He's a competent man."

"Pleased to meet you," said Meade. "At ease, private," he said to Ned. Ned proudly ended his salute to the general and then saluted his cousin. Brian loved Ned's Union soldier act. He was quite good at it.

Meagher began. "President Lincoln has had it with McClellan's indecisiveness. He wants some fire-eaters to turn around the rebels. They nearly captured Washington, you know." Actually Brian didn't know, but he kept his mouth shut. "This is where General Meade and the rest of us come in. We're going to turn the war around, but we've got to find out where Pickett's troops are. We know they are somewhere around Gettysburg."

"Sir, haven't they been seen by our men in the gondolas?" asked Ned.

"No, the tree cover is too dense. Besides, the rebs have been shooting them down."

"Bollocks!" exclaimed Ned. "Savages. I thought we had a gentleman's agreement. They use their balloons and we use ours as well. Everyone dresses up like newspaper men and photographers and nobody gets shot."

"Well, those days are gone. People are getting shot down on both sides."

Brian shot Ned a glaring look.

Meagher cut in. "We need you two to go into the woods, find out where they are, get back to us, and report their positions. With your backgrounds in Indian fighting and trapping, you're naturals for this assignment."

"Can I wear me uniform?" asked Ned.

"I wouldn't," said Meade. "I would dress like Brian. That way you'd have a better chance of surviving if you got caught. Plus, you'd blend in with the scenery better."

"Can you legally do that, General?" asked Meagher." He is a U. S. soldier."

"Not if I give him a furlough." Meade turned to Ned. "You are hereby on furlough from the Union army. Unfortunately, it is to be spent in the woods near Little and Big Roundtop at Gettysburg, Pennsylvania"

"Yessir," said Ned.

"Any questions?" asked Meade.

"No, sir."

"Keep this to yourselves, boys," he admonished.

Ned saluted, and they left the car. As they returned to their seats Brian said, "No one ever gets shot down."

"Well, I thought it was true. Bloody rebel savages. What a fine kettle of fish. Ah well, I feel safer on the ground anyhow."

"Is it true the South almost captured the White House?"

"Aye. Where have you been? Studying at the University of Mars?"

"Look, during exam time you don't have time for such niceties as reading the newspaper."

"Ah, the poor pressed student. Nothing like learning as an excuse for ignorance," mused Ned.

"Oh, you're a fine one to talk! You get us into a war on the side that's losing. In a year I can save lives with these hands. Now they're going to be crawling around in the dirt in the forest, looking for people who want to shoot us. What a great way to spend my last summer off!"

"Well, we might be losing now but we'll win because we're right," said Ned defiantly.

"Isn't that what Napoleon said at a place called Waterloo?" asked Brian as he slumped into his seat.

"Very good. You are becoming quite a scholar. I'm proud of you."

Reno approached Ned and said, "On your feet, private."

"Sorry, sir, I can't. My legs stopped working."

"Stopped working?"

"Yes, sir. Ever since General Meade put me on furlough."

"Furlough? So soon?" Reno asked incredulously.

"Aye, sir. Rank has its privileges, but the privileged outrank the rank." Brian guffawed. "Be a nice officer and bugger off, sir," said Ned, as he closed his eyes and feigned falling asleep. Reno stared at Brian in disbelief.

"Don't look at me. I'm just a civilian. Believe me, I've known him a long time and this is the best I've ever seen him behave. He can be quite violent and unpredictable, especially when he's sleepy."

Reno shook his head and marched down the aisle. The enlisted men stifled their laughter until he exited the car. Ned opened one eye and said, "Sanctimonious shitheel."

The car erupted with laughter. Brian took off his hat and playfully began to beat Ned with it, yelling, "That'll teach you to get me in a war, you crazy Irish bastard."

The train steamed towards Gettysburg.

44

They sat at the summit of Roundtop and still couldn't figure out where the Confederates would come from. They bunkered at a place called Hell's Kitchen and changed into their buckskins. Brian still refused to carry a gun. Ned proudly pointed out his new Springfield rifle.

"Fifty-eight caliber and about as accurate as a Hawken, but lighter. Who needs accuracy when you're shooting miniballs that big? Well, shall we go up for a look?"

Nervously they entered the gondola. They had decided against dressing as journalists in case the balloon went down behind Confederate lines. The gondolier expertly mixed flames and gas and they were aloft in a matter of minutes. Brian had to admit it was exhilarating but he didn't care for the idea of being shot at.

"This is bloody marvelous, old Brian. It's like being an eagle. We should take one of these to Montana some day."

Before Brian could answer, the gondolier toppled over as a shot rang out from below.

"I suppose we found the rebels," said Ned darkly.

"Shit!" said Brian as he bent over to help the fallen man. He had been shot directly in the femoral artery from below. Then a second shot wracked the man, entering his back and exiting from his chest. The fifty-eight caliber ball had pulverized his heart. "Bastards are using Enfields. As you can see, they are quite deadly." Brian looked up as Ned dropped his Springfield and stood on the dead man's chest.

191

"Have you no respect?" Ned was standing on tiptoe, clutching his gonads, perched on the dead man's torso. "What are you doing?" asked Brian.

"Protecting the family jewels," said Ned quietly. Another ball shattered the floor two inches from Brian's left leg. He joined Ned atop the dead gondolier. They stared at each other fearfully, waiting for the next shot from below. They looked like mirror images. Finally Ned cackled and said, "You look like a bleedin' chimpanzee staring at himself in a mirror while holding his bollocks."

Brian managed to laugh. Another ball hit the dead man from below. "I don't suppose you know how to fly this thing, do you?" he asked Ned.

"Can't say that I do," replied Ned.

"Great. We'll probably just keep going up. We'll be the first men to land on the moon."

"Oh, I don't think you need to worry about that."

"What do you mean?"

Ned pointed up. There were three, slowly growing holes in the balloon. They were slowly coming down over enemy lines. Fortunately, it was getting dark. With luck, they might land after dark—assuming they didn't crash or blow up first.

45

The general paced in front of his tent. If only they could figure out where Pickett was! He was only twenty-three-years-old, and he had risen in rank faster than any other officer in the history of the U. S. Army. Finally, he would make Libbey proud of his "Autie" He would prove to his father-in-law, a stern judge from Michigan, that his daughter had married the right man. He was an excellent horseman, and loved the moment when troops would charge at the enemy. He never heard the volley of shots aimed at him and his men. He never heard the cries of the wounded. All he could hear was the thunder of hooves and the sounds of their bugles as they stormed toward the enemy. At those moments he felt invincible, like a winged avenger. He would yell, "We've got 'em on the run, Wolverines! Charge!" His men either loved him or hated him, but they never doubted his courage. He was always visible at head of his troops, with his white, floppy civilian hat, bright red bandanna, and long, curly blonde hair. They would have followed him into hell—and often did. Eleven horses were shot out from beneath him during the course of the war. Historians would belittle his intelligence, always pointing out that he graduated at the bottom of his class at West Point; but in fact, he was very bright. He studied just enough to get by. He would have two hundred and ninety-six demerits by the second month of school. (Three hundred meant expulsion.) He invariably ended the year with two hundred and ninety-nine. His classmates liked him, as he was always interesting to talk to, had a great sense of humor, and was a renowned prankster.

His best friends from his class returned to their homes and became officers in the Confederate Army. But he was a staunch Democrat, and though opposed to Lincoln's policies, he was first and foremost a soldier. He would carry out his orders. Tomorrow he would crush the rebel's armies, if he could find them. He was musing on the irony of all this when his sergeant interrupted his thoughts: "General Custer, General Meade wants to speak with you at his command post."

"Thank you, sergeant." He petted his horse and headed to the tent.

46

J ust before they crashed, Ned caught a glimpse of Big Roundtop and the last rays of the sun as it sank in the west. He then triangulated the rebel fire had come from a spot south of them.

The gondola hit the roof of a barn, tipped, and dumped them unceremoniously into a haystack. Next the gondola slid off the roof, tipping their supplies, Ned's gun, and the poor dead gondolier out onto the ground. They grabbed their supplies and started to run towards the woods. "She's gonna blow!" gasped Ned. The dried wood, the haystack, and the gases in the balloon—now collapsed on the gondola—exploded in a fireball that levitated them off their feet and launched them into a pile of manure. Both had the wind knocked out of them. Brian couldn't hear out of one ear; his left eardrum was punctured. He looked over at Ned and laughed. "You look quite distinguished with hog shit on your face."

"Aye, you look somewhat like an unwashed heathen yourself. Can you still run?"

"I think so. I can't hear very well, though. I think the explosion ruptured my eardrum. Luckily it'll heal."

"Not if you keep talking so loud. Every Confederate in the county is going to be here in about ten minutes. I think it would be better for us if you whispered—or even better, shut the fock up and follow me. Of course I realize silence is impossible in your case." Brian crossed his eyes. Ned stifled a laugh and they ran into the woods. They found a deserted den and crawled in. The farm was swarming with Confederate troops. Luckily the explosion obliterated their tracks. After an hour the enemy troops left. Ned and Brian waited and calculated where the troops had come from, silently painting their faces black. Brian put on his Sioux war vest. Ned quietly laughed, "Now that's a sight! You look like Uncle Tom himself, dressed up as an Indian. Hah! The Confederates won't know what to do with you—a white man the color of a slave, dressed like a Sioux. It's a bloody shame you didn't bring your Hawken. We might need it."

"I told you, I'm a noncombatant. I'm not going to kill again."

"That's quite noble of you. I am certain the rebs will understand. Should we get surrounded, maybe you could point your bean at them—I'm quite convinced that will overwhelm them with fear."

"Your feeble attempts at humor are pathetic."

"I disagree with you, but I see your vocabulary is improving"

"Who's Uncle Tom?" asked Brian.

"Jaysus! Don't you read? Haven't you heard of *Uncle Tom's Cabin?*" Brian had heard of the story, as it was very popular just before the war, but hadn't read it.

"A bleedin' doctor, yet hopelessly illiterate," mumbled Ned disgustedly.

Brian stared off into the distance and put his fingers to his lips. A lone Confederate soldier cocked his Enfield rifle, giving away his position. Ned silently sneaked out of their den and circled around behind the sentry. Brian prayed that Ned would get the rebel first, and suddenly wished he had his gun with him. The silence ended with the sound of wood thumping bone.

"Come out, lad, I pole-axed him with the butt of me Springfield. We'll be back at camp before he wakes up."

They quietly made their way south, skirting the Confederate troops, and made it back to camp at 3:30 in the morning. The Union sentry nearly shot them, but Ned talked their way out of the potentially deadly confrontation. At 3:45 a. m. they were standing at attention in front of Colonel Thomas Meagher's tent. They told Meagher of the rebels' position. Thomas thanked them." Good work, lads. Tomorrow we'll turn this bloody war around."

They went back to their tent but couldn't sleep. They washed the charcoal from their faces. Ned put on his Union uniform. Brian actually felt patriotic, seeing the proud Irishman wearing his new country's brand-new blue uniform.

"You look nice, Ned."

"Thanks, lad. Why don't we go to the front and watch the action? We might as well get to see the results of our little excursion."

Brian left his buckskins on. He didn't want to be mistaken for a Union soldier. Maybe he could convince Meagher to allow him to assist in surgery at the hospital tents; he had noticed they were always busy. Amputations seemed to be the most common operations. He and Ned found a spot on the far right-hand side of the front; they knew the rebels would come from the left. They settled down behind an entrenchment and fell asleep.

47

They awoke before dawn. No sign of the Confederates was visible. Ned stretched and yawned and said, "Hoka hey."

"What's that mean?"

"Sioux battle cry. It's a good day to fight, a good day to die...something of that sort."

"I hope it's not prophetic."

"No chance. I'm not shooting unless I have to. I've done my part. I'm going back home a decorated war hero...Thomas will see to it. Live to be eighty-five, make a deathbed confession, the whole works."

"I like that plan," said Brian." I'm going back too as soon as possible, to get ready for school. Maybe I'll get some experience in surgery before I go."

"I'm proud of you, lad. Me favorite pupil. You've come such a long way, a doctor and all."

"Thanks, Ned. You've been an inspiration to me. I doubt I would have gone to school if you hadn't always goaded me about my ignorance. By the way—how much education have you had?"

"Well, to be honest, I was pushed ahead three grades at the elementary level. I graduated from the University of Dublin at the tender age of eighteen. I was working on me doctorate in Greek history when Thomas and I ran afoul of the law because of all of our ranting against the crown. My family had to emigrate to America, and I actually taught at Harvard for a year before deciding to head west."

"My God! You'd never guess with your language and behavior among the mountain men."

"Aye, it's an old Irish trick–crazy like a fox, so to speak. If you act a little less educated than you really are, you can relate to the common man and they can teach you a lot, you know. Those uneducated mountain men taught us how to survive up there." Ned talked on and on. Brian was once again impressed by the depth of Ned's knowledge.

Just before dawn they began to talk about how much they missed their wives. They longed to marry again but none of the white women they had met could match White Fawn and Laughing Bird. Brian was surprised to see a tear form in Ned's eyes when he talked about her and their unborn child. Old Ned was human after all.

Brian told him how much he missed White Fawn and especially Sweet Child. They grew morose and silent.

Ned, typically, brightened and said, "Well, we got the bastards that did it now, didn't we? Hah! That was sweet revenge."

"What's that?" asked Brian, cupping his ear.

"Keep your voice down. You look like a decrepit old deaf Sioux medicine man!" Ned laughed.

Suddenly his smile was cut in half as his jaw exploded. Brian felt searing pain in his left arm. He watched in horror as the top of Ned's head burst into a geyser of white bone, pink brain and scarlet blood. His friend pitched backward as if in slow motion. He stared blankly at Brian and mumbled, "Me tee, my ma."

Brian grabbed him and promised, "I'll get them to her, just *please don't die!*" But He knew it was hopeless. He tried to cover the awful bleeding wound with his bandanna. Ned lost consciousness. Brian held him in his arms as he convulsed. He whispered, "I've got you, old friend, Brian's got you...See you in heaven."

Ned's face began to contort, like an infant searching for its mother's breast. Brian had seen this before in patients with devastating brain injuries. They always seemed to revert back to infancy just before they died. Ned's face began to shimmer because of the tears in Brian's eyes. He held him tightly. Finally Ned's seizure stopped and Brian released his grip. Ned couldn't hurt himself anymore. Ned stopped breathing, covered in blood, his eyes glazed over. A second shot hit him as he died.

This time Brian saw the source—a sniper in a tree about fifty yards to their left. Gently he closed Ned's eyes, took Ned's gun, carefully aimed and killed the soldier. Brian's mouth contorted into a feral grin when he heard the tree branches snap as the Confederate sniper's body fell to the ground. He put the gun down to hold Ned one last time vowing, "Now I'm going to get the rest of them."

Brian started to moan. Slowly he looked around and began to scream, "No...no! Why did you take him, God? Goddamn you. Some God you are! No, not Ned, not Ned!"

Then he took the gun, reloaded, and went over the top. He had stopped yelling. Instead he said quietly, "I'm gonna kill every one of you Confederate sons of bitches."

He started to run to the rebel lines.

48

Custer had mustered his troops to charge. Out of the corner of his eye he saw some commotion to his right. "God, not another suicide!" He had seen it before on both sides. Usually it was some poor young kid away from home for the first time in his life. His brother or best friend had been killed next to him the day before. The soldier would lie in his tent and cry all night. The next morning they always charged the front lines. It was all so senseless, he thought.

Usually the opposite side would hold its fire, since every soldier knew that, "there but for the grace of God go I"...But once a man came close enough to be a danger, they would open fire. Then the man would be cut to pieces in the ensuing fusillade, each soldier silently cursing himself rationalizing that he had put the man out of his misery.

Custer noticed however, that this man was different. He wore buckskins and charged in a serpentine fashion. He was no suicide; he was intent on killing everything in his path. Sensing opportunity, Custer wheeled his horse toward the buckskin clad fighter, for the man had caused a breech in the Confederate lines. His men followed, wheeling into the midst of the rebels. Soon his men were firing point-blank, running their sabers into the Confederates, cutting a wide swath of destruction. The Confederates were on the run.

Custer turned back to the man. He was covered in blood and pink matter. He was disheveled; his eyes were glazed, and he was surrounded by six dead Confederate soldiers. It looked as though he had shot the first, bayoneted another, then turned the Springfield around and bludgeoned the next. He had probably taken that man's Enfield, shot one more and bayoneted yet another. He was kneeling over the last dead rebel.

Custer couldn't figure out what he was doing. The Confederate's head was hidden. Suddenly bile rose in his throat as he realized the crazed man was scalping the dead soldier.

"Halt, I say! We don't do that in the Union Army."

The man growled, "I'm not in your goddamned army!" and continued scalping the dead Confederate.

Custer drew his pistol and aimed at the crazed man in buckskins.

Brian looked up and saw a Union officer in blue wearing a white hat and red bandanna, but the combination of tears, blood, and sunlight in his eyes obscured the man's face. He vaguely could make out the outline of a gun pointed at him. He suddenly wondered why he was scalping a dead man, and dropped the knife in disgust. He was dizzy and his left arm hurt.

Custer saw that the fighter in buckskin was wounded, and then Brian passed out.

"Sergeant, get this man back to the surgeon. He's been shot. Get his name when he wakes up."

General Custer wheeled his horse and charged back into the fray.

49

Civil war surgeons described for the first time a phenomenon that has continued into modern warfare: most superficial wounds are caused not by shrapnel but by pieces of bone from a nearby soldier who had been killed. Brian's case was no different. When he regained consciousness, he was vaguely aware of the screams of wounded men around him. The noise of rapid sawing surrounded him as surgeons amputated limbs.

Soldiers were given bite blocks to chew on, alcohol and laudanum to deaden the pain. It was awful.

He was aware of two men probing his left arm. Surprisingly, he felt little pain.

"God, it looks like they're using gold for miniballs," said one surgeon.

"No, look carefully. There's bone attached to it," said the other.

"It's a tooth! Shit, we're going to have to amputate. He'll get gangrene for sure."

"No, you won't," said Brian.

"Look, I'm a surgeon and I know I have to amputate or you're going to die."

"I'm a medical student, and I say no. I have rights, you know."

"You're going to be a doctor? You're out of your mind, man. What kind of a doctor would kill six men?"

"I saw my best friend nearly decapitated by a Confederate sniper. I went completely berserk."

"I think you're still berserk. You know we have to amputate. Teeth are covered with bacteria."

"I'll take my chances. I've got some herbs in my tent."

"They didn't teach you that in medical school."

"No, I learned that from a Crow medicine man."

"You really sound daft to me."

"Just the same, put a drain in it—and by the way, that tooth is my property."

"No, it isn't. It's the property of the U. S. Army."

Brian told him the story of Ned's gambling and his promise. Reluctantly they put a gauze dressing on his arm and packed the wound. The pain was horrendous. The surgeon finished dressing the wound and gave him Ned's tooth with the gold filling intact.

"Good luck. I'm sure you'll be back with sepsis and gangrene."

"Thank you, sir, but no thanks for an amputation." Brian got to his feet. "Where do they take the dead?"

"They haven't gathered them up yet. The casualties are the worst of the war for both sides."

Just then Colonel Thomas Meagher thundered, "Where is he? Where's McCaffrey?"

"Over here, Sir," said Brian.

"Where's Ned? Have you seen him?"

"Sir, Ned was mortally wounded just before the battle began."

"Ah, Jesus. Not Ned! Dear Mother of God, no!" He began to sob in front of the bewildered doctors. "Can you take me to him? We must find him and bury him with honor, not in some mass grave."

"I'll find him, but we need a dentist."

"We don't have dentists here," said one of the surgeons.

"Then you'll do," said Meagher.

206

"But sir, I have to take care of the living. You can't expect me to remove teeth from a dead man!"

Meagher drew his revolver and aimed it at the surgeon.

"You'll come with me now, sawbones, or *you'll* be a dead man."

"Yes sir."

Brian led them to the entrenchment. He couldn't believe the carnage. Union and Confederate soldiers lay atop one another like a pile of cordwood. Smoke was everywhere, and the stench was unbelievable. Flies seemed to envelope the area. The cries of the wounded etched their way into Brian's soul.

When they found Ned, Brian looked away. Colonel Thomas Meagher retched and collapsed. The surgeon went about his task reluctantly as mini-balls whizzed around them. A sergeant said, "Beggin' your pardon, sir, but you shouldn't be out here."

"Mind your business, soldier, and start shooting back or I'll court-martial your bloody 'arse right here."

With that, Meagher pulled out his pistol and began blazing away at the Confederates, yelling "Bloody rebel bastards!"

The surgeon finally removed the last of Ned's teeth and gave them to Brian.

"Thank you, sir," said Brian.

"In a way, I was glad to do it. Just make sure his mother gets the gold."

"I can guarantee that," said Brian.

"Not if you get gangrene and die. I want to check that wound every twelve hours."

"Yes, sir," replied Brian.

The sergeant and Colonel Meagher covered Ned's body and carried him back to camp. They placed him apart from the others.

"Sergeant, get him a good coffin and bring him to my headquarters. Tomorrow we'll bury him with full military honors. Tonight we'll have an Irish wake in his honor."

Brian went to his tent, removed his bloody war vest and buckskin, and re-dressed his wounds with herbs. The pain quickly subsided and the bleeding stopped. He washed up. That night General Meade and Colonel Meagher got roaring drunk—as well as Brian. They talked into the night, telling one hilarious Ned story after another. General Custer joined them but did not drink, as he neither drank nor smoked.

The next morning they buried Ned at the summit of Big Roundtop. Meagher had ordered a marker made for him: "Here lies Sergeant Ned O'Grady, who served his adopted country with honor and bravery. He was a good son."

American and Irish Republic flags draped Ned's coffin. He had been dressed in a new blue uniform and was given a twenty-one-gun salute. Afterwards, Thomas and Custer delivered moving eulogies and the priest gave him absolution for his sins.

Custer then took Brian aside and said, "I want you to be my scout."

"Sir, I would rather serve my country assisting in surgery, if you don't mind."

"I'll see to it that you can assist in the afternoons and evenings, if you wish, but in the morning you will be my scout."

Brian knew that Custer would not take no for an answer. Besides, he liked and respected the man after talking at length with him the night before. He did this for two months. Custer was wildly successful and he never hesitated to give Brian much of the credit.

Brian's wound never became infected and he gained considerable surgical experience. He left in September to finish his last year of medical school.

George said, "When you're done, I expect you back here as an army surgeon."

Brian promised to return as soon as he graduated.

His last year of school was a breeze for him as it consisted mostly of surgery. With his wartime experience he was as adept as some of his teachers. He graduated with honors. The dean offered him a position as an instructor in surgery at the medical school. Brian thanked him but rejoined George Custer's unit as a surgeon until the end of the war.

After Lee's surrender, he watched with amusement as Custer took the table on which the surrender was signed and carried it aloft over his head, shouting with glee. The man was mesmerizing; he enjoyed life to the fullest. In a way he reminded Brian of a combination of Sitting Bull and Ned—a strong leader and a great warrior with an unbridled zest for life.

He accompanied George Custer and wife Elizabeth to Washington for the victory parades. Brian, like everyone else was captivated by "Libbey": she was a perfect match for George. They were deeply in love and devoted to one another.

Brian stood near the reviewing stand and watched Custer, who was a superb horseman, pretend to lose control of his white steed. The horse galloped ahead of the others, George's golden hair flowing. Sparks flew from the stallion's hooves as Custer galloped past the president with unrestrained glee on his face.

He wheeled the stallion around and rejoined the other generals, who were not quite as amused as the press and President Johnson. They all passed the reviewing stand, Custer for a second time. Once again he galloped down Washington Avenue.

Brian thought to himself, "Some day he'll be back—but he'll be the one on the reviewing stand."

The press loved George and Libbey. They were the ideal couple—a dashing war hero and his beautiful wife. Washington groveled at their feet; they were invited to all the victory balls and celebrations, and Libbey made sure that Brian escorted Washington's most beautiful debutantes.

When all the celebrations had died down, George summoned Brian and asked him what his future plans were. He said, "I think I'll go back to St. Louis and either continue my father's practice or teach surgery at St. Louis University. But first I have to go to the Dakotas and fulfill a promise: to return Ned's gold and his uniform to his mother."

"That's noble of you, but watch out for Red Cloud and Sitting Bull. They are terrorizing the Dakotas and the Montana Territories."

"I can take care of myself. Sitting Bull's my friend."

George Custer gave Brian his white stallion and helped put them on the train for St. Louis.

50

When he arrived in St. Louis, Brian liveried the white stallion and returned home. He checked in with his tenant, Dr. Welsh, and made sure that his father's practice was continuing. He did notice that some of the patients had left his practice but didn't think too much of it. After all, his father was a tough act to follow.

He visited with the dean, who once again offered him a position teaching surgery at the medical school. He replied that he would think about it—but first he had to go to the Dakotas to fulfill a promise. He didn't elaborate, but the dean somehow understood.

He took his buckskins and war vest to a man who specialized in cleaning old clothing. He never looked into the sack containing them as they were still covered with Ned's blood. He went to a jeweler with the bizarre request that the gold be melted out of the teeth. At first the jeweler was apalled, but after hearing Brian's story about Ned and his mother's inheritance, he reluctantly agreed to the grisly task.

Brian bought a sealskin container and placed Ned's gold, his uniform, and his medals, as well as his own medals, into the bag. He had it sealed and waxed to make it waterproof. He then purchased a map of the Dakotas and booked passage to the Dakota Territories on the train for himself and his horse.

Once again he marveled at the speed with which they could travel. He thought of Ned's hatred for the railroads, yet the train would get his legacy to his mother quicker.

Brian disembarked at the Dakota Territories, saddled the horse, and headed out into the cold October sky. He had a pretty good idea where he was headed and took a direct course toward the Platte River. The going was slow. The weather turned ugly and soon it began snowing. By the time Brian reached the Platte, the snow was two feet deep and the river frozen.

He crossed in the general vicinity of where Ned's mother's cabin would be located. When he was within fifteen yards of the opposite shore, the ice began to moan and creak. Fissures began to fan out on the surface. The stallion became wild-eyed and Brian could feel the horse shivering beneath him. Suddenly the ice around him shattered and they sank into the icy current. He managed to grab the sealskin bag as they went under, the current dragging them down. He clutched the sealskin bag with one hand and the bridle with the other. The horse swam gallantly under the ice. He held on doggedly, but knew that soon he would freeze or drown.

The horse finally reached firm footing near the shore and they broke through the ice. The force of breaking through the ice flung him out of his saddle but while was falling off he managed to grab the horse's tail as it struggled ashore. Just before he reached shore he lost his grip on the bag and fell back into the icy water. He slowly tried to get to his feet and staggered back to the river. He had to get the bag before it was carried away. He couldn't believe that he was diving back into this icy grave.

Down he went and saw the bag wedged against a boulder. He came up for air. The air was so cold that his lungs felt ready to explode. Then he went back down and managed to recover the bag. The current tried to pull him back underneath the ice. He had to swim back toward the hole he had come from.

He finally made it, staggered ashore, and began to pass out. The cold was overwhelming. He could feel ice forming on his beard and eyebrows. He was shaking uncontrollably. He was so close and yet so far! But he thought he could see smoke coming from what appeared to be a chimney in the distance.

Brian crawled to his horse and grabbed for the stirrup but couldn't raise himself onto his back. Gradually he felt himself being dragged gently by the steed towards the house. He managed to open one eye and look over his shoulder. He heard a strange scraping noise next to him and realized that it was the sealskin bag, now frozen bouncing off the snow. He *couldn't* die now—but he couldn't stop shaking. He vacantly began to wonder how long he could hold on.

When he awoke he was in a dry warm bed. He was still shivering. As he looked up he saw the face of a kind, old woman with red hair. She looked like Ned.

"Who are you? Where am I?" he asked the old woman.

"Eileen O'Grady," she said with a smile. "Why don't you leave go of your bag, lad?"

He looked down. His hand was still shaking and he was still clutching the sealskin bag." Did my horse make it?"

"Aye, he did. And he saved your life indeed. I've got him hobbled in the barn with a warm, dry blanket and fed him some hay. He's a fine animal. You never would have made it without him, you know."

"I need to rest, but I've something to give to you," said Brian.

"How nice," she smiled. "But get some rest for now, lad. You look quite peaked."

Brian fell into a deep sleep. Although he was still shivering, he could finally relax. He knew that he had fulfilled his promise.

51

When Brian awoke, sunlight streamed through the windows. The snow on the ground shimmered in the sunlight. It was still early November, a last respite before the endless cold set in.

He got up. He noticed that his right ear was frostbitten; his left little toe was black and blue, but probably wouldn't fall off. He washed and shaved. Eileen had warm coffee, eggs, biscuits, and bacon for him. She scurried happily about her kitchen. She asked, "What's your name?"

"Brian McCaffrey."

"As I live and breathe! You're Ned's dearest friend."

"Aye, ma'am, and he was mine. I take it you've heard the news?" he asked cautiously.

"Yes," she said softly. "First I received a telegram from the U. S. Army, but I hoped that somehow it was a mistake. Then Thomas came by after the war and told me everything. I miss Ned so. He…he was such a good son." Her voice cracked. Brian got up and hugged her as she quietly wept for her dead son. Brian was on the verge of tears himself. They held each other for a long, long time. Finally she looked up and said, "You were with him when he died. Did he suffer much?"

"No, ma'am. He was laughing when he was shot. His last words were to bring his gold to you. He didn't feel a thing."

"Ah, that's a blessing. A mother's worst fear is that her

215

child will die before her."

"He went quickly in the service of the country he loved." He gave her another hug and gently said, "I'll be right back."

Brian returned with the bag and opened it. First he gave her the gold. He had had it amalgamated into one large nugget. It was worth over four thousand dollars.

"Merciful Mary! It's more than enough money to take care of me for the rest of me life."

"That was always his intention."

"How did he keep it safe?"

"Oh, he always managed to keep it with him. He was always hiding it somehow," he laughed.

He quickly changed the subject by presenting her with an American flag and Ned's blue uniform. Eileen began to cry again but smiled brightly when Brian said, "He looked so dignified in his uniform! When he wore it he was bursting with pride. I never saw him so happy as when he was wearing his uniform."

Finally Brian produced the medals. Thomas Meagher had promoted him posthumously to sergeant. He gave her his sergeant's stripes, a Medal of Valor, and a Distinguished Cross. He had thrown in his own medals as well, as she would never know the difference. She gathered them up and held them to her bosom.

"I'm so proud of him. A distinguished soldier. Who would ever have guessed? He was such a sweet, obedient child. I always thought he would be a priest some day."

"*Ned?*" thought Brian to himself. Instead he said, "Yes, he was a devout man. I'm sure he's in heaven as we speak."

"Not that he didn't have a stubborn streak, and he was frightfully intelligent. I think his intelligence is what got him in trouble at the University. He loathed repression and the English continually ground us down with their imperious heel. His father was no help either, for he was always railing against the Crown. We had to leave or they would have been hung for sedition. They sent poor Thomas, Ned's cousin, to Tasmania. You know they offered

Ned a position at Harvard but he turned it down? He and his father wanted to see the frontier. After his Da died working for the railroads, he was a changed man. He began to hunt more often and drink more, and I know that he had his share of fisticuffs. It's in our blood, you know."

"Yes, I know, ma'am," Brian said quietly.

"I thought he would go back and teach Greek history again, but then the frontier got in his veins and he couldn't leave it. He was good to me. He would visit as often as he could although he didn't seem to write often. He'd rather talk to me personally. He was very fond of you. He was so proud of you becoming a doctor, and all."

"Well, I wouldn't be a doctor if it weren't for him. He was my mentor and he never let me forget it."

"Ah, that's my Ned. He wouldn't let you forget him, would he now."

They laughed. She was so pleasant and sweet. Brian ended up spending the winter with her. She was the mother he had never had. One day he confided that he felt so guilty that he had been talking loudly before Ned had been shot, and that he had often blamed himself for Ned's death. He also felt guilty for being alive when so many other people had died around him.

She hugged him and said, "Shush, now. You shouldn't blame yourself. You shouldn't feel guilty. We're survivors, you know. God saves some of us to work here on earth for a reason. Perhaps Ned's reason for being on earth was to teach you and make you a great doctor. His memory will be preserved by the human lives you save."

Suddenly Brian felt better. All the guilt about Ned being killed instead of him finally left him. He embraced Eileen and said, "Thank you. I think I finally have a purpose in life. I'm going back to teach students and young doctors the art of surgery."

They had many other lovely, long talks through the winter,

but finally spring came and it was time to leave. She baked him bread and gave him pemmican. Just before he mounted his horse, she gave him a locket containing a lock of red hair. He knew it was Ned's.

She said, "Keep it with you. Whenever you feel down or you feel like you're losing your purpose, he'll keep your spirits up."

He thanked her and kissed her gently on the forehead. "Thanks, mom."

"Bless you, my son. Come back and visit me again. It was lovely having you here. You made it much easier for me."

Brian mounted up and forded the Platte at the spot where he had almost died. When he reached the other side, he looked back. Eileen was smiling and waving gaily at him. He blew her a kiss. She did the same and he rode off, unable to look back.

After he had gone a few miles, he considered heading north toward the Black Hills. He wanted to see his old friend, Sitting Bull. But he had heard that Red Cloud and Crazy Horse had massacred the soldiers at Fort Fetterman that winter and decided against it.

He spurred his horse back east. He promised himself to write George Custer and thank him for giving him such a reliable horse. Not many horses were strong enough to have made it through the ice of the Platte River.

52

When Brian arrived in St. Louis he returned home. Dr. Welsh sorrowfully told him the sad news that Bridget had died of puerperal sepsis after childbirth. The baby, however, was fine, and they had named her Bridget. There had been no complications until the day after delivery when fever set in. She was dead in forty-eight hours.

Brian took it amazingly well. Then he asked Dr. Welsh if he washed his hands between examining women in labor.

He answered haughtily, "No, of course not."

"The midwives do, and they have far fewer complications. There are also reports from Boston and London that when strict handwashing technique is applied between patients, complications of sepsis are far less frequent."

"Surely you can't suspect me to be the cause of her death?" said Welsh angrily.

Brian coolly said, "If you expect to practice with me, you'll wash your hands in iodine solution between patients."

Welsh said he would consider it.

Brian put his shingle up on the house and soon his practice began to thrive. His father's old patients returned and he was gratified to see them. Many of them told him the same thing: Dr. Welsh was a cold, uncaring physician who charged twice what his father had.

After examining the books, Brian called Welsh in and told him to leave. The doctor was dumbstruck and angry, and called Brian a "pompous ingrate" who needed far more experience before he could lecture him about washing his hands and how to treat patients.

They parted angrily.

Brian visited Bridget's husband John Ryan and offered his condolences. The boy Liam, was now becoming a young man. He wanted Brian to take him hunting the first chance he could get. Brian promised he would, and the boy bounded out for a night of carousing. He father sadly shook his head. "I can't control him. Since his mother's death he no longer listens to me. She could at least make him behave—but he looks at me as if he weren't even my son. He loves his little sister, though. I think that she is the only reason that he stays here."

Brian said, "I'll take him hunting and talk some sense into the boy. He's a good lad. I lost my mother when I was young. I know what he's going through. Don't worry. He'll be all right in time."

They shook hands. Brian kept his promise, taking the boy into the woods and teaching him how to stalk game, how to shoot, how to respect the environment. He taught him the ways of the Crow and Sioux. He taught him to respect his father and gradually the boy did come around.

But Liam did not attend the University to study law as his father wished. He went aimlessly from job to job, trying to find himself.

Meanwhile Brian had accepted the dean's offer and begun work as an instructor in surgery. Soon he was an assistant professor. He wrote papers, taught students and interns, and set up the first surgical residency program at St. Louis University. Soon he became head of the Department of Surgery. Nothing he had done before prepared him for the infighting of medical politics, the massive egos and strong wills of doctors.

His first order of business was to establish strict handwashing technique guidelines at the hospital. A furor among the medical staff erupted, a meeting was called by the dean. Brian informed them that as surgeons he expected them to wash between examining women in labor and prior to deliveries.

Doctor Williams, who had delivered more babies than any of the other physicians, staunchly refused, saying that he had years of experience and that he was not a surgeon. Brian then asked him if he sewed up vaginal tears after childbirth. Williams answered yes.

"Then you're practicing surgery—and you will adhere to our policy or I'll see to it that the only thing you deliver around here is the mail."

There were astonished gasps and some laughter. Williams became more indignant. Finally the dean stepped in and said, "Let's try it for six months. If the death rate goes down, then it will be a strict policy."

The death rate did indeed plummet. Soon every mother in St. Louis wanted her child delivered at the University Hospital. Their success was so great that they had to open a new wing just for delivering babies. They decided to establish a special training program called 'Obstetrics,' which would remain in the Department of Surgery where Brian could continue to oversee its activities.

When the new wing was established they had an opening ceremony. Brian gave a very brief speech and they christened it St. Bridget's Hospital for Childbirth.

The years went by. Brian was becoming immensely successful and was renowned as the best surgeon in St. Louis.

When he found time to read the papers, the news was filled with Red Cloud's war and wild stories about Sitting Bull and Crazy Horse. They were accused of killing miners and settlers in the Dakotas and Montana Territories. The Bozeman Trail had been closed, and the cavalry had left Fort Smith in Montana—whereupon the Sioux promptly burned it to the ground. All around was a strong sentiment to take revenge on the Indians. Brian knew what would happen next.

53

The newspapers were soon filled with stories of Custer's exploits in the Indian Territories. He and his men had tracked Black Kettle's Cheyenne down the Washita river. Attacked before dawn, they had killed some of the warriors and a hundred and fifty women and children in a predawn raid. Most of the warriors had escaped to a higher ridge and Custer had to hastily withdraw, leaving some of his men trapped behind. The Eastern press was furious that innocent women and children had been killed. An inquiry ensued and Custer was severely admonished.

His next mistake was to throw General Ulysses S. Grant's son into the stockade at Fort Abraham Lincoln for drunkenness. Grant had never liked George in the first place, but this was the final straw.

Brian had received a letter from him soon after this. He had never known Custer to be so disconsolate. In the letter he said he was a soldier, not a politician, and had only been doing his duty. He wrote that he loved the plains, loved hunting, loved wildly riding across the prairies chasing buffalo and shooting elk and deer...In his heart he knew that if he were an Indian he would do the same as Sitting Bull and Crazy Horse, for there was nothing more exhilarating than the hunt on the wild Montana prairie. But since he was a soldier and under orders, he had to fight the Indians' threat from the West.

Next Brian read in the papers that Custer had been court-martialed for desertion. He had grown lonely on the plains, and had ridden back East to visit his beloved Libbey. He appealed his court-martial but it was futile. He was demoted by the Army and scorned by the press.

In 1873 the economy of the United States was faltering. The Civil War had sapped the country's resources. A depression ensued, and banks started to fail. Luckily Brian's own bank was solid and his inheritance remained intact.

Custer was directed by General Sheridan to lead an expedition into the Black Hills to investigate rumors that gold had been discovered there. He returned with the news that the Black Hills were full of gold. Once again Custer was the hero of his country and revered by both military leaders and the press. But when miners began combing the Black Hills, Sitting Bull and Crazy Horse declared war. The inevitable was coming to pass.

Brian received another letter from Custer who was upbeat again. He said that Libbey had joined him at Fort Abraham Lincoln; that they were doing well and spending days riding out on the plains; that Libbey loved the West and loved being with him. He had never sounded so happy.

Once again poor Custer had gotten enmeshed in politics and had backed an unsuccessful attempt to oust the Secretary of War who was one of President Grant's favorites. Now Grant was furious, and had recalled Custer to Washington to testify before Congress—just before General Terry and the Seventh Cavalry were about to counterattack the Indians in the Territories.

Brian had just finished a difficult operation when a nurse approached him and said, "Dr. McCaffrey, there's a very important man waiting in your office to see you."

He grumbled to himself, thinking it would be a board member of the hospital expecting preferential treatment. When he walked into his office, there sat George Armstrong

Custer in full military regalia. George bellowed, "Well, look at the world-renowned surgeon. I've come here for your services."

"You look pretty healthy to me," Brian said, smiling.

"No, I don't need surgery. I want you to accompany me when we go after Sitting Bull and Crazy Horse."

Brian said coldly, "No, they're my friends. I won't lead you to them."

"I'm not asking you to lead me anywhere. I've got Crow scouts that can take me to their tepees if I want. I need skilled surgeons. This is going to be a bloody battle."

"I thought you had been recalled to Washington."

"I have, but General Terry assures me that he will not conduct an Indian war unless I'm leading the Seventh Cavalry. He's already telegraphed Grant saying that we can't begin to fight unless I'm leading. I'm going back to Washington to charm my way out of this; on my way back, I want you to join me."

Brian considered the options. He did have a vacation coming up and down deep, he hoped that he could somehow get Custer and Sitting Bull to sit across from one another and work out a peaceful solution.

"I'll go with you, but I'm not going as a combatant; I'm going as a surgeon, and I will treat wounded Indians as well as your soldiers."

"Brian, I have no personal emnity toward the Indians. I'm a soldier following orders, and I do what my superiors tell me. If an opportunity to discuss peace develops, I'll be happy to discuss it. Meanwhile, I've got to get on the train and talk to Grant and Congress and get myself out of this mess. I expect to be back in three days and I want you with me."

They went out into the hall. Nurses and doctors stared at the war hero and surgeon, trying to act uninterested in the scene in front of them. Custer jauntily walked away, smiling at the nurses.

225

Brian began the task of getting someone to cover for his office and making sure that his postoperative patients would be well cared for. He went home, packed his instruments, got out his buckskins and his Sioux war vest, and prepared for the journey west.

54

Fort Abraham Lincoln was a very busy place before the expedition departed, and the men were restless. They were tired of drills. They wanted desperately to fight. Generals Terry, Gibbon, Custer, and officers were planning their strategy. Libbey Custer made their quarters into a homey but elegant place in the midst of the desolate outpost. The day before they departed, George Custer and Libbey rode off together on the plains for a picnic. Brian envied them as he watched from the ramparts and saw them laughing gaily as they galloped away. What a happy couple! Brian felt a deep longing for a wife that would make him as happy as George Custer.

That evening the decision was made. Terry would head east and north into the Dakotas, then turn south into the Big Horn region. Custer and his troops would proceed south to the Rosebud and follow the Little Big Horn to the Big Horn river; there they would rendezvous with Crook, who would be coming up from Wyoming. Then the three forces would comb the valleys of the Big Horn and Little Big Horn until the Indians were surrounded and brought to their knees. The "Indian problem" would be over forever. They hoped that their victory would coincide with the celebration of the centennial of 1876 in Philadelphia. The country had been planning a grand exposition for three years. The giant exhibition halls would be packed with people from all over the

227

country when the news of the victory would be announced.

Custer had his own agenda. The Democratic National Convention was only two weeks away. The morning of their departure was bright and sunny and hot; the horses pranced anxiously. The wives stood raptly in admiration of America's greatest mounted fighting force. They looked so young and brave and confident in their blue uniforms. Their sabers glinted in the sunlight. Their carbines looked menacing as they prepared to leave the gates. Nothing could stop them.

Terry offered Custer a Gatling gun that could shoot hundreds of rounds per minute. Custer smiled and said, "Thanks, but my boys won't be needing it. It's too heavy to cart around and it will only slow us down. This time we won't let them escape."

When the gates opened, the men kissed their women and the drums began to beat. A bugle sounded. The garrison band began to play "Garryowen." Custer could hardly contain his excitement. He stood tall in his stirrups, pointed his saber to the opening, and announced, "Boys, it's time to rid America of the Indian threat to Manifest Destiny. The Black Hills will be ours. Let's go get 'em!"

Off they went. Brian felt both proud and ashamed of his country as he followed them out the gates. The Crow Indian scouts were in the lead with Custer. To his right and left were his brother, Tom, and his cousins, Autie and Boston. The Custer family, he hoped, would bring victory and gold to their financially strapped nation.

Brian wished Ned could be with them; he would have loved the military pageantry of it all. Brian felt sorry for the Indians. He knew they would be defeated, herded on to reservations, and victimized by greedy Indian agents who always became wealthy at their expense. Brian still wanted to get Custer and Sitting Bull to parley before the slaughter by the U. S. Cavalry began.

Custer was uncharacteristically quiet, with a somber expression on his face as they crossed the plains. He looked much older. He wore his hair short instead of in its usual long, curly mane.

Brian struck up a conversation with Major Reno. Reno had matured and had become an able leader respected by his men. They laughed about their first encounter on the train, and Reno expressed his sadness at hearing of Ned's death. "To tell you the truth, I admired his spunk and humor. At the time I was humiliated—but I was acting like a horse's ass."

"You? Never," interjected Major Benteen. He was a tall intense man with prematurely white hair—his reward for leading several bloody battle charges during the Civil War. He too was a competent and skilled leader, whose men respected and feared him. His troops would follow him anywhere, regardless of the strength of the enemy.

Brian rode next to Dr. O'Neal for several days. He was a small man but Brian could tell that he was a dedicated, competent army surgeon with a fine reputation. He hoped that none of these bright young soldiers would need their services.

The troops' morale was high. They knew that this would be guerilla warfare, far different from the stand-and-charge attacks of the Civil War. They were veterans, hardened from the Washita and other Indian skirmishes in the Black Hills. They knew how to fight renegades and were used to using trenches and creek beds to their advantage. They couldn't wait to try out their new carbines, the best and most wanted weapons in the military arsenal.

They didn't know, however, that Crook's men in Wyoming had been attacked that very day by Crazy Horse, leading an overwhelming army of Brule, Hunkpapa, Sansarc, Blackfoot and Sioux—supported by Cheyenne, the best horsemen in the world. Crook had hastily beaten a retreat into Wyoming with his surviving men. The U. S. force had already been cut in half and they didn't even know it.

A hundred miles to the south, Sitting Bull stood on an outcropping, marveling at the size of his encampment. Never before in the history of the Sioux had all of them united to fight. He was gladdened by the addition of the Cheyenne, whom he feared and respected. He knew through his scouts that the blue- coats were

coming. His scouts had told him that a large force of cavalry, led by
General Terry, were on their way. The warriors below were celebrating
their victory over Crook. Yet in the face of this he had a strange sense
of foreboding. What would happen to his people if they lost? Their
children would die on the white man's reservations, never learning
their proud history or their religion, and the freedom of the buffalo
chase. We *must* win, he thought to himself.

He asked One Bull to assist him with the Sun Dance. When he
was younger he had looked forward to the torture of the Sun Dance, for
it gave him a powerful vision. As he grew older, he disliked the
starvation and thirst, as he would have to stare into the sun as he
received one hundred knife slashes to the arms. He hoped that a vision
would come. Visions, too were growing hard to come by as he got older.

Later, Sitting Bull stared into the sun. The cuts no longer hurt.
Blood was congealed on his aching arms, suspended by ropes to the
ceremonial pole. The flies bit him ceaselessly on his arms and face. He
grew agitated; no vision had yet filled his spirit. After thirty-six hours
of staring into the sky, he collapsed. The men left him. Then he closed
his eyes—and the vision came. A great cloud of dust came from the
north, towards their encampment. Out of it came white soldiers, but
they were hanging upside down from their horses and they had no ears.
It was a strange vision, Sitting Bull awoke with a start, smiling. The
Great Spirit had given him a sign. The soldiers were upside down
because they were dead, and they had no ears because they hadn't
listened to the Sioux's warnings to stay out of the Black Hills.

His men came to him and he told them of his vision. A great
celebration ensued. Not only would they survive, they would be
victorious over their hated white enemy! All they could do now was
wait. Crazy Horse and Gall and the other leaders thanked Sitting Bull
for his vision and rushed to their camps to tell their warriors the good
news.

55

Generals Terry, Gibbon, and Custer arrived at the Rosebud. Terry and Gibbon and their men would head west and attack from the north in four days. Custer would take his men south to the Little Big Horn to try and find the Indian encampment and drive them north towards Terry. By then Reynolds would have arrived from the west, Crook would have found George's men, and they would join to trap them all. It seemed like a perfect plan.

As they split their forces Terry yelled to Custer, "Slow down and save some Indians for us, George!"

Custer laughed and waved gaily at his friend. "Don't worry, there will be enough for all of us," he replied. But as they rode off, his expression became grim and determined. The Sioux wouldn't escape him this time.

Brian was mystified by Custer's energy. The man would not slow down. They rode eighteen hours a day, far into the night. At this rate, they would be at the Little Big Horn in two days. Reno and Benteen occasionally cast worried glances at one another. They didn't like this one bit. The men and horses were becoming tired. Neither man liked Custer, and didn't bother to hide it. Custer knew it, but knew also that they would fight to the death no matter what.

Finally, they camped at two a. m. above the valley of the Little Big Horn. Everyone was exhausted—except Custer. He sat on a log, conferring with his officers, and finally fell asleep with a cup of coffee in his hand. Brian didn't even bother to unroll his bedroll, but collapsed on the ground. It was still warm at night. He awakened when he heard Reno and Benteen arguing with Custer that the pace was killing the horses and the men would be too tired to fight. Custer maintained that if they arrived early, they would have the element of surprise on their side. After all, he said, it had worked before at the Washita.

Reno and Benteen grumbled and walked off to confer amongst themselves. When they were out of earshot, Curly, George's favorite Crow scout, told him that he had seen a trail of broken grass more than a mile wide, indicating that a large Indian encampment had moved through the Valley in the last few days.

"It could have been a buffalo herd, for all you know. Relax, Curly. My boys will annihilate them."

"Sir, that was not a buffalo herd. It was full of Indian sign. There are no buffalo around for miles."

"Curly, I plan to surprise them and wipe them out. The sooner I do it, the sooner I can telegraph headquarters about our victory. You see, there is a great meeting of white men—the Democrats. Once they hear of my victory, I will be a shoo-in as the next presidential candidate. Soon I will be the Great White Father, and Grant and his drunken Republicans will be out of a job. Serves 'em right for court-martialing me."

"I'll give the Crow all the Montana Territory. It's all yours. All you have to do is find them for me. Then we will get the Dakotas and the Black Hills and all the gold and my country will be rich again. Can't you understand that?"

"Yes, but you must slow down. The men are too tired to fight."

"Don't worry about my boys. Get some sleep."

Brian tried to roll over and talk to Custer about a peaceful solution without bloodshed—one which would make him a hero as well. But he was simply too tired to move and fell asleep.

When he awoke, he saw Custer peering through a long brass scope at the valley below them. It seemed empty. There was some smoke in the distance. Curly and his scouts had returned from a long night of reconnaissance. Custer didn't like what he was being told. "I don't believe that there's as many Indians down there as you think."

"Sir, there are at least a thousand warriors down there."

"I can only see one camp and it couldn't possibly hold that many hostiles. Look for yourself."

"They are hidden around the bend in the river."

"You're always overestimating the enemy, Curly. Be brave"

Curly seemed visibly shaken. The other Crows seemed agitated.

"We'll surround them and send them running to the north, right into Terry's forces…that is, if they survive," Custer laughed. "My orders are to engage the enemy. We can't let them get away. This is our moment in history."

Brian had never seen Custer so angry.

"Sergeant, tell Majors Reno and Benteen to get over here *now!*" From their vantage point he told Reno to cross the creek feeding the Little Big Horn to the left and charge south into the camp. He instructed Benteen to stay on this side of the river and head toward the camp so that if the Sioux crossed the Little Big Horn to escape Reno, he could cut them down as they tried to cross the river. Custer himself planned to stay behind the foothills, come up from behind the camp to the south, attack their flanks from behind, and drive them north back toward Reno.

On the surface, it seemed like a brilliant plan. Unfortunately, Custer did not know that he was heading straight for a huge concentration of warriors, hidden behind the bluffs and cottonwoods on the other side of the river. He told the men to put their sabers in the scabbards so that the sunlight wouldn't glint off the swords. He cautioned them to put their metal cups and canteens in their packs, so that the utensils wouldn't clang as their horses approached the camp. The troops solemnly split into three forces. They were brave young men, hardened young warriors, but they were haggard and exhausted. Nevertheless, none showed fear. It was six a. m. and already the valley was turning into an inferno. Benteen and Reno walked off grumbling and shaking their heads. They mounted up.

Custer was wearing his buckskins instead of his blue uniform. He had his usual red bandanna on, and his floppy white hat. He seemed serene now. After all, he was going to be president after he was through with the Sioux. Brian rode up and asked to speak to him. Custer arched an eyebrow. "What is it, doctor?"

"Can I take you to Sitting Bull? I will carry a white flag and I am wearing a Sioux war vest. Sitting Bull promised that his men would never attack me as long as I wore the vest."

"I'm sorry, Doctor. It's too late for talk of peace. Those men are murderers of our people."

"But, sir."

"McCaffrey, I didn't bring you here to parley. I didn't bring you here as a scout. I didn't bring you here as an advisor. I'm not asking you to fight them. I brought you here to be a surgeon. You care for my men, and I lead them. Is that clear? If you want to take care of wounded Indians, that's fine with me too. But don't interfere with my battle plan. That's all, Doctor."

Custer wheeled his horse away, led the column of men behind the ridge, and disappeared down into the valley. Brian shook his head and followed. He wanted to talk to Dr. O'Neal, but he had left with Reno's men. Brian was followed by a young Crow named Red Tail.

Suddenly, as they made their way down the narrow trail, Brian's horse stumbled and threw him. He hit his head on a low-lying branch and was knocked unconscious. Red Tail stayed with Brian, trying to revive him.

56

Sitting Bull, Crazy Horse, and the young warrior Gall sat in the Hunkpapa camp. They could see the children and squaws playing in the river. Now at about ten a. m., the temperature was already nearly a hundred degrees. They had feared an attack at dawn, as was the U. S. Cavalry's custom. Another day of waiting. Crazy Horse complained that his men were becoming increasingly restless. Gall said nothing. Sitting Bull counseled the younger men to be patient: "They will come tomorrow or the next day."

They went over their plan again. Sitting Bull would remain in the camp with some of the older warriors to protect the women and children. Young braves would act as couriers so that he could direct the battle, yet still could lead an escape route into the mountains if his vision did not come to pass. The two young leaders left for their camps to keep their men calm. Sitting Bull went into his lodge where his wife and children waited and played with them. Then he sent them out and began to pray for victory. At about one o'clock, the squaws and children who were playing in the river saw a great cloud of dust from the north. Some of the warriors were fishing. Then they saw the blue coats of Reno's men and heard the whine of bullets, which began plunking around them into the river. They scrambled ashore and ran to the camp screaming, "The soldiers are coming!"

Gall's men mounted, and charged toward Reno. Benteen was still out of sight and couldn't tell that the battle had begun; he plodded toward the south on the opposite side of the river. Reno's advance was suddenly halted when his scout's brains splattered on his chest and face. He was devastated. Then he saw hundreds of Gall's men coming towards them. Clearly he was outnumbered and outgunned. He pulled his men back and fought back into the timber, shielded by a breastwork of dead horses and logs. Arrows whizzed by. To his horror, not only was he badly outnumbered but the Indians somehow had obtained repeating rifles. "Where the hell are Custer and Benteen?" he fumed. They were fighting against hopeless odds. He hated retreating, but it was his only choice. His men were being cut to pieces and their wonderful new carbines were jamming at an alarming rate.

As Reno and his men holed up, Gall wheeled his horse back to the main camp as Benteen had finally decided to cross the river. Gall's men decimated them as they tried to fight the raging current. Finally they too had to retreat. They headed back north, crossing the river above Reno, and came up from behind to lend him support. Now two-thirds of Custer's forces were pinned down.

Crazy Horse, watching from a distance, figured that another force would come from the south—probably be Two-Stars Crook and his men. Instead of attacking Reno and Benteen he led his unbelieving men away from the battle up behind a hill, hiding his men from a force that he knew would attack from the south.

Just as he thought, two hundred and seventy-five blue coats started crossing the Little Big Horn south of Sitting Bull's camp. The white soldiers always attack from two sides. He had guessed right. Custer was leading his men straight into a death trap, and didn't even know it. Worse, he was ecstatic. He raced towards Sitting Bull's camp. Custer ordered his courier to fetch

Benteen from across the river and bring plenty of ammunition. He yelled "Come on, boys! We've got 'em on the run."

Soon the Indians started killing his men with repeating rifles. Custer was furious. "Stupid politicians armed these savages with Winchesters to use for hunting buffalo and they're killing my men." He fumed and fought gallantly. He began to race up and down the battle lines, encouraging his men. He then decided that the only course was to ride right through the camp and to the hill above the encampment. He could then hold off these red bastards, he thought, until Crook and Terry showed up. "Where's Reno?" he wondered. "He should be here by now."

They fought their way up the hill, taking heavy casualties. Now they were safely headed towards the high ground. Gall and Sitting Bull's men were below. Custer had the higher ground—he had outsmarted them, he was sure of it.

Suddenly his men were being shot at from behind and above. They were only fifty yards from the top. He turned and saw Crazy Horse's men above him. In that instant he knew he had been outmaneuvered. His own carbine jammed. He threw it down, took his pistols out and began blazing away at the thundering horses and men. All he could hear was the noise of their hooves and the screams of the Indians. They sounded like a buffalo herd. His men still fought bravely on.

"Don't quit, boys!" he yelled and began to laugh.

He knew that he had been mortally wounded by a bullet in the chest. He hacked at Indians with his knife. He felt an explosion in his head and fell backward. He could feel them raining blows on him. He just saw blackness, then felt peace. His last thoughts were, "Libbey...boys, I'm sorry." It was over in less than twenty minutes: two hundred and seventy five of America's best fighting men were dead.

The Indians rode away shrieking victory cries to tell Sitting Bull that his vision had come true. Silently the squaws moved among them, taking their guns and knives. Some of them mutilated the dead soldiers, cutting off their ears because they hadn't listened. The hot winds blew away the flies and the cries of the few dying cavalrymen. Occasionally there would be the sound of a muted pop of a Colt pistol as the last of the dying, parched men put a bullet into his head to avoid the pain of the torture of the squaws.

The wind stopped. The sun began to set behind Last Stand Hill. When Brian awoke his head throbbed. He and Red Tail rode down into the Valley. In the distance they could hear the celebration of the Sioux to the south, and occasional rifle shots from the north. It was dusk when they forded the Little Big Horn. The valley was eerily quiet. The prairie grass had been dancing in waves with the hot winds, but now it was suddenly silent. The grass took on a pink hue and was still. There were dead horses and men in blue coats with no ears lying upside down on the hill. The only sound was the buzzing of flies and the shrill cry of a hawk. The carnage was worse than anything he had seen in the Civil War. There was no one to treat, no one to save.

They went over to the last knot of men lying next to one another or on top of a fallen comrade. They were just boys, lying dead in the prairie grass. Some of them died with their knives in the breeches of their carbines, trying to dislodge the cartridges that had expanded and fatally jammed the chambers of their brand-new carbines. The guns had been useless against the Indians' repeating rifles. There were arrows everywhere. Brian recalled Ned's words that the Indians had an easily replenishable source of ammunition:all they had to do was pick up already used arrows and shoot them again. The irony of it all was not lost on Brian. Wars weren't won by the latest guns that the white man could develop. They were won by the people that knew the land.

He took off his vest, and began to wave it at the ravens picking at the fallen men. Then he saw Custer. He looked as if he had fallen asleep. He had some blood on his chest and a small black hole in his left temple. His eyes were closed and his arms were folded. He had a serene expression on his face. He had not been mutilated in any way, nor had any of the men around him:it was as if the Indians had left them alone because they had fought so bravely.

He knelt down and ran his fingers through Custer's blond hair and said, "Goodbye, old friend." Then he covered him with a blanket.

They rode to the north, skirting the few Indians that had Reno and Benteen pinned down, and joined them from the rear. O'Neal was haggard and frantically trying to tend to the wounded. Reno seemed befuddled, still covered with blood and brain tissue. Benteen was furious. "Where's George Custer and his men?"

Brian quietly told him that he and all of his men were dead three miles to the south.

"We didn't hear any shooting. Are you sure he's dead?"

Brian said matter-of-factly, "I saw him myself. George Custer, his men, and all of the relatives that served with him— all are gone."

"God, if Terry and Gibbon or Crook don't show up we'll be dead by morning. "

They decided not to tell the other men, as they were already devastated. They were wounded and thirsty. Five of the men had been killed trying to bring back water for the wounded from the river.

Brian joined O'Neal trying to save the remainder of the wounded. All were suffering horribly; they were in great pain and cried out for water. Brian and O'Neal knew it was hopeless. The men would die anyway, although water would ease some of their agony. He put on his war vest and four volunteers joined him as they went to the river for water. He gently poured it into the parched mouths of the wounded men. The look of gratitude in their eyes brought a bittersweet feeling of warmth, compassion, and sorrow into his heart. One by one they died in the night. 239

PADDIES

A few survived. He wondered how they would get out of this hot, deadly valley of the Greasy Grass. Somehow they would have to get to the Rosebud, onto a paddlewheeler, and back to the safety of a military hospital. Brian couldn't sleep. His head still throbbed. His hands were covered with blood, iodine, and fragments of gauze as he worked desperately by the light of a single lantern. "Jesus, I hate war. All of this just for a stupid mineral called gold," he muttered. O'Neal heard him, nodded his head, and grimaced as he pulled an arrow out of a screaming soldier's thigh.

57

The Indians returned at dawn. Reno muttered, "They're like a bunch of damn ghosts. They just materialize out of nowhere. How in the hell are we going to beat these people?" Sure enough, they seemed to materialize out of the mist coming from the river. No one spoke. They hunkered down. Neither side fired. The sounds of two horses came from a distance. Brian recognized one Indian as Crazy Horse. The other one was Gall. They gave several hand signals and more Indians materialized from behind the cottonwoods and rocks.

One of the men said, "Major, maybe we ought to just surrender."

"Shut up, you fool!" Benteen whispered. "Did you see any mercy out there yesterday? Now they're going to finish us off. Just fight for your life—it's all you got left before one of 'em cuts your heart out. They want to send you to the land of the dark spirits, son. Maybe if we're lucky, Crook, Gibbon, or Terry or somebody will finally save us." Brian knew he was right.

Gall rode out of sight into the mist. Crazy Horse sat on his horse just out of range, scanning the hillsides and thickets ahead. He motioned to his left and several Indians on foot started to flank the left side of the hill. Benteen's men positioned themselves to thwart their advance. Crazy Horse let out a whoop and they rode toward them." Fire!" shouted Reno. The noise made the wounded men jump.

Brian's head felt like it would split from the combination of hitting his head, being up all night, and the noise of the gunfire. Arrows whizzed by and clattered off the aspen trees. The whines and screams of

241

miniballs, bullets, and scared men filled the air.

Reno and Benteen had managed to use their ammunition sparingly through the night in order to repel the first wave of Indians that came in the morning. The soldiers, armed with carbines, would fire until their guns jammed. Instead of all firing at once, they staggered their shots so that one group could pick out its casings and reload while another group fired. At the side of their positions they had men with pistols and double-barreled shotguns to catch those on horseback who charged into their midst. Above them on the high ground they were protected by the best shots in the company, armed with Sharps rifles that could kill a buffalo at three hundred yards.

They dug in. It worked brilliantly. For once they were killing more of the Indians than vice versa. Reno had conceived a plan for the sharpshooters to shoot the horses out from underneath the Indians. Once they were down, the men with the shotguns and repeaters would finish them off.

After three unsuccessful waves of attacks, Crazy Horse and Gall called their warriors back. It was about ten in the morning.

A short, squat man rode up on his horse and began talking to them.

Brian asked Benteen for his field glasses. It was Sitting Bull. He turned to Benteen and said, "I'm going out to parlay with them. I know two of their leaders." He still had his vest on." Anyone have a white flag?"

"Why not?" muttered Benteen, "We can't keep this up much longer. George had most of our ammunition."

At the river's edge, Sitting Bull said, "Let them go. The white men have fought bravely. The ones we let live will tell the others of our victory and they will leave us alone forever."

Gall said nothing. Crazy Horse said, "You are becoming soft, Sitting Bull. Do you think those white dogs would spare *us*?"

"No, but I want them to spread the word of our fierceness to keep the soldiers and the miners and the settlers out of our country. Maybe now they will think before going back on their word. Besides, enough fighting. They are pitiful. Let us leave and have a great hunt and celebrate our victory. The spirits have told me that a buffalo herd is on the other side of the mountains."

While Crazy Horse pondered his words, a man wearing a war vest and carrying a white flag walked stiffly towards them. His shoulders drooped; his clothes were bloody. He had a bloody bandage over his head. Some of the Cheyenne charged at him and struck him with their Coupe sticks.

"Enough!" thundered Sitting Bull. "He wears my vest! If one of you violates my word, I will his cut his heart out and feed it to the ravens!"

Brian walked up to them. "What are you doing here with the white soldiers, 'Man-Who-Rides-Buffalo'?"

"I came as a medicine man to heal the soldiers—and your men, as well."

"So you have completed the study of the white man's medicine! Can you cure my limp?"

"No," said Brian quietly.

"I didn't think so. What are you going to do for us?"

"I can treat your men's battle wounds. I have become an expert at treating bullet wounds."

Crazy Horse laughed. "You should come see for yourself how few of us need your help. We do not need the white man's help. We're going to let you white dogs go. Tell the others to stay out of our country. The next time, no one survives." He turned his horse and rode back to camp. Gall did likewise, a cold look of complete derision on his painted face.

"Hoka Hey!" he yelled, and raced across the plains.

"They are proud of their victory," said Sitting Bull. "Come ride with me."

They rode along the river bank and slowly up the hill where George and his men were lying. "Was that Two-Stars Crook?"

"No, that was my friend, George Armstrong Custer."

"We thought it was Two-Stars. He looks different to us than Custer."

"His hair was cut before the battle."

"Strange how a man's hair can change his look. He fought very bravely. The men around him were very strong warriors."

"They were his brothers and cousins and favored soldiers."

"Blood brothers fight for one another like a grizzly defends her cubs. So this was the great Custer! Crazy Horse said he laughed in their faces when they took him."

"I would have expected that of him. I figured he would fight furiously to the end."

"Why did he ride his men so hard? They could barely walk after they got off their horses, let alone fight. The battle was over in less time than it would take to light a pipe. We did not even need our guns…our horses could have overrun them if we wanted. He was a foolish leader. Did you know him well?"

"Yes, I liked him very much. He was loved and respected by his men. You know what he loved to do most?"

"Kill our women and children."

"No, he loved to chase the herds and ride into their midst. He was crazy, like you, me, and Ned."

Sitting Bull shook his head. "There aren't enough buffalo left for us, let alone for your people. We worshiped the buffalo; your race just kills for the tongue and hide, and lets the meat rot for the coyotes and ravens. It is so foolish."

"I know we are a wasteful people with no respect for the land," said Brian.

"Maybe this will teach your people to respect us and our land."

"You know that won't happen," Brian said. "Now more soldiers will come."

"I know. But for now, we will celebrate our victory and hunt one last time before I go to the Grandmother's Country."

"Canada?"

"Yes. They leave us alone and there are more buffalo. Our people can't live on your reservations and take your hand-outs. We will lose our spirits, our religion and our dignity. Before I leave you, old friend, I need to know one thing. Did you bring him to us?"

Brian reddened and said, "No. As I told you, I came as a medicine man for both sides. The Crow scouts led him here."

"I know. I'm sorry I tested your words, but I had to hear you say them. It makes me feel glad that you are still our friend."

"I am. He was my friend too. I had hoped before the battle that I might have sat between you two, and let you both speak of peace and smoke together to prevent this. I was a fool."

"That is the sad truth, my friend, but at least you had hoped for a better thing for all of us. I am glad that you still keep a good heart. Has your heart found another woman?"

"No, I've just about given up."

"A man needs a good woman and children. We are becoming old men, my friend. How is Ned?"

"He died in our war."

"Such craziness," Sitting Bull sighed sadly. "Come, let us embrace, old friend. There is little time left."

After the two said their goodbyes, they gave each other a sign of peace. Both men smiled sadly at the irony of it all.

"Keep safe in Canada. I will tell no one where you are."

"Thank you, brother. Stay safe with the white devils. Are you sure you won't come with me?"

"No, thanks. I like warmer weather. I can't chase buffalo on horseback anymore, my bones get too sore. "

"Yes, I wish I had the wisdom of my age, and the body and loins of a young brave again."

"Well, I'm not that old yet," smiled Brian.

"You will be soon, my friend."

They rode off in opposite directions. When Brian got back, the men were peering out anxiously waiting for another attack. Brian rode up with his flag and said, "Let's get out of here. Sitting

245

Bull has decided to spare us as long as we tell Crook and Gibbon and Terry to stay out of their country."

"Fat chance," said one of the soldiers.

"Where do they think they can hide?" said Benteen.

"I'd say any damn place they choose for now," said Brian.

Slowly a few of the men ventured out to drink from the Little Big Horn, one soldier covering the other as they drank. No arrows or shots came in their direction. It was as if the enemy had been swallowed up by the mountains. Around noon they saw dust from the north end of the canyon. "It's Terry!" shouted one of the men.

When Terry and his men rode up the shock of what had happened registered on their faces. "Where's George?" he demanded.

"He's lying dead on a hill about three miles to the south," said Reno.

"George dead? I can't believe it…I can't believe it!"

"Believe it, sir. He led us into a monumental ambush. We were foolishly deployed and hopelessly outnumbered," said Benteen.

"Major Reno, what's your assessment of the situation?"

"I agree completely with Major Benteen. It was an egregious mistake."

"I wouldn't use such big words at the Court of Inquiry, Major. The brass likes things plain and simple."

"How many survivors are there?"

"There are thirty men without wounds, and twenty-one who are wounded badly. "

"Wells, take your men to the top and see if you can see where the bastards went. Don't engage them, just have your scouts trail them and use double-backs to keep us informed. Every courier should be covered by two other men. Any questions?"

"No, sir."

"Move out, now! Major Howard, take your men to the hill. We've got to bury our men. Sergeant Morris, take your men with

246

them. It's going to take a long time to bury all these poor boys. O'Riley, you and your men double back and find Reynolds and his men and get back here. Let's set up perimeter guards in case they decide to come back. Where's Hollihan?"

"Here, sir."

"Take fifteen of your fastest men and horses and four of the Crows back towards Fort Union. Have them get a steamer to go up the Yellowstone as far as the Rosebud so we can evacuate the wounded to Fort Union."

"Aye, sir."

"Hayes, get those wagons up here and be gentle with the wounded boys. Get me some more medical men up here now, God dammit!"

Around four p. m. Gibbons' men showed up and they began to evacuate. Brian had wisely removed his vest when Terry's and Reynolds' men came in sight. He was in no mood to explain his appearance to the general. Benteen and Reno told Terry in private how Brian had convinced Sitting Bull to spare them. Brian told them that he hadn't, that the Indians had already decided to set them free and to tell the rest of the white men to tell their leaders and the press to stay out of the Black Hills and the Montana Territories.

Slowly the hospital wagons arrived and began to carry the remaining wounded out of this valley of death. Brian had been relieved by an army surgeon named Telsrow. Another surgeon, named Wilson, relieved Dr. O'Neal. Brian collapsed with O'Neal on top of some blankets and fell asleep as they bounced along the trail. He slept a dreamless sleep. Just before he fell asleep he remembered the look of Terry's crestfallen face as he muttered, "Why didn't you wait, George? So many dead!...God dammit! How are we going to tell Libbey?"

Three days later they reached the Rosebud. The steamer was ready for them. The stacks were billowing smoke. The wounded men were quickly loaded on board. Curious settlers crowded around to look at the survivors. Some of the women crossed themselves as they heard the moans of the wounded. Reporters from the Bozeman and Helena press were already there, shouting questions at Reno and Benteen. Both men ignored them and pushed their way up the gangplank.

Brian stepped on board as Staff Sergeant James Riley informed the press that "Yes, two hundred and seventy five men were killed, including General George Armstrong Custer. The number of survivors remains uncertain, and some men will die en route to Fort Union. Those are all the details that I can give out for now. Good day, gentlemen."

He clambered aboard and they shoved off. The captain of the steamer set a record—sixty-seven hours to Fort Union. Twelve more men died on the way of their wounds and sepsis. When they arrived at the army hospital Brian and O'Neal told the army surgeons each man's injuries in great detail. Many of them would need amputations.

Dr. James Abramson, the surgeon in charge of the hospital, complimented Brian and O'Neal on a job well done and informed them not to talk to anyone about the details of the battle: they would be summoned to a Board of Inquiry about the debacle. He explained that Grant was furious over the disgrace of the Seventh Cavalry's loss.

"Sir, may I make a candid observation?" said Brian.

"Certainly, Dr. McCaffrey."

"Piss on the President and all the other morons running this so-called civilized country."

O'Neal shrugged his shoulders and said, "He's been under a lot of stress, Doctor."

He and Brian soon found themselves quickly emptying the contents of a bottle of whiskey in the nearest saloon. The place was strangely quiet and somber. The patrons of the bar cast furtive glances at them, but none approached them, for it was obvious they wanted to be left alone.

58

Two days later he took the train back to St. Louis. He politely told his friends and the nurses that he couldn't talk about the battle until he had testified at the Board of Inquiry. When the day came, he walked into the Drake Hotel in Chicago to face the Board.

When asked if he felt that Majors Reno and Benteen had acted in a cowardly way, he answered, "No. They saved their men by retreating in the face of a superior enemy" he said.

One of the military lawyers asked, "Are you implying that the Indians were superior to our men?"

"Not in the military sense; they just had superior strategic positions. They outnumbered our forces and fought very well. The soldiers complained to me about their carbines jamming."

"Doctor, you were absent during the first part of the battle due to a fall from a horse, is that correct?"

"Yes."

"You were absent for a period of time the next day. Is that correct?"

"Yes," replied Brian evenly.

"You are a friend of Sitting Bull. Is that correct?"

"Yes," said Brian tensely.

"Did you alert Colonel Custer in any way as to Sitting Bull's whereabouts?"

"Of course not. Are you implying that I helped Colonel

Custer ride into an ambush after he was informed by his scouts and fellow officers that he was outnumbered?"

"We're weighing all possibilities, Doctor McCaffrey."

"Counselor, I was a friend of George Custer. I went as a volunteer to help his men should they become wounded. I went there at his insistence and at my own expense."

"Doctor, we are here to find out the truth."

"The truth is that George was overly excited about finally catching the Indians. He didn't want them to escape. I had seen him and his men fight during the civil war when they were outnumbered and they prevailed. He just didn't believe the scouts and he figured his men could fight their way out of anything. His mistake was splitting his forces up and attacking when the men were exhausted."

"Are you an expert on tactical warfare, Doctor?"

"No. I'm an expert at listening to boys and young men scream in pain from gunshot wounds. I've seen men with half their faces blown away. Counselor, have you ever seen a man that's been gut-shot? They sit there looking at their wounds in disbelief. They are always thirsty and hot. They can feel their hearts starting to beat out of control. They keep trying to change position to make the pain go away. Morphine, and laudanum won't make the pain go away. Did you ever see a man with a wound in his chest, Counselor?

"No, I'm not an expert in tactical warfare; I'm just an expert at watching men die from so-called 'tactical warfare'."

The attorney eyed him coldly. "What did you say to the Indians the day you rode out to parlay with them?"

"Counselor, I've already given you a written statement to that effect. In essence, we talked about letting our men go. They had already decided to let them live."

"So you're not taking credit for saving our men?"

"No. It was Sitting Bull's decision."

"Sitting Bull? Surely you jest."

"No, he wanted us to know that his men meant business

250

about keeping the Black Hills. He also knew that other troops were headed his way."

"Do you know where he was headed with his people?"

"I can't say."

"Can't say or will not say? We know he has already escaped to Canada."

"Good."

"You could have told us."

"Am I a defendant here or not?"

"I am simply saying that you could have known of his plans since you were his old friend and you talked with him. He could have told you of his plans. We could consider your silence on this matter as a treasonable offense."

"Counselor, if I could read Sitting Bull's mind, maybe I could have told the military where to look for him. Unfortunately, I was concerned about the welfare of our wounded soldiers. The various tribes apparently scattered after the battle. Who could have found them? Besides, our side could have lost again. Or worse, we could have ended up massacring a bunch of old men and squaws and children, while leaving the warriors to escape and fight you again."

"Doctor, your attitude is not very respectful towards the military."

"No, counselor. I respect the military. I just don't like you "

"Doctor, in your opinion, then Majors Reno and Benteen acted professionally and bravely in the line of duty?"

"That's correct."

"Do you think George Armstrong Custer was solely responsible for the defeat of the Seventh Cavalry at the Battle of the Little Big Horn?"

Brian thought it over and sighed, "Yes, that is correct."

"Why, Doctor?"

"Only George knows the reasons."

"What do you think, Dr. McCaffrey?"

"I think he wanted to be a hero. I think he wanted to be president of the United States. I think he honestly believed his men could beat anybody."

"Thank you, Doctor. You are dismissed."

Afterwards, Reno and Benteen were acquitted of all charges and the blame was laid solely on Custer's shoulders.

He visited with Custer's wife Libbey, who was understandably upset with his testimony, and tried to make amends. She carefully told him that the press had pilloried George as a fool that had killed hundreds of young men because he didn't obey his own orders. Brian calmly told her that Custer's orders were to engage the enemy and to defeat them, and he had done his best to do that. He was clearly outnumbered and had fought bravely. She angrily told him that she would spend the rest of her days defending George's honor.

"Libbey, I'm sorry. He was a great man and a great warrior. He fought bravely. He loved you. I loved George. I loved his spirit. We'll all miss him. He was not a bad man. He just wanted to serve his country."

59

After the inquiry, Brian returned to his practice at the university. With Reno and Benteen acquitted, the blame was placed squarely on Custer's shoulders. Terry never publicly blamed Custer for the defeat, but his silence was damning. The press had a field day at Custer's expense.

Brian's colleagues would ask about the battle and he tried to fill them in on the details. He noticed that he didn't seem to have as much interest in medicine as he had had before. He was forty-six-years-old, rich, educated, a widower, with few friends. Most of the people he knew were either dead or spread out over the frontier.

He continued to teach and operate, but at the age of fifty he decided that he had had enough of being up all night and teaching and dealing with people's problems; he decided that he wanted to travel. He went to London and Paris and New York and marveled at the museums and theaters. The atmosphere, hustle and bustle of the big cities intrigued him—but down deep he knew that he wanted to be back in the mountains again.

Brian's hair was turning gray and he was developing a paunch just like his father. He still liked to hunt and fish, but sleeping on the cold ground had lost much of its appeal. His joints ached after long days of riding looking for game outside of St. Louis. He tried to take Liam on these trips, but the boy was now thirty years old and was always too busy to go along. He visited with his few remaining friends in St. Louis, but they had little in common any more. He learned from Bridget's husband that the boy seemed to have no purpose; he had finally quit working at the docks and had departed to explore the West and prospect for gold.

"What a useless trait to inherit," mused Brian to himself.

After reading that Sitting Bull had re-entered the U. S. and was going to give a speech in South Dakota at the opening of a railhead, he decided to go visit his last living old friend. He thought of visiting with John Johnston, who was now a sheriff in Red Lodge, Montana. They could talk about the old times. The country was different now.

Inevitably, he headed West. The train ride westward astonished Brian as the unsettled country had become replete with buildings at the railheads. He watched with fascination and disgust as so-called 'sportsmen' would shoot buffalo from the train as they rode by the herds which, by now, were so much smaller. He desperately missed the days of riding in their midst and taking them down at close range for survival, not for sport. He felt like an old relic.

He would sit in the smoking car with his cigar and Scotch and tell the so-called sportsmen of the old days when he had to track buffalo for miles rather than shoot them from the platform of a rail car. Many of them would listen politely and ask questions. Others would nod and changed the subject to politics as they felt uncomfortable about killing the great beasts with ease with their modern weapons.

They finally reached Minot, South Dakota, where Sitting Bull was going to dedicate the railhead. Sitting Bull had now become quite a figure in Western folklore. Many Americans believed that he personally had killed Custer. This was reinforced when he relived the battle in Bill Cody's traveling Wild West Show. Brian wondered how the old warrior felt about himself. He guessed that he needed the money for his family and people and would do anything to support them.

The day of the ceremony, Brian was sitting in the audience when Sitting Bull was introduced. He shook hands with the governor. He spoke in his native Sioux tongue and a young Sioux would then interpret the great warrior's words. There were many settlers in the crowd anxious to get a look at the man who had outwitted the U. S. Cavalry. When he finally spoke, the crowd grew silent. His words were plain and simple:

"You white men have killed my people and lied to us."

The interpreter did a double-take and translated his words as, "I am happy to be here for this grand celebration."

"Your railroads have slaughtered the buffalo and ruined our hunting grounds."

The young man translated, "We are thankful for the railroads which have brought goods and settlers to our people. "

The white men cheered.

Sitting Bull's expression did not change. Brian began to smile. The old man would never be their lackey. Sitting Bull finally concluded, "You are nothing but pigs and some day the Great Spirit will come and give us back all that is rightfully ours."

Brian began to laugh out loud as the people around him began to stare at him strangely.

"We look forward to working with the Great White Father and work for continued peace and happiness between our people."

The crowd erupted in cheers. People near Brian stared at him as he continued to laugh even louder at the interpreter's last remark. Sitting Bull saw him in the crowd and smiled. Then he bowed and again shook hands with the governor.

Afterwards, Brian went up to him. "That was quite a speech," he said in Sioux.

"A man should say what he feels," smiled the old chief. "Did you see the look on that young fool's face when he first heard my words?"

"It was priceless," said Brian.

"I guess that's the only fun I have anymore. I am always under surveillance by your government and the agents. They are afraid I'll lead another uprising."

255

"Why did you give the speech?"

"I get money for my people if I speak and tell your people what they want to hear. Today I felt like having fun with your people's ignorance. How are you doing, my friend?"

"Good. I quit being a medicine man. I am just traveling now, before I am too old."

"It is a pity that youth is wasted on the young. Have you found a new woman yet?"

"No."

"That is too bad. A man needs a good woman."

"Are you still with two wives?"

"No, I just keep one. I just need company now. I'm afraid that I'm not much of a bull anymore."

"Is it true that Crazy Horse is dead?"

"Yes, he surrendered and went to the reservation under Crook's command. The whites were afraid that he would escape. Crook had him arrested and when he saw he was going to be placed in a cell, he fought and was killed. They say that Little Big Man helped the soldiers. I too will probably die that way, but I have always tried to keep one step ahead of the agents and soldiers. I don't want to fight anymore. There is still some hope that we will get the Dakotas back. I have been offered eight million dollars for a reservation."

"Are you going to take it?"

"No, I'm going to ask for twenty million to be paid out over several years so our people can continue to survive."

"That's a lot of money."

"It's nothing compared to the gold that they will take from the hills and what price can you pay for a people's way of life?"

"None, I guess."

"True, my old friend. Would you like to see my people and wife and children?"

"Yes."

He spent a month with them and became saddened by their

dependence upon the Indian Agents for meager food supplies and the barest of essential clothing. They were no longer allowed to have guns. They were useless to them as there was little game left. Instead of elk and deer and buffalo, they ate pork and beef and corn and beans. They were a proud people who were being systematically destroyed by a bureaucracy.

They parted for the last time.

Brian rode a stage to Red Lodge, Montana and visited with Johnston. Johnston told him that Del had died. He was now a successful lawman but really didn't have too much to say. He told him that Jim Bridger had died at the hands of the Mojave Indians and that Carson had also died from pneumonia.

He went to Helena and visited with Governor Meagher. Brian spoke to him about the plight of the Indians. Meagher told him that he felt sorry for them but the 'mindless savages' deserved their fate if they didn't take up farming and learn the white man's way. Besides, it wasn't politically prudent to champion the cause of a people who had tortured and scalped friends and relatives of his constituents.

Ned's old house was bought by a young couple. She was a teacher and he was a miner. He went by the old school where Ned had taught. It was abandoned and had been replaced by a new, large school to accommodate Helena's burgeoning population.

He decided to buy a new rifle: a Winchester 40-60 lever action. He bought some new buckskins and blankets along with moccasins and two mules. He wanted to see the Yellowstone country that Ned had told him about.

He bought a new bedroll, plenty of jerky, cigars, and whiskey and headed into the wilderness.

60

After a month in the wilderness in the Yellowstone country, he felt good again. He noticed that he just didn't have the strength that he had as a youth, and sometimes he would get short of breath. One day he developed some chest pain, and a pain down his left arm as he led the mules out of a deep canyon. Another time he experienced it while chopping wood. The second time he felt weak and nauseous. Luckily he had brought his medicine bag and had taken some nitroglycerin and the pain went away. He had had several patients that had complained of pain three or four times a day and took nitroglycerin and lived for years, so he wasn't overly worried. He would get more nitroglycerin the next time he was back in civilization.

At dusk his mule's hair stood on end as it came to a stop. Brian unsheathed his Winchester. He could hear a man yelling and the unmistakable roar of a grizzly bear. The mule wouldn't budge. He dismounted, double-checked that the Winchester's magazine was full, and put on a sling of cartridges and crept towards the commotion. He approached downwind of the bear. He could see the man patiently being observed by the bear. The bear shook the tree. The man's horse lay dead and his rifle lay useless on the ground below. He approached as close as he dared.

The first shot hit the bear in the chest but he continued to rage and shake the tree. The second shot was wide. The bear looked around for him but didn't see him hiding behind a log. The next shot hit the bear behind the ear and dropped him on his side. Brian shot him three more times in the chest. The bear didn't move. Neither did Brian. He reloaded the Winchester.

The man began to clamber down the tree yelling, "Thank God you were along, mister!"

That voice. Could it be him? "Stay up there for another ten minutes until we're sure he's dead. They sometimes get a last swipe at you."

"Uncle Brian?"

"The same, Liam. What are you doing out here?"

"Trying to find myself, I guess. And you?"

"The same."

"Maybe we could join up for awhile; it's a lot safer."

After they dressed the bear, they sat and talked and ate. After dinner, he offered the boy a cigar and a drink. The boy took the drink but passed on the cigar. "No, I want to try a chew rather than smoke it."

Brian gave him a plug to chew on. Soon the young man turned green and threw up on Brian's foot. The boy was embarrassed and apologetic. Brian told him the story of how he had thrown up on the Liver-Eater's moccasins and they laughed into the night.

They traveled together for weeks. He told him Ned stories, war stories, and Indian stories. He taught him how to survive in unexpected storms and how to hunt elk and deer and bear. He taught him how to cook and dress them. He never told him that he was his father.

Soon it was fall. The boy told him that he had decided to go back to school. Brian smiled and said, "A man can always use an education."

"I guess I'll finally take up law, just like my dad."

"Good lad."

"So long, Uncle Brian."

"Good luck, Liam."

The boy headed east. The old man headed for the Little Big Horn. He wanted to winter with Plenty Coupes on his reservation.

The night after the boy left, he sat at the campfire. He missed him. He looked forward to seeing his old friends the Crows. Maybe he would find a young wife to keep him happy in his old age.

The pain started in his stomach and went up into his jaw. This time he began to sweat profusely. He reached for his medicine bag and took a nitroglycerin. The pain eased up. He was too tired to hobble his mules. He crawled into his bedroll. He fell asleep instantly. He felt warm and happy and was floating towards a bright light. He could see himself lying below next to the campfire. The mules were feeding peacefully by the stream. He didn't know if this was a dream or if he was dying. He had had patients tell him of similar experiences after high fevers and going under chloroform. He really didn't care; he just felt happy. Out of the light he saw a man wearing buckskins, riding a horse. "Well, lad, do you know where you are?"

"Ned?"

"The same."

"Am I dreaming?"

"Hard to say."

"Is this heaven?"

"Could be, or we're both dreaming."

"If this is heaven, it sure looks a lot like Montana. Only it looks like the old days, when it was full of buffalo."

"Aye, they're back. Enough for all of us. The fighting's all over. We and the Indians live peacefully here. There aren't any damned railroads here, either. Would you like to see your wife and children?"

"Sure. This can't be heaven…it's a dream. Besides, this can't be heaven because you wouldn't be here so soon."

The figure in the light just smiled and said, "Ah, you'd be surprised, lad. Follow me."

They rode off towards the white light. He hoped he wasn't dreaming.

261

EPILOGUE

Dear Reader;

I suppose the end of our story is somewhat unsettled. Did Brian die that night or was it a dream? I leave it up to you to end the story as you wish. Eventually they all passed on.

Sitting Bull was murdered on December 15th, 1890 by the Indian police because of the Ghost Dance Uprising. The Indians believed that if they practiced the Ghost Dance, the white men would all die or leave with their railroads and the buffalo would come back to their sacred land.

Sitting Bull was buried in a pauper's grave in South Dakota. The last to die was John Johnston. He contracted pneumonia at Red Lodge, Montana at the age of 89. Since he was a Union soldier, he was sent to the Wadsworth Veteran's Hospital in Los Angeles. He soon died there. The last of the mountain men was ironically buried in a cemetery near the hospital in, of all places, downtown Los Angeles.

Ned and Brian would sometimes grow restless and their spirits would soar over the mountains of Montana. Brian would show Ned the valley of the Greasy Grass where the Little Big Horn slowly meandered through the battlefield. They would stand on the ridge where Crazy Horse surrounded George and shake their heads. It was now covered with white markers for the fallen soldiers. They would sometimes be joined by the spirits of Sitting Bull and Crazy Horse and listen to the tourist's endless questions to the caretakers of the battlefield. After a while they would soar over the Yellowstone and look down lovingly at the young herd of buffalo and elk, the geysers, canyons, waterfalls and the lakes. Its beauty had lasted, thanks to the white man finally realizing that beautiful places deserve to be kept sacred.

Finally, they would soar over the Madison range and sit on the banks of the Madison River. Brian would lay his head on the ground and listen. He could actually hear the grass grow there in the spring. They would smell that sweet mountain air mixed with the scent of wildflowers. The winds hummed their beautiful symphony to them mixed with the muffled roar of the river as it carved its way through the valley. They would watch rainbow trout rising to the caddis and salmon flies. They would watch deer swim across the river and antelope warily coming to the river's edge to drink its pure, cool water. They would sit and talk for hours, reliving old times, constantly kidding and teasing one another.

Sometimes at night, if you listen carefully, you can hear Brian say, "It's still beautiful, isn't it, old Ned?"

"Aye, lad. it's 'home'."

JAMES PATRICK MULROONEY
July 4, 1995

Patrick Mulrooney was born in 1943
in Ohio and earned his M.D. at OSU
in 1969. When not busy in his
radiology practice or with his family,
Dr. Mulrooney enjoys his log cabin in
Montana watching sunsets and
writing.

3/04   8   1/04